ONLY A DUKE WILL DO

TO MARRY A ROGUE, BOOK 2

TAMARA Gill

COPYRIGHT

Only a Duke Will Do
To Marry a Rogue, Book 2
Copyright © 2017, 2020 by Tamara Gill
Cover Art by Wicked Smart Designs
All rights reserved.

ISBN: 978-0-6489050-6-6

ONLY A DUKE WILL DO

TO MARRY A ROGUE, BOOK 2

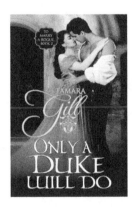

Without a Season, Lady Isolde Worthingham captured the Duke of Moore's heart at a country dance. But on the eve of her wedding, a scandal that rocked the ton and sent her fleeing to Scotland alone and unwed, leaves her perfectly planned future in a tangle of disgrace and heartbreak.

Merrick Mountshaw, the Duke of Moore loathes the pitiful existence he hides from the ton. With a scandalous wife he never wanted, who flaunts her many indiscretions, life is a never-ending parade of hell. When the one woman he loved and lost returns to London, he knows he can no longer live without her.

But vows and past hurts are not easily forgotten. Love may not win against the ton when a too proper Lord and Lady play by the rules.

CHAPTER 1

Mountshaw Estate, Wiltshire 1805

Isolde Worthingham, the second eldest daughter of the Duke of Penworth, spooned syllabub into her mouth and grinned at her betrothed, a man she had known for only one year, yet it felt like she'd known him her entire life. Merrick Mountshaw, the fourth Duke of Moore, was a gentle soul, much like herself, and suited her more than she'd ever dreamed. So much so it was almost like they'd been made for each other.

He smiled back, his eyes sparkling with humor. How was it that in only a few hours they would be married, finally promised to each other before God and all those they cared for most in the world.

Excitement thrummed through Isolde's veins. She'd waited for what seemed forever for this day to arrive. How lucky she was to be marrying for love, something that she and her sisters had promised to uphold after witnessing such a union from their parents' own match.

And she had found it with Merrick. The last dinner

together as an unmarried couple carried on around them, and was enjoyable and hearty. The conversation was of nothing but the forthcoming nuptials and the joining of two great families of southern England. The event of the Season some said.

It did not surprise her that the wedding was titled as such, with half of London having traveled to Mountshaw, Merrick's ancestral home, to attend. Everyone who was anyone would see them state their vows, their promises to each other, tomorrow. She couldn't wait.

Merrick took her hand, pulling her from her thoughts, placing a lingering kiss on the inside of her wrist. Warmth spread across her cheeks, and she bit her lip.

"I cannot concentrate on this dessert when there is something all the more delectable at table," he whispered, leaning close.

She laughed, looking about and hoping no one heard his words. "You tease, Your Grace."

"With you, I tell only the absolute truth." He smiled and answered a question from her brother Josh across from her. It was always pleasant sitting next to Merrick. In fact, she preferred it to the other end of the table, where she would hardly be able to see him between all the fruit and flower arrangements lining the great expanse. And if she sat away from him from tomorrow onward, she wouldn't have the delightful feeling of his boot rubbing up against her silk slipper.

There is no hope for the man. I've ruined him.

She inwardly chuckled at the thought. Once one of Town's most-loved rogues, Merrick had been quite a sought-after gentleman, not that Isolde had known anything about him until last year, when they'd met. She watched as he spoke with her brother about having some celebratory drinks after the women retired. Merrick was animated in conversation; his strong jaw teased her to stroke it, to drag him down for a kiss by lips that still distracted her when she looked at him. He was, in her estimation, perfect.

And she loved him so very much. He enjoyed life and all it offered, always imagined the best of any bad situation. The duke cared for his friends as much as his tenant farmers and staff. He was unlike anyone she'd ever known. The best of men.

Isolde sipped her champagne, the bubbles tickling her tongue, and the day's tension slipped away as the dinner progressed. Everything was ready for the wedding. The flowers were set, the trestle tables were on the lawn, waiting for the servants to set them for the wedding breakfast tomorrow morning. Her trunks sat packed in the entrance foyer for their trip to the Continent, and her wedding gown hung against her armoire. All Isolde had to do was try not to blubber uncontrollably as she promised her heart and soul to the man beside her, something she would absolutely fail at.

Isolde leaned over toward him, gaining his attention. "Must you, Merrick? I can hardly concentrate on this meal as it is, never mind having your foot dancing along my leg."

"It is only fair, as I've not been able to concentrate for months." He winked, picking up his glass of wine and taking a sip. She watched him, entranced when he licked a droplet of the drink off his lips. He caught her watching him, and understanding dawned in his gaze, hot and full of promises.

He picked up her hand and kissed her fingers, paying homage to the square diamond he'd given her in celebration of their betrothal. The ring had been his grandmother's, and now it was hers, and God willing, their son's wife, one day.

Heat pooled in her belly with the tantalizing stroke of his mouth against her body. The thought of the wedding night left her breathless, and she took a fortifying sip of champagne.

"I love you," he said, loud enough for all to hear the endearment.

"And I you." Her response was automatic, natural, and she blessed the day her best friend, Miss Hart, had introduced them at a country dance one year earlier. From that day forward, Merrick had been attentive and unrelenting in his pursuit of her, and she reveled in the fact she'd brought to heel one of London's devilish rogues.

Her father, the Duke of Penworth, cleared his throat, watching them with mirth. Her dearest papa all but glowed with pride. "I would like to propose a toast to the Duke and the future Duchess of Moore. May your life be full of love, good health, and happiness."

Her father smiled, and she noted the sheen of unshed tears in his eyes. He'd always been an emotional man, and they loved him all the more for it. "Moore has proven himself this past year to be a determined and honorable young man, and was I not assured he'll do nothing but strive to make my beautiful daughter happy, I would not have allowed the union to go on. But tonight my heart is full and joyful. Isolde has chosen well. It fills me with contented pleasure knowing you will forever be safe and blissful. So please raise your glass to the future Duke and Duchess of Moore."

The chorus of cheers burst from the table, and Isolde smiled at Merrick when he kissed her hand a second time. She looked around the long, marvelously decorated table, smiling her thanks to all her family and the few close friends who were present.

Her gaze halted on her best friend, Miss Leonora Hart—Letty to her. A frown marred her usually perfect forehead, and her lips were thin with displeasure. Letty looked distracted, worried even, and Isolde paused, promising to find out what ill her friend was feeling before the night came to an end.

Perhaps it was because Isolde was about to be married and Letty wasn't going to have a Season in Town due to finances at home. Her father, the local vicar back in Surrey, was not fluid in funds, and had refused the Duke of Penworth's offer to give his daughter a Season. Isolde had thought his decision very unkind, and unfair for Letty, and not being able to help had made the situation even more frustrating. And Letty's father's decision was final. He was not a vicar swayed by persuasion.

She would speak to her father again about the situation before she left for her wedding trip to Paris and Switzerland. Letty was practically her sister, after all, having known each other since they'd been in braids. There was nothing Isolde didn't want more for her friend than to have the happiness she herself had right at this moment with Merrick.

Finally, the dinner came to an end and the men stayed behind for their port and cheroots. Isolde made her way to the withdrawing room, ready for the night to be over so the next day could finally begin. Her wedding day... How amazing that sounded.

CHAPTER 2

One year earlier, Cranleigh Country Dance

Merrick, the Duke of Moore, leaned against the wall of the assembly rooms in Cranleigh and watched his life turn upside down before his eyes. What a marvelous creature the woman with dark-as-night hair was —a town beauty, probably of modest fortune from the look of her gown, but captivating in every sense of the word.

She will be mine...

For the past fortnight he'd been staying with his good friend from Cambridge, the Marquess Wardoor, and had agreed to attend the country dance as a bit of a lark. But who's laughing now? Certainly not I.

He walked toward the door that opened onto the front gravel drive, the rooms claustrophobically hot. Was it only he who was afflicted with this prickling heat? Surely not. He pulled at his cravat, though his gaze never left the woman who seemed to have captured his soul in mere minutes.

She was the most breathtaking angel in the world.

The lady laughed, a rich, intoxicating sound, not a frivolous giggle. Her plain friend joined in her mirth, and his heart stuttered to a stop in his chest. He frowned, not fully at ease with the way his body responded to the woman. Yes, she was pretty, but modestly dressed, not his usual type of dark-haired beauty who wore silk of rich colors and deep shades.

This woman's gown was a light blue muslin, her hair pulled back into a style he'd seen about Town, but without the adorning jewels or hair combs. She needed no ornaments to accentuate what was there for all to see.

Beauty personified.

I must meet her.

Walking through the crowd, he stopped to speak to people, not wanting to look too desperate. Slowly he edged his way to her side, but if he was expecting a warm welcome —the honor of his presence with gushing statements and breathlessness— he was sadly mistaken. He received none of those. In fact, he received no welcome whatsoever.

Merrick frowned. The angel continued to speak to her friend, completely unaware that he stood beside her, all but begging her to forget Society's rules and turn to greet him— allow him to introduce himself.

It was a novel experience, being ignored, and not one he was comfortable with. Most people cared to know what he thought of different subjects. They wanted to know if he was attending an event, and if not, what were his reasons and should they follow his lead? They clamored for his opinion on the latest on-dit and such, but it would seem, not this country miss.

If her ignorance of him was anything to go by, she didn't give a fig as to his opinion, or his presence.

His friend, Lord Wardoor, caught his eye and walked over, bowing before the two women. "Miss Hart, Lady Isolde Worthingham, may I introduce you to my friend from Cambridge, His Grace the Duke of Moore."

Merrick snapped his mouth shut. She was the Duke of Penworth's daughter! The women curtsied, both casting speculative glances at him, and, for the first time in his life he couldn't form words.

His angel spoke first. "Your Grace, it is a pleasure to meet you." Her voice was articulate and clear.

He cleared his throat. "My lady, Miss Hart." He bowed, clearing his throat yet again. "Are you enjoying your time in Cranleigh?"

"We are, Your Grace. Our time here has been the best of fun."

He nodded, unable to tear his gaze from her. She blushed, and his heart thumped loud enough he was sure she would hear. How awkward. "Will you dance with me, Lady Isolde?" She cast a knowing look to her friend and nodded. "Why thank you, yes."

He led her onto the floor, her perfect hand resting delicately upon his arm. Even through the material he could feel her touch. It marked him, burned a brand into his soul that he was sure would never be replaced by another.

He pulled her into the dance, taking delight at her gasp that turned into a laugh. "Do you like to dance, Lady Isolde?" She met his gaze, her eyes bright with mischief. "Isolde, please. And yes I do, when one's partner is affable and pleasant.

What about you, Your Grace. Do you like to dance?"

They were pulled away for a moment by the steps of the dance before they were reacquainted again. "My name is Merrick. And yes, I do now."

She grinned up at him, a rose-color blush making her more delightful by the minute. The feeling that he should never let this woman go thrummed through his veins. "May I call on you when you return to Town?"

"I'm not returning to Town immediately, but home before

the Season starts in earnest. When I do, I would like for you to call."

He twirled her, the hem of her gown brushing the tops of his boots. He could smell roses and leaned close, wishing he could kiss the little freckle that sat against her neck—a tempting morsel if ever he saw one. "It is done then."

"What is?" She smiled up at him, her gaze flicking to his lips. The air between them thickened with unsated desire. Yes, it was desire he felt for this woman, since the moment he'd laid eyes on her. Had Wardoor not urged him to attend this fete, he would never have met this delightful creature.

Fate...

"My life." He pulled her closer than was necessary, wanted her to see, to read in his gaze what he could not voice at this time, no matter how much he wanted to.

"Your life, sir?" She smiled, and he was lost. "How can your life be done?"

"No, you're right," he said. "Not done at all, but only beginning. With you."

For the remainder of the night Merrick did not leave her side. For a daughter of a duke she held no guile, did not lift her nose before the gathered throng and throw her wealth and powerful family against their modest means. If anything, he thought she was trying to fit in more, be another one of the guests, a country miss out for a country dance.

And he adored her for it.

---

*F*rom the moment he'd seen her he'd known she was extraordinary, and he'd wanted her. The dance had marked the start of their courtship, and he had not ceased until she'd agreed to be his wife.

And now, in only a few hours, that wish would come to fruition.

It could not come soon enough.

The touch of a silk glove on his arm pulled him from his musings. Isolde wrapped her arm about his and pulled him close to her side. "What are you thinking about? You have the oddest look on your face." She smiled up at him, and he wanted to lean down and kiss her. Hated that propriety refused to allow open displays of affection. Once they were married, he would let Society go hang and kiss her whenever and wherever he wished.

"I was thinking about the night we met. Do you remember?"

She chuckled, taking a sip of champagne. "I do. It was the best day of my life. Well…" She paused, meeting his gaze. "It was the best day, but something tells me tomorrow will surpass it."

Unable to keep from touching her, he kissed her hand. "I love you so very much. I promise to be the best husband I can be and make everything you ever wanted come true."

Tears pooled in her eyes, and he wiped one away that dared to mar her beautiful face. "I hope they're happy tears."

"You're incapable of creating any other type."

---

*L*ater that evening, after all the ladies had taken themselves off to bed, Merrick, along with the Duke of Penworth and Isolde's brother, the Marquess of Worth, partook in a few celebratory drinks. More than Merrick should have had if his uneven vision of the staircase was anything to go by. He was foxed, well and truly foxed. He clutched the banister and staggered to the second floor landing. That he made the floor, without toppling backward and breaking his neck, was a marvel.

The house was quiet as he made his way past Isolde's bedchamber—an overwhelming urge to cross the threshold ran through his mind, but the sound of a footman downstairs, sliding the bolt across the front door, kept him from diverting his course.

This time tomorrow night she would be his, and he pacified himself with that thought. They had the rest of their lives to be together. He could wait another few hours.

Making his suite, he noted his bed had been pulled down for the night by his ever faithful valet. The fire had long burned down to nothing but ash, and a chill marred the air. Stripping quickly, he staggered, falling over, and with a crack, his head hit the edge of his bed. Merrick swore, rubbing his skull, his head now thumping. The room spun, and he blinked, trying to focus his vision. It didn't work, but he dragged himself into bed, not bothering to climb under the sheets.

The room rocked, and for a moment Merrick thought he might fall out of bed. Nausea spiked in his gut, and he groaned. He would never drink again. Never, ever again.

---

*M*errick woke with a start at the sound of the door clicking shut, before the bed dipped to his side. "Shush." A finger pressed over his lips and a slight figure to his side straddled his hips.

He mumbled, the words foreign and chaotic. Was this a dream? A lithe figure straddled his legs and the intoxicating fragrance of roses filled his senses.

Isolde...

"Is this a dream?" He smiled, unable to open his eyes. For

some absurd reason his lids were like stone and wouldn't cooperate. It meant only one thing—this was a dream, and a very good one by the feel of it.

He clasped Isolde's slender hips, reveling in the feel of her form so close to his. The juncture between her legs rubbed against his cock, and he hardened with need. For months, he'd wanted to sample every morsel that made up his betrothed. To taste her sweet flesh, to give and receive pleasure.

"We're not married yet." He laughed, the loud sound making his head spin faster.

She laughed, a husky sound that was full of need, a temptress in his bed. The sound was odd, not Isolde's usual laugh, and he opened his eyes only to see complete darkness in the room. "You should go back to your room—" This is only a dream. No one can harm anyone with such a dream.

She cut off his words with a demanding kiss, a kiss that left him in no doubt where this rendezvous would end. Her tongue swirled with his, and he lost all thought of being gentle, of taking his time, of savoring the moment. Her fingers tangled in his hair, holding him to her and taking everything he could give.

"This is the best dream, Isolde. Thank you for this gift," he said, fumbling for her shift and lifting it over her body before throwing it to the ground. He wanted to feel with his hands what temptations she had to offer him, to learn the dream version of his love as much as he'd learn her true form on the morrow.

Her ample breasts rocked against his chest, her nipples beading into hardened nubs against his palms. He leaned down, taking one into his mouth, laving at the nipple, kissing it until it peaked like a sweet meat.

Isolde moaned, and his breathing hitched. Her hips swayed in a dance of desire, rubbing against his shaft, and he gritted his teeth. Her breasts, full and heavy in his hands, were larger in this dream version of Isolde than the real-life one. He chuckled, halting a moment as nausea spiked through his gut.

"Hurry," she whispered against his ear, before taking his lobe into her mouth and biting it gently.

His body roared with need and he rolled her beneath him, hooking her long, perfect legs about his hips. "Impatient, my love?"

"Oh, yes," she moaned, her feet pushing his ass and his cock toward her core.

He growled at her begging and clenched his jaw, trying to halt the overwhelming need to push within her heat and take her. His alcohol-induced brain fought for clarity, but too many whiskeys had dissolved all clear thought. None of this is real in any case, so why did it matter?

"Isolde, you have no idea how much I've wanted you like this. The past twelve months have been the longest I've ever lived. To be so close to you, yet denied our joining, has been a never-ending torture." He took a calming breath. "I'm foxed, my love. In fact, not only can I not see you, but I feel like I could topple from this bed at any moment. Are you sure you would not like to postpone?" What am I saying? Postpone sleeping with Isolde? The alcohol had obviously impeded his mind.

"Make me yours," she purred, rubbing herself against his member, sending the blood in his veins to pound.

"Blast it." He slid into her, heedless of her gasp of pain. He desperately tried to pull his self-control together, to stop and allow her time to catch her breath, but when her hands clasped his nape, her bottom lifting a little, allowing him to deepen his stroke, there was no going back.

He breathed against her neck, placed small reverent kisses across her skin as he started the smooth glide and dance of making love to his future duchess. She was the sweetest thing he had ever held in his arms, welcoming, needy and warm, her core so tight he fought not to lose himself before bringing her to climax. But it was no use. For so long he'd wanted her in his bed, to hear her delectable sighs whispered against his ear. It was too much, and Merrick allowed the pleasure to coil through him before losing himself within her. His dream version of Isolde was magnificent, and it left him longing to sample his bride in his wakeful hours.

"I've wanted this for so long, Merrick. What a pity it wasn't my name that you moaned. But never mind, I shall have that too, eventually."

The words acted like a bucket of cold water and nausea spiked through his gut. "Isolde?" The answering chuckle was the final death knell. Leonora.

"Have you guessed yet who your dream lover is, Your Grace?"

The word no reverberated about in his brain. Merrick stumbled from the bed, his hands grappling for the chamber pot in the dark. He wretched into the container, over and over again, his mind seizing on some way to change the last moments in this room to anything but what they'd been. Oh God, he'd finished in her.

With the cuff of a nearby shirt he wiped his mouth, slumping on the floor. "How dare you."

The door to the chamber opened, spilling light throughout the room, revealing the woman on his bed. "Oh, I dare, Your Grace, and it seems my dare has paid off."

---

*I*solde sat up with a start, hearing the light knock on her door. She frowned. Who'd need to see her at this late hour? With the wedding tomorrow, she had excused herself early last night, wanting to look her best. To be all that she could be for the man she loved.

She smiled at the thought of Merrick and climbed out of bed, grabbing her shawl and wrapping it about her shoulders before opening the door. Nothing but a darkened hallway, sporadically lit with the moonlight that came through the windows that ran one length of its side. Farther along, toward Merrick's room, a candelabrum burned low on a hall stand and would soon be snuffed by its own melted wax.

She stepped into the hallway, looking about but seeing no one. Isolde pulled her shawl closer about her shoulders when a shiver ran down her spine, the chill of the night air colder than she thought it should be this time of year. Turning to go back into her room, a crackle underfoot made her look down to see a small missive folded neatly on the floor.

Her name was scrawled across it, and she picked it up, breaking the seal. Unable to read it where she was, she walked into her room and lit the candle by the coals still glowing red in the fire grate. The writing was unfamiliar, and the letter even more so.

Lady Isolde,
I'm sorry to write this letter, My Lady, but you need to know the truth of the man you're marrying. As a good Christian woman, I believe people deserve happiness, and yours would not be complete within a marriage of lies and deception. I beg you to go to the Duke of Moore's room where, unfortunately, all will be revealed. Sincerely very sorry for you.

*I*t was not signed. Isolde walked back out into the passage, and she looked toward Merrick's room at the end of the hall, the double golden doors closed with no light visible from beneath its threshold.

Her stomach twisted into knots. The truth of the man you're marrying? What did that even mean?

She stood still, debating if she should go and see if he was still awake. Show him the missive and ask why she was being warned away from him in such a way. Again, she read the note, scrunching it in her hands and wishing it to Hades. Who would write such a thing to a bride the night before her wedding? A cruel hoax that wasn't the least amusing. She trusted Merrick more than anyone. He would never hurt her.

She would not sleep at all, lest she speak to him, so Isolde walked toward his room and stopped when a door farther along the passage opened. Her father stepped out into the corridor, his brow rising when he spotted her.

"Isolde, what are you doing at the duke's bedchamber door?" He came up to her, looking at her with a mixture of mirth and censure.

She ignored his question, holding out the missive. "Father, was Merrick in good spirits when you left him tonight? He wasn't experiencing concerns over our forthcoming marriage, was he?"

He shook his head, confusion clouding his eyes before taking her note. He read it quickly. "Not at all. In fact, he was in high spirits." His words trailed off when a feminine giggle sounded from behind Merrick's door.

Isolde swallowed the dread that threatened to bring up her dinner. Surely she was hearing things. An animal outside or a servant belowstairs, but when the noise sounded again, this time followed by a groan, Isolde's dread turned to horror. She met her father's gaze and would forever wish she had not.

The duke's visage took on a murderous edge. "Isolde, go back to your room," he said more firmly than he'd ever spoken to her before. He pushed her toward her room. "Now," he finished in a voice that brooked no argument.

Isolde stood her ground. In no way was she going to leave until the truth of the situation was revealed. "I have a right to know what Merrick is about, Father." She took a shuddering breath, her heart pumping a million miles too fast. "No matter what it is. Please open the door."

Her father made some unmentionable comment that at any other time would've shocked her, but not tonight. What she was about to see might kill her. Ruin all her hopes and break her heart. Her papa turned toward the ducal chamber like a man going into battle. He grabbed the handle, swinging the door wide and giving them the perfect view of Merrick's bed. Or at least the perfect view of the woman sitting up in Merrick's bed. Naked and hair mussed from bed sport.

The blood drained from her face, and the room spun. She stood, mute, shocked to her very core, as Letty smiled her way, triumph written across her every feature.

"Ah, Isolde, I see you received my note," Leonora said, smirking.

Isolde had once thought her friend pretty, but not anymore. Tonight she was the ugliest creature on earth. She had given her the note so she would walk in and witness them together? What friend did such a thing?

The door handle was cool, and Isolde held onto it like a lifeline as her attention refused to shift from the two people who had ruined all her dreams. Her best friend since childhood and the man she loved had made love, enjoyed each other like a married couple.

It cannot be true... This is a nightmare...

Her gaze blurred, and her stomach lurched. Isolde raced to a nearby potted plant and heaved up everything she'd consumed at dinner. The smell of earth filled her senses, and for a moment she thought she would faint. But the sound of her father's voice, a ducal roar that was scathing, startled her from succumbing to the malady.

"Get out of that bed...now!" her father demanded, going about the room and lighting every candle he could find. Never had such disgust resonated from her nonchalant parent.

Not Merrick. Please not him.

Her betrothed scrambled to his feet beside the nightstand, his chest as bare as Letty's and heaving just as fast. Merrick held up a hand. "I'm sorry. I... I don't know what's happened here."

The lump in Isolde's throat threatened to choke her, and the pain that tore through her would surely maim. Tears ran freely, and she wiped at them without a handkerchief. "Why?"

"Oh, my darling, Isolde. I'm sorry." He looked toward the bed, stepping quickly to its side and wrenching the sheets up to cover Letty. "Let me explain. Please," he said, swaying and grasping the post of the bed to stabilize himself.

Was he drunk? Did he think to buy himself out of this mess by claiming to be in his cups? How could he be so cruel? Isolde moved to stand beside her father.

"I don't understand it myself," Merrick said, meeting her gaze.

"Pray, tell me, Moore, what the hell you think you're doing compromising your future wife's closest friend?" Her father spat the words, his face mottled in anger. "Explain yourself, boy, before I take you outside and put a bullet through your cold black heart."

Merrick rubbed his hands through the hair on the back of his head, his face as pale as a moonlit night. "I…"

"I will not ask again," her father said, his patience clearly running out.

Merrick shook his head. "What I have done is unforgivable. My only excuse, as feeble as it will be, is that I thought Miss Hart was Isolde. I thought it a dream."

"Clearly not," Isolde whispered. Merrick took a step toward her, and her father stepped between them. She was glad of it. At the moment, Isolde did not wish Merrick to touch her, to come within a foot of her. How dare he treat her with so little respect? Had they not been caught, would he still have married her on the morrow with not a whisper of him ruining her friend the night before?

"Isolde, you must believe me. I didn't know it was Miss Hart. I would never do this to you."

He strode toward a chest of drawers and quickly pulled on a clean pair of breeches. Unmoved, she noted his hand shook as he fumbled with the buttons, but nothing he said or did could change what she'd seen this night. What this meant for them. He pulled on a shirt that had been absently discarded over a chair, ruffling his hair to further disarray.

Yet, if they kept what had happened here tonight between those present, marriage was still a possibility. No one ever need find out and, in time, Isolde would one day forgive him his mistake.

"I love you, Isolde. Please give me a chance to explain." A kaleidoscope of horror went around in her mind. Her betrothed had slept with another, and on the night before their wedding. A slap across her cheek would've been less painful. She wiped her nose with the back of her hand, failing to care how inappropriate the action was for a woman of her station. The room was claustrophobic and had an odd smell to it, like sweat and something else she'd never experienced before.

She strode to the window and pulled up the sash, breathing deep the crisp night air. Although it didn't take away the wrenching pain that threatened to consume her, it did provide some clarity to her mind.

"How long?" she asked at length, turning to face the two people who had once been her world.

Merrick's gaze darted between her and her father before he answered. "Just this night, but Isolde, I didn't—"

"Since the night you met at Cranleigh," Leonora interrupted, shrugging. "It was very wrong of us, but we couldn't allow our last night together to go without sampling the pleasures we've found in each other's arms. I'm in love with Merrick, as he is with me. We're very sorry, Isolde, but it is what it is. You must move on from this." She paused, smiling sweetly. "I do hope we can still be friends."

"How dare you, Miss Hart, that is utterly untrue," Merrick said. "She lies, for reasons that are unfathomable to me." Merrick glared at Letty. "If you have any sense at all, any heart, you'll speak the truth of the situation instead of spewing these vile falsehoods."

Isolde shut her mouth with a snap, not expecting so much honesty. Yes, she wanted the truth, but brutal truth with a hint of conceit was beyond her limits at this moment. She took a calming breath. She would not be sick all over the Aubusson rug. *How will I survive this?*

She straightened her spine and fought to pull herself together. She was a duke's daughter, a woman of independent means, with sound moral character. Never had she done anything scandalous. All her life she had done what she was told, had acted properly in every circumstance, although she'd never been taught about one like this. She would not crumble before the two people she'd trusted most in the world. The two people who'd betrayed her in the worst way imaginable.

They'd had enough triumph over her this eve. They would not get any more. "Were we ever friends, Letty?" she asked, reverting to the childhood name she had always used for her. "A friend would not do something so deplorable." Her lifeless voice was void of emotion, and she hated them for making her sound dead.

"For a time I think we were, Isolde." Leonora met Merrick's gaze. "The game is up. Isolde knows our dirty little secret. It would be best if we all accept our fates and resume life as normally as we can." Letty crossed her arms over her chest, nodding for good measure.

Never had Isolde experienced the vile, unpleasant emotion she believed to be hate coiling through her. But she did now. She hated Letty or Miss Hart, as she would forever term her.

"You will release my daughter from the marriage contracts and henceforth she is no longer betrothed to you. Do you understand, Your Grace?" her father said, his voice quivering in anger.

Isolde calmed the panic that warred within her at the thought of losing Merrick. "Father, maybe we should allow Moore to explain fully what happened here. Everyone is assembled for the wedding. We cannot just walk away now."

Her father was unmoved. "You will renounce any claim on my daughter and free her from this union," her father said, taking her arm. "I will have my lawyer deal with the legalities forthwith."

"You will marry me tomorrow, Isolde. Your father cannot set me free from a union I want as much as you. I love you. Please..."

His dismissing of the situation as a mere misunderstanding that could be thrown out along with yesterday's coals, poked her temper. She shrugged free of her father's grip and marched over to Merrick.

He lifted his chin, but his eyes were wild with fear. "Marry you without an ounce of explanation?" she said, fighting the tears that threatened. "If you cannot explain away this betrayal to my satisfaction, from this day forward, should we meet in a ballroom, or see each other in London, you will turn about and leave, walk in the opposite direction. You will be dead to me, Merrick. For my love of you will be dead."

For I am dead… The words whispered through her mind and again, the image of Merrick's tortured visage blurred before her. She swiped at her cheeks, hating the fact she was crying before two people who had no care for her, in any way.

"Miss Hart tricked me, made me believe it was you who came to my room. I couldn't see. I didn't kno–"

She hit him. The crack of the slap echoed loudly in the room, and remorse swamped her the moment she'd done so. Never in her life had she hit anyone. Damn them both to hell for making her someone she was not.

Merrick didn't say a word. He just looked at her, his eyes brimming with tears. "Please. I can't live without you. You're my everything."

"I am nothing to you." She shook her head, despair rippling through her like a tremor. "Trickery? Being foxed? That is your excuse? How could you do this to me?"

Merrick shook his head, no words forthwith. Isolde turned to Miss Hart, a woman whom she'd considered as close as a sister. "And you," she seethed. "We've supported you in Society, given you friendship, considered you a member of our family, and this is how you repay that debt?"

"I didn't know I owed you anything," Miss Hart said, raising her brow.

"You did not, but loyalty doesn't cost anything. I would never have done this to you."

"I love Merrick, and now that your betrothal is at an end and I am well and truly ruined, I will marry him. I, Miss Hart, a vicar's daughter, will be the next Duchess of Moore."

"The hell you will be." Merrick's fist clenched at his side, and Isolde feared that he would strike Miss Hart, but after taking a deep breath, he seemed to acquire some semblance of control. "I will never marry you, Leonora."

"You will marry Miss Hart, and it'll take place tomorrow. You can deal with any legalities when you return to London." Her father turned a disgusted look at Miss Hart. "Get out of that damn bed and get dressed before I remove you myself. Have some respect for yourself and others."

Miss Hart quickly did as he bid, not bothering to hide her nakedness from those in the room. Isolde's cheeks burned. When had her friend become so crude? When had she stepped away from all that was good and proper, to become this vile cheating woman who'd do anything to get what she wanted?

A duchess's coronet.

Her friend over the past months had been acting odd. It all fell into place now. What Leonora had said was true. Merrick had been sleeping with her friend for some time, declaring sweet love to Isolde, while making it with someone else. Any wonder she'd often caught her friend glaring at her, looking mulish whenever she was in Merrick's company. Miss Hart was jealous, and rightfully so, it would seem.

Merrick paled, looking to her father. "I cannot marry Miss Hart. I love Isolde."

The unmasked dread in his voice was surprising. Either the cheat was a brilliant actor, or at least some part of him cared for her a little. As a friend perhaps, as it was obvious he did not desire her enough to ruin her. They'd been betrothed for a year. And there were times when they'd been alone. He could've had her if he wished, and she wouldn't have stopped him had he tried.

But he had not.

"You will marry me, Merrick, and I wish for Isolde and her family to stay and watch."

"I would rather die than stay and see you marry the duke."

The comforting presence of her mother came up beside her, taking her arm. "We will be leaving at dawn. You may marry the Duke of Moore tomorrow or next week, but we shall take no part in it," her mother said, her voice stern.

"You will," Miss Hart said, lifting her chin in defiance. "Or I shall tell everyone that the Duke of Penworth has been taking advantage of me for years. Touched me inappropriately as a child and passed me about to all his friends as a toy. I will say that when Merrick heard of this little arrangement, he wanted to partake in it as well."

"How dare you." Isolde's father blanched, his eyes wild with anger. "We have given you everything you desired when your own father was unable to. How dare you slander us with such little regard to what your words could do to a family who has loved and cared for you."

"Pfft," Miss Hart said, her visage one of disdain. "If my story will win me the Duke of Moore as my husband, I will have no regrets. But I am the daughter of a respected vicar, even if he's poor. People shall believe me, not all, but most, and it will be enough to ruin both your households."

"To hell with my reputation and what costs this would have to my name. I will not marry you, Miss Hart. I loathe you."

"You will, Moore, because if you do not, your denial of me will hurt Isolde, and you'd never wish that now, would you." Miss Hart smirked, meeting each of them with a level stare.

Isolde wanted to believe Merrick, but she could not deny what her own eyes had seen. "I wish you both very happy," she choked out, trying to take a calming breath.

"Isolde…" Merrick's voice trailed off as her mother pulled her toward the door. The passage beckoned like a savior; anything would be better than the room they now found themselves in. A room she'd once longed to see now made her wish she could burn it to the ground.

"You know what you mean to me." Merrick's voice broke on a sob, and Isolde paused at the threshold.

The image of them both naked left her physically ill, but so too did Leonora's words. Who to believe? Merrick seemed genuinely upset, but Leonora may have tired of being a secret, playing to the Duke's rules, and had forced Merrick's hand. Had he been playing her a fool, too? Or did Leonora trick them both? Nothing made sense, and all of it was cruel. Heartbreakingly so. She had trusted them. Never did she believe either capable of inflicting such pain. But they had, and now she didn't know what to do. How could he have done this to me?

"Isolde, please don't…please don't leave me. I love you."

Her father followed them to the door. "You, Miss Hart, have proven yourself tonight to be the worst kind of person. You have no qualms in bringing people down whose only fault has been to love you. We shall attend your farce of a wedding tomorrow to the Duke of Moore, because I shall never let anything hinder my children's prospects or allow lies, such as you sported tonight, to tarnish my family's impeccable reputation." The duke turned to Moore, shaking his head a little. "You, Moore, shall marry Miss Hart without any fuss, if only to make some small amends to the woman who loved you and witnessed that love thrown in her face as something worthless and dispensable. After the ceremony tomorrow, we shall take our leave and never have anything to do with one another again."

"Take Isolde back to her room. I shall fetch a maid to make up a tisane to help her sleep."

Her mother nodded, and Isolde did as her parents bid. The solid wooden door of her room loomed before her, and with it came a little relief. Isolde sat before the hearth, only a flicker of warmth coming from the blackened coals. The embers slowly died, and so too did her heart.

Tears streamed down her cheeks, and it was only when her mother patted her face with a handkerchief did she realize how much she was crying. "Mama, what am I going to do?"

"Shush, darling. Do not tax yourself any further. All will be well, although not tonight, not tomorrow, or even six months from now, but one day you'll be yourself again. I promise you."

Thinking of Merrick, she started to cry, great gasping sobs that hurt her chest and made it hard to breathe. "I've lost him. And I love him still." Her voice broke at the realization.

Her mother shushed her, pulling her into an embrace. "I know, darling. I know you do. But there is nothing for it now. You will have to return with us to Dunsleigh."

Isolde thought of all she had lost, not just Merrick, but her future, their plans. Their trip away to the Continent, Paris, Rome, and all the delightful places in between that they were going to visit, crumbled in her chest like her heart. "He's really going to marry her, isn't he?" Even saying such a thing sounded absurd, and yet it was the truth. The truth as she would know it from tonight onward.

"Yes, he is." Her mother's face was a mask of concern and pain. "I'm so sorry, darling. You did not deserve this."

Isolde strove to calm down before her sobs woke her

sisters and they started with their meddling questions. Her body hiccupped for breath; her eyes, so swollen and sore, hurt when she blinked.

"Come, you must sleep." Her mother helped her stand, and Isolde didn't fight her decree. Tiredness would succeed over her mind and, for a sweet moment, she'd forget what had transpired this night. It was enough to make her lie down and try.

She settled under the blankets. The maid knocked on the door and her mother ushered her into the room, taking possession of the glass of whisky and a cold compress. Isolde downed the drink in one gulp, grateful for the burning amber liquid and the cooling cloth against her eyes.

The tears started afresh when the comforting embrace of her mother wrapped around her, pulling her close and holding her as if to never let her go. Not since she was a child had her mother acted in such a way, and some of the despair left her, knowing she had the support of her family. She would need them in the months to come.

She took a shuddering breath. How could a night once filled with so much excitement and anticipation twist into such despair and horror? Rolling onto her side, the ring Merrick had given her pressed into her cheek.

She held out her hand and looked at the cluster of five round diamonds, each of them encased in a bed of silver and sitting on a band of gold that was etched into a leaflike pattern. The ring had been Merrick's grandmother's, and it had been the most beautiful gift Isolde had ever received.

But no longer. Now it represented a fractured circle of trust, pulled apart and unfixable.

She yanked it off, unable to throw it no matter how much she longed to. She reached over and placed it on the cabinet beside her bed, looking at it as it twinkled prettily under the candlelight. The ring and its beauty were as fickle as its owner.

"I'm not going back to Dunsleigh, Mama."

"But darling, I think this is the best option for you, considering the circumstances." Her mother rubbed her back.

"I'm going to stay at Avonmore. I cannot remain here and watch their union while being looked upon with pity." At least in Scotland she could escape members of her Society and their false sympathy. And seeing Merrick married would surely bring her to her knees. Of that she was sure.

"I will talk to your father about it and, although I cannot promise, I will try to give you your wish."

Isolde sighed in relief. "Thank you. That is all I ask." She closed her eyes and tried to clear her mind of her whirling thoughts—horrible thoughts of Merrick and her friend in a compromising position. Of the sounds that had greeted her upon approaching his room.

She swallowed the bile that threatened and prayed she had the strength to get through this pain. And yet, how could life go on when your soul mate married someone else?

It cannot.

*errick stood at the altar before the priest, Isolde's brother at his side, no longer acting as a witness, a close friend in support and joy, but a sober reminder of a future that was no longer in his control.

He loosened his cravat, his body uncomfortably warm in the small church. The guests who had arrived for his and Isolde's wedding were all gathered behind him, and yet none of them were aware of what was about to transpire.

Instead of the long-awaited wedding uniting two great

families, now he was about to marry a woman he'd never looked at in anything other than friendship. It didn't bother him that Miss Hart was only a vicar's daughter. If he'd loved her, he would've married whomever he chose. But to marry anyone other than Isolde, the woman who held his beating organ in the palm of her hand, was the veriest of torture.

Isolde's brother mumbled something unintelligible beside him, but it wasn't hard to decipher. Isolde's family was upholding the threat that Miss Hart had dispensed on them all. To think that in only a few short hours his life would become something he'd never thought possible. It was unfathomable. No matter how much in his cups he had been, this whole situation was his fault.

How had I not known...?

A woman started playing the piano, and he turned to watch as Miss Hart glided toward him, the triumph on her face not slipping as the startled gasps of the gathered guests exploded in the small church. She walked proudly toward him, in a gown of the lightest blue silk, her chin high.

This cannot be my reality.

He sought out Isolde and met her gaze. The pain he read on her sweet face tore him in two, and he wanted to go to her, comfort her, and assure her what he'd done was a mistake. A trick played on them both by someone they had trusted. But he could not. The threat hanging over Isolde would ruin her family. Merrick did not care for his own reputation as the Duke of Moore, which could be rebuilt. But he would protect Isolde's with his life, even after this farce.

He noted her eyes were red-rimmed and a little swollen, no doubt from copious tears. He fisted his hands, his own vision blurring, hating himself for the cad he'd been. What had possessed him to drink so much? He turned back around and faced the priest. In fact, thinking over his night with the Duke of Penworth, he'd not drunk that much, and yet he'd been extremely dizzy and tired... Had Leonora put something in his drink he did not know of?

Miss Hart came beside him and placed her hand upon his arm. The priest's lips thinned in disdain before commencing the service. The man had been displeased when woken early this morning and notified of the change and what was expected of him with accompanying funds to sweeten the agreement. Merrick's stomach roiled.

He would have his lawyers look into the legalities of this marriage once he returned to London, but for the moment, it kept Miss Hart from ruining them all and allowed Isolde to leave with some morsel of respect to start her life again.

Without him...

His stomach heaved at the thought, and he shut his eyes, breathing deep, lest he vomit on the altar. A selfish part of him never wanted to see Isolde again, for to see her marry another—as he was doing—would kill him stone dead. The thought of some other man kissing her sweet lips, of touching her in any way, drove him to the point of madness.

The priest cleared his throat, and Merrick realized he'd been asked a question. Taking pity on him, the priest repeated the words, and Merrick answered, feeling Miss Hart beside him relax a little.

The remainder of the ceremony quickly followed, and he was glad of it. The sooner this travesty was over, the sooner he could try to forge some semblance of normalcy to his life.

Although, when he looked down at Miss Hart, reading the triumph in her cold gaze, normalcy would not be in the cards for him from this day forward. Not after her escapades of the night before, which had shown what she was capable of. The loathing was unsurmountable. Never would he be able to treat her with respect such as he should. They would be husband and wife, but in name only. He would not forgive her this treachery or his own stupidity.

"I now pronounce you man and wife," the priest said, smiling a little to buffer what the words meant to Merrick.

He turned to the congregation, not able to look at Isolde, and with a strength he'd not thought he possessed, walked his new wife down the aisle and outside. There were no claps of congratulations. No smiles or happy tears. Just shocked visages of those who'd witnessed something that they had not had the time to process. Merrick understood the feeling well, for he, too, could not believe what had transpired.

Nor would he ever.

CHAPTER 3

Five years later—Avonmore, Scotland

Isolde sat on a large tree stump overlooking Loch Lochy and clasped the latest letter from her family. Today marked the five-year anniversary of living in Scotland. Could it have really been that long since she'd left Dunsleigh for Avonmore after what had happened with Merrick? She pushed the thought of him aside and broke the seal, wanting to hear what everyone had been up to the past month.

Avonmore Estate loomed behind her and gave her comfort, but it wasn't filled with the sounds of her family, of her sisters bickering, or of discussions over the latest on- dit or a risqué new gown design from France. Her home here was quiet and peaceful, but lonely. Situated on the loch's shore, Avonmore was a medieval dwelling, made up of large dark gray stone that looked imposing on the green landscape and yet indoors, it was anything but hostile; it was beautiful, comfortable, a home fit for a duke.

Since her arrival, she'd made amendments to its gardens that had softened the home's harsh exterior, making it less daunting and more appealing to the eye. Her father, God rest his soul, had bestowed it upon her in his will, and she would be forever grateful for the gift. She looked over the loch, marveling at the beauty of the highland country. She would never leave. Scotland was her home now, and she was content. Well…almost.

She looked back to her letter, the latest from her mother, and continued to read. It seemed her brother was coming to visit. She smiled at the thought of her little brother, now the Duke of Penworth. A strutting peacock always came to mind when she thought of him, grand and full of airs over his stature. Bless his heart, she could only laugh at some of the antics he got up to.

He was always such fun when he came to see her, and a tremor of excitement raced through her veins at the thought of someone to talk to. Elizabeth was happy and settled and lived not far from here, only a two days' carriage ride. Isolde often contemplated going to visit her sister, who also called Scotland home, but with a young son and expecting their second child any moment, she didn't wish to impose on them too much.

The sound of crunching stone beneath boots snapped her attention behind her. She folded the letter and tucked it into her pocket just as her friend Anne, the Countess of Kinruth, came from behind a large bush. Isolde waved in welcome and stood, meeting her along the graveled path.

"Good afternoon, Anne. I didn't expect to see you so soon, what with you preparing to leave for London." Isolde noted her friend's bright eyes and reddened cheeks and wondered what had her in such a hullaballoo.

Anne beamed at her. "Oh, Isolde, I'm so happy, in fact I could boast to being the happiest woman on earth, I'm sure."

Isolde laughed at her friend's excited natter. "Then don't leave me in suspense. What has happened?"

"I'm going to have a baby. Clayton and I are pregnant." Momentarily shocked and not without a pang of jealousy, Isolde nevertheless clasped her friend in a fierce hug. Knowing of Anne's struggles to have a baby, she prayed for the child to be a boy to continue the family name, but as long as it was healthy and the mother came through the ordeal well, what did it matter?

"I'm so happy for you, dearest. Oh, I'm beyond excited for you both." She pulled Anne down to sit on a nearby stone bench. "Clayton must be so pleased."

"He's very happy. And with us traveling to London, this news has come at a good time."

"Do you think you will be back here for the birth or will you stay in Town for your confinement?"

Isolde desperately wanted her to return, but Avonmore, like Anne's estate, was some distance from Society, from everything, really. It would be safer if they remained in Town until after the birth. It was wholly selfish on Isolde's behalf to wish for her friend to have the babe here, and she chastised herself for even considering it. All that was paramount was Anne's wellbeing, not her own loneliness.

"I will stay in London at our family home, Kingston House. It is probably best and safest for all concerned, to be near a doctor." Anne paused in thought and then grasped Isolde's hand in excitement.

"You must come to Town for the Season, Isolde. I demand it of you. You're more than welcome to stay with us in London, if you do not wish to stay at your own family's residence." Anne's eyes widened in enthusiasm. "Please say you will come. I'll not be showing for some months yet. There will be plenty of time to turn a few gentlemen's attention toward you before I'm locked away to miss all the fun."

Isolde laughed, gesturing for Anne to walk along the stony loch's shore. "I'm sorry, dearest, but I cannot. I find London not to my taste these days." Nor the idea of seeing Merrick again, happily married and flaunting his great escape from her before all of Society. She shook the depressing thought aside, hating herself for still being affected by such a deception. "But you must promise to bring back your little babe so I can spoil him or her rotten. And know that I will miss you both dreadfully while you're away."

"And us you, my dear." Anne rubbed a hand over her still-flat belly. "Are we on for dinner tomorrow night? It'll be our last before we leave."

"Of course, and now we can make it a celebratory affair," Isolde said. "But please ensure your cook does not serve any Scottish delicacy. As much as I love Clayton and his Scottish ancestry, I do not wish to eat boiled pig gut."

Anne nodded. "I concur."

Isolde watched her friend as she chattered about the latest on-dit going about Edinburgh, and what fashions were the most popular in London this Season. An overwhelming sense of longing consumed her. Had she married Merrick, she too could've had a child by now and been a mother, just as she'd always wished.

She sighed. Perhaps she had paid her penance for being young, naïve, and blind, and it was time she moved on with her life. Allow a gentleman to court her, fuss about her skirts, and propose marriage in a darkened garden, as so many of them did.

Maybe it was time to let go of the past. There was nothing stopping her from traveling to London to enjoy the Season. Only her own reluctance to see her former fiancé, and surely she shouldn't allow that to prevent her. She'd never been a coward, so to act one now was maddening. It would be easy enough to write her brother and tell him to postpone his travels…

"Anne, I think I'll change my mind and come with you to London," she said, making a decision on the spot. "I haven't seen my family for so long, and with you gone from here, there will be nothing for me to do."

Her friend clasped her arm, hugging her. "Oh, how wonderful! We'll go to all the balls and parties and have the most enjoyable time one can have. It'll be grand."

"And you won't mind if I stay at my family's home in Town? I should probably see them as much as possible before I return to Avonmore."

"I understand, of course. We shall still see each other as much as we do now." They continued along the shore until they came across the small path that led back to the house. "I'll be glad of the company, as Clayton will no doubt make the most of being back in Society and spend much of his time at his club."

"He's devoted to you, Anne. I doubt very much you'll see any less of him than you do now."

Anne smiled sheepishly. "I suppose you're right." She laughed. "Now, you must organize yourself immediately, as there's no time to lose. We'll be leaving the day after tomorrow."

Isolde nodded, deciding to limit what gowns she took and instead purchase a new wardrobe upon arrival in London. "I'll have my maid start on it right away." She paused. "And you're sure Clayton won't mind me accompanying you about Town."

"Never! Clayton will be overjoyed you're coming, truly. He's forever boasting his neighbor is the Lady Isolde Worthingham."

Isolde snorted. "Yes, your friend the lady spinster of Scotland. What's not to boast about?"

Anne's eyes went wide at her words. "The title of lady spinster of Scotland will soon be forgotten. With your lovely ebony locks and dark emerald eyes, you're too beautiful. The ton will eat you up like a sweetmeat."

"Set the ton ablaze? Now that would be worth traveling all those tedious miles to accomplish." And if Merrick happens to see the flames, then so be it...

Anne all but bounced beside her. "La! The day after tomorrow cannot come soon enough."

Excitement thrummed through Isolde's veins. It was time. This diversion was just what she needed. After Leonora's horrible trick had resulted in Merrick jilting her, she'd locked herself away in Scotland, hoping Society would let her be, and for the most part they had. But even Isolde had to concede that over the past few months she'd been finding it awfully hard to remain at Avonmore, no matter how much she loved the estate.

She longed for company, to see her family, and to socialize. She hadn't even had a debut like so many of her friends had. After meeting Merrick at a country dance, they had been betrothed within months of that night, and a coming-out hadn't been necessary. But it was time to face her past, return to town, and possibly find a husband for herself.

"I think now that I've decided to go, I agree with you." The thoughts of balls, of parties, and friends she hadn't seen in an age, were something to look forward to, and she hadn't had anything to look forward to in a very long time. And London was big enough that her and Merrick's paths may never cross, since married men tended to stay in the country.

Or ignore his presence as best as she could if he was gracing Society this year.

*T*he miles to London were tedious and long. By the time the fields had given way to wooden cottages and then the stately stone homes of London, even Isolde's excitement at seeing her family had waned.

Thoughts of getting out of the jarring vehicle were all that occupied her mind, no matter how much Anne's enthusiasm hadn't diminished since the moment they'd set off. Her friend's mind was on nothing else except what fun they would have, how many parties they would attend, and who they would see. Not to mention, all the baby preparations she was to begin once she made Town and commenced the shopping on Bond Street.

The smells of London, of coal mixed with the polluted waters of the Thames, soon accompanied them in the carriage, removing any hint of the fresh country air they were used to. The stench of rubbish in the streets rose, and Isolde frowned as she watched children play and search through the putrid piles, hating that people had to live in such squalor. She turned, looking at Clayton asleep on Anne's shoulder, smiling at the fact he could sleep with her constant conversation buzzing in his ear.

As they entered central London, the streets became tree-lined thoroughfares. Children and nannies played in parks amongst the grass verges, and families of the highest echelon went about their business, whatever it may be.

Isolde relaxed into the leather squabs, looking forward to being back amongst Society. For all her talk that she hadn't missed what had once been her second home, and as much as she loved Avonmore, she had to admit she'd missed London terribly. This sojourn back to Town was just what she needed.

She shut her eyes, remembering the night before her wedding to Merrick, the what-ifs and how her life could have been so different had he not broken her heart. She, too, could've had children playing at the parks they now passed, be one of the parents teaching her children to ride a horse and converse appropriately with others.

Even after all this time, how could it hurt so much? Isolde tried to push the pain from her mind as it loomed with its dark clouds and thunderous memories that always left her forlorn and angry. In truth, she hardly remembered what had been said; only images remained in her mind—damaging and hurtful—even though she fought every day to erase them, they remained as vivid as a painting on canvas.

And it was not something she ever wanted to see again. That Merrick had slept with someone else was not her fault. A woman of eighteen, she'd been naïve and blind to his true nature, to a man's fickle cock. But no longer. Now, she was a woman of three and twenty, past hurts left where they should be—in the past—and a future that loomed as bright as the whitewashed buildings surrounding them.

The carriage rocked to a halt, and Isolde smiled, excitement that she would soon see her family replacing her melancholy. Not a few feet from her were her sisters, her mama, and brother, all waiting for her arrival. Anticipation thrummed through her veins. Yes, coming home was the best choice she'd made in a very long time.

Clayton woke with a start as the door was pulled open by a waiting footman.

"It seems you are home, Lady Isolde." The Earl of Kinruth jumped onto the cobbled sidewalk and held out his hand to help her step down.

The house in Hanover Square was a large home built in the Georgian style. Double-fronted doors with a lion clasping the knocker between its steel jaws had greeted the family for as long as she remembered. Isolde looked up and smiled at the Worthingham coat of arms that was carved into the stone wall.

Home...

She turned and smiled at her friend, who remained in the carriage. "Thank you again for bringing me to Town. I'll call tomorrow, and we'll make plans."

"It was entirely our pleasure. We love having you with us," Anne said, smiling.

The front door flew open, and a gaggle of screams and laughter sounded. A lump formed in her throat at hearing her family after such a long absence. Isolde was pulled into fierce hugs from her mother and her sisters, barring Elizabeth, who had remained in Scotland.

"You're here! Oh, my dearest child. Come, come inside and tell us all your news. We've missed you so dreadfully." Her mama clasped her arm, holding her tight.

Isolde turned back to Anne and the bemused Earl of Kinruth and quickly introduced her family to her northern neighbors, before taking her leave and going inside. The house hadn't changed; the same servants greeted her, and the same portraits hung where they'd always hung. Nothing had changed except her.

Older and wiser were good things to be, she mused. Well, wiser at least. She didn't want to be too old just yet. There was a Season to be had and possibly the finding of a husband. She allowed her family to pull her into the parlor where catching-up and gossip reigned supreme, and time held no sway.

---

*T*wo days later, refreshed from their journey, Isolde and Anne, accompanied by Lord Kinruth, decided on an afternoon ride in the park. Over the past five years,

Isolde had taken up the sport, for Scotland held little else for women to do, other than shoot or fish. All of which she'd become quite fond of and accomplished at.

Hyde Park was bustling with carriages. Gentlemen and ladies strolled the graveled drives and grassy meadows. The day was warm, but not hot enough to make the emerald green riding gown she wore uncomfortable. The delightful little hat that sat sloped on her head gave her an air of mystery. Anne loved it, too, and yesterday had demanded that they not leave the milliner without it. Of course, Isolde could not disappoint her friend.

Through the clearing, Isolde could see Rotten Row, and an urge to go faster than the leisurely stroll assailed her. "Anne, I think I may go for a run on the Row. Would you mind?"

Anne shook her head. "You'll cause a scandal, Isolde. Ladies don't gallop."

Isolde grinned. "Perhaps I'll start a new trend."

Her friend laughed. "Perhaps you will." She paused. "We'll come with you and wait beside the track. We can continue on toward the Broad Walk when you're finished."

"Thank you." Isolde turned her mount toward the track and noted the moment her mare anticipated a run. She'd missed Pace, her beautiful sixteen-hand mare, and riding her again was another delightful homecoming.

The Row was somewhat deserted, a surprise since the park seemed quite busy with the mingling ton. Some distance ahead, two riders raced down the straight. She walked Pace while waiting for their private war of speed to end.

To the side, she could see a father teaching his young son how to sit comfortably in his saddle. She chuckled when she noted how the father led by example. A London dandy came to mind as she watched the man sit proud in his saddle, a superior lift to his chin.

She looked away, but not before catching sight of his profile, outlined in the afternoon sun, and something about the gentleman seemed familiar. Isolde narrowed her eyes, trying to better see him at this distance, but to no avail. She shook the thought aside, supposing it could be one of her brother's friends whom he'd brought up to Avonmore during one of his trips. Although she couldn't remember any of them being married or having a child.

Her mare pranced, digging at the ground with her front hoof, her patience running out. She patted her mount's long neck. "All right, girl, let's give you a run, shall we?" Isolde sat low in her seat and gave the horse free rein, pushing her into a gallop within seconds.

Pace did not disappoint, strong and fast, and one of her father's prized possessions, her mare was always a satisfying ride. She coaxed the horse on, gaining speed and laughing as her hair came down about her shoulders, pooling against her back. But, just as she'd hoped, her perfect little hat didn't move. It had been a fine purchase, after all.

The Row was soon eaten up, and she smiled at the two gentlemen who watched her with awe-inspired features. Both the gentlemen nodded in appreciation when she turned to trot back toward Anne and Clayton.

Isolde laughed, patting the horse once again, promising to do this as much as possible before the Season came to an end. How freeing to have the wind in my hair and speed beneath my feet. And handsome gentlemen smiling at me with appreciative glances.

London is just what I need. Distraction and life.

---

*M*errick looked over his shoulder and toward Rotten Row at the pounding of an approaching horse. His gaze took in the powerful lines of the animal and the small feminine rider atop it.

"Now, William, look at the lady riding that mare." Merrick pointed toward the track. "Even sitting sidesaddle, see how she is leaning low over the horse's neck when the horse is galloping." He looked away from the enchanting sight and caught his son's eye. "Not that I think you're ready for such speed, but it doesn't hurt to see how it is done correctly."

"I like my horse, Papa. Can we trot?"

He smiled, reaching over and tweaking his little boy's button nose. His wife thought him mad to teach their son to ride at only four years of age, but had his own father not taken the time to teach him, he wouldn't be the competent rider he was today. "Very well."

"Trot, Papa. I want to go fast."

Merrick laughed. "Are you holding on tight?"

His son nodded, wiggling down in his seat. "Can we show Mother when we go home? I want to show her."

"We'll go to her directly, and she will see how accomplished a rider you are." Not that he imagined Leonora would care to see such a feat from her son. In fact, over the past four years, Merrick had deduced Leonora saw Will as more of a hindrance than the sweet little boy he was. There was no room in her life for children or their hobbies.

William nodded, his eyes bright with excitement at showing his mother. "Thank you, Papa. Thank you."

Merrick smiled, hiding his unease that it would be a chore to get Leonora to come look. Hating to disappoint the lad, he would do everything in his power to ensure the outing took place, if not today, at least soon.

The sound of a woman's voice, cooing to her mount as she walked past, made Merrick turn in his saddle. His eyes widened, and he swallowed upon recognizing her. He'd not seen Isolde since her quick trip to Town two years earlier, just before her sister Elizabeth's elopement with the Earl of Muir. He'd dreamed of hearing her sweet, lilting voice again.

If only one more time.

She looked in his direction, and he realized the moment she recognized him. Like a curtain being pulled across a sunny window, so too did her face shutter to reveal no emotion at all. How he hated himself for hurting her that, even now, five years after his marriage, she loathed him still. Believed him capable of such faithlessness.

"Wonderful ride, Isolde. If only I could join you," a dark-haired woman said, walking up to Isolde, a gentleman close by her side. Merrick nodded at the gentleman, having known Lord Kinruth since Cambridge.

"Moore," the viscount said, waving and walking his horse over to him. They shook hands. "It has been too long, my friend. How are you these days?"

"Very well, and yourself?" Unease coiled through Merrick's blood at the horrified shock written across Isolde's visage at seeing him again. He couldn't blame her. The memory of that dreadful night filled him still with disgust and loathing. Years may have passed since then, but it was still as fresh in his memory as if it had happened only yesterday. Isolde's less-than-pleased countenance at seeing him could only mean that it was a painful wound for her as well.

"Let me introduce you to my wife." The viscount gestured to the dark-haired woman accompanying them. "This is Anne, Lady Kinruth, and our good friend, Lady Isolde Worthingham."

Isolde shifted in her saddle, her face paling. "We are acquainted." Her words hardly audible.

"You are?" The viscount beamed. "Oh, jolly. How wonderful that we all know one another. We shall not have to be so formal. Pray tell us, how do you know each other?"

"Well, as to that," Merrick stammered, unable to think of any further words.

"The duke and I have known each other for some years. He married a former friend of mine, Leonora Hart. Her father was the vicar at Dunsleigh, our estate."

Merrick met Isolde's gaze, and shame washed through him.

Isolde cast a glance at his son, and Merrick took the opportunity to introduce them to him, selfishly wanting to keep her close by for a little while longer. "This is my son, William, the Marquess of Olson and future Duke of Moore." Isolde's knuckles turned white about the reins, and her mount shook its head in protest.

"Your son? How happy you and the duchess must be." Ice dripped from her words, and the chill of them struck the center of his heart. but she turned to look at William, and her face softened, reminding him of how she used to look at him. "It's very nice to meet you, my lord."

Merrick cleared his throat, not sure words were possible. Never had he met a truer lady. After all that had passed between them, that she spoke to his son without censure or repulsion doubled his respect for her. His gaze took in every exquisite detail. The green riding attire revealed a figure he had dreamed about for nigh on six years. Even riding sidesaddle, he could see the long length to her legs, remembering that when she was in his arms, her mouth came up to the base of his chin.

She and I fit together so perfectly.

All the suppressed desire and love rose within him at seeing her again, and he cleared his throat. He turned to Will and made the appropriate introductions.

His son bowed slightly in his seat. "It's a pleasure to meet you all."

The resounding chuckle from Isolde made his heart ache. "The pleasure is all ours, my lord." Isolde adjusted her seat but didn't meet Merrick's eye. "I see you're out riding, too. Are you having lessons?"

"I am," his son replied. "Papa is teaching me."

She smiled, and it was as if the sun had come out. For so long he'd lived in darkness with Will being the only beacon of light. Not that he deserved happiness, after what he'd done to Isolde. It was only fitting that he was the laughingstock of London. The only duke in the realm who had a wife who enjoyed everyone else's company but his own. Not that he cared. From the moment he'd married Leonora, he'd not been able to stomach the lying wench. "I thought it was time he learned to ride in the capital. Today is his first time with his pony in the city."

"When the time comes, that is our thought as well. We must teach our children how to go about correctly and safely while in London," Lord Kinruth said, smiling at his wife.

Isolde's horse stomped an impatient hoof to be gone. "Yes, I agree. All children should have lessons."

He nodded, smiling as his son trotted down the row with his groom by his side, his little chin lifting in self-pride. How Merrick loved him. Loved him more than he ever thought he would, considering who his mother was. From the time the little swaddled child had been handed to him, moments after the birth, Merrick knew nothing would ever part him from the little soul, not even his mother, who at the time had demanded the figure-ruining monster be removed from her suite.

"He's lovely, Your Grace," the countess said, her smile warm.

"Thank you." Merrick didn't often hear praise for his boy,

all due to the lad's vulgar mother and her antics about town. There was only so much his name could protect, and even some things were too large of a scandal to hide. He looked back at his boy who was now kicking his mount, trying to make it go faster. The little pony's legs, however, refused to go faster than a trot. "And I fear it won't be long before he's demanding a horse instead of a pony."

"Watch me. Watch me. Watch me."

The earl laughed. "Of course, Lord William. You have our full attention."

"Thank you for taking an interest," Merrick said, swallowing hard. "It's usually only me who takes the time to teach him such things, and he never gets to show off his learning to others."

"We're in town for some months, and I'm always up for a ride in the park or a drink at Whites, Moore. Do not be a stranger to us," Lord Kinruth said.

"I would like that." And oddly it was true. Since his marriage to Leonora there were few whose company he kept. The ton still invited him to their events where he laughed and drank, as if nothing was amiss—he was a duke, after all— yet there were always the whispers that he'd broken the trust of one of their own. He'd been the worst of men, toward a daughter of a duke, no less. He would never be forgiven, and certainly the ton would never forget.

"Where is Her Grace, Moore? At home? Looking after the rest of your offspring?" Isolde asked, her face a mask of undivided attention.

Lord Kinruth and Anne looked on with interest.

Isolde met his gaze, and again he was struck by the innocent question. "Her Grace is busy about Town and doesn't ride very often. She is at home."

Isolde's brow rose. "She used to like riding quite a lot. I'm sorry to hear she no longer does."

Merrick frowned, unsure if what Isolde was saying coincided with her feelings. He could not read her at all. Not as he used to. He gnashed his teeth. "How long are you in Town, Lady Isolde?"

"For the Season only. I've come down from Scotland."

"You were in Scotland this whole time? I thought you may be—" She sent him a warning glance, and he stopped his line of questioning. "Where in Scotland were you staying?" Her lips thinned in distaste at his continual questioning.

"At Avonmore, my family's Highland home. Father bequeathed it to me in his will."

"Ah yes. I know of it." The benign talk was enough to make him go insane. Damn it to hell, he wanted her to look at him with something besides hurt and betrayal. What he wouldn't give to change their past, to make it just as they had planned. What he wouldn't give to have her forgiveness. "Well, as much as I've loved our little reunion, we must be on our way. Good day to you, Your Grace."

Merrick watched her canter away, Lord Kinruth and his wife bidding him a hasty good-bye before turning to follow Isolde. Her leaving him yet again reminded him of the day her family had bundled her into the carriage and driven away, taking his heart with the equipage.

"Damn it all to hell," he mumbled.

His son gasped. "Daddy, you said a naughty word."

He sighed, having been so focused on Isolde he'd not heard his son ride up beside him. "I apologize. That was very bad of me. Now, let's see if we can get this pony to step into a canter without you kicking the poor beast to death."

CHAPTER 4

*I*solde took a deep calming breath as she rode away from the man who was now her past, but had once been her future. The sight of him again, his fierce dark eyes that gave little away, taunted her emotions. His perfectly straight nose, strong jaw, and chiseled cheeks that showed his aristocratic breeding to perfection were not something she'd thought to see so soon. The disastrous final night they had spent together under the same roof bombarded her mind, and she fought to control her constitution.

Their time had passed. Best that she place him within that box as well.

Anne and Lord Kinruth bid good-bye to Merrick but then stopped quickly to converse with another gentleman before joining her. She could see that they'd not known the history between her and Merrick and probably wanted to hear more.

Anne trotted up to her, her eyes bright with wonder. "I must admit, dearest, I did not realize you and His Grace were so closely connected."

"I am heartily delighted you know His Grace so well. We

shall be a very merry party this season, once the duchess joins us, of course," Lord Kinruth said, looking pleased by the turn of events.

Isolde composed herself enough to answer. "It has been years since I've seen the Duke of Moore and his duchess. I think it would be best if we go on as before and not force a friendship that neither of us wish for."

Anne nodded. "If that is what you wish, dear, of course we shall not meddle." Anne looked back at the gentleman from whom they'd just parted. "Now you must let me tell you whom we just ran into. A gentleman acquaintance of ours. Blake Marlborough, Marquess of Wardoor. He's back from the continent, as he has a home in Paris. He's here for the Season."

Isolde ignored her friend's shrewd gaze. She had decided to come back to London to try to find a husband. A man who she could trust and have children with. It was only right that her closest friend would try to matchmake. "I know Lord Wardoor. I met him a few years ago at a country dance. I'll be glad to see him again, but not today." She fiddled with her reins, not wanting to remember what a good friend Wardoor was to Merrick and that it was, in fact, Wardoor who'd introduced them. "I hope you don't mind, but I must be off home. I promised Mama a good catch-up today before the Season goes into full swing and we won't have enough time to breathe, nevertheless gossip."

"I understand your wish to spend time with your mama. If you wouldn't mind, may I send our groom to accompany you? Clayton has promised me a little longer ride today, since it's to be my last, and I'd hate to have to cut it short."

Isolde smiled, happy that her friends would soon be a family. "I don't mind, and I thank you." She paused as his lordship beckoned the groom over to them. "Will you be attending Viscount Chudley's soiree tomorrow night?" she asked.

"Yes, we will."

"I shall see you there then." Isolde rode toward the gates that led onto Park Lane. The slow trot toward home calmed her nerves. However, seeing Merrick again had taken all the enjoyment out of her day. Now, she wanted nothing more than solitude in the quiet of her room, where she could think. Why could Merrick not have stayed in the country like other married men were wont to do? Once, he used to enjoy the country more than the city. Isolde sighed; she would just have to resign herself to the fact that this Season they would be in each other's social sphere and would need to make the best of that bad situation.

Her ruse that her mama wanted to see her was just that, a ruse. Although, upon arriving home, her need for peace was short-lived when her younger sister, Alice, knocked loudly on her bedchamber door before throwing it open and storming inside.

"Mama said you borrowed her pearl and gold necklace. I wish to have it threaded through my hair tomorrow night. I think it'll make my light curls more vibrant. What do you think?" Alice frowned. "Is something the matter, Isolde? You're very pale."

Isolde sat up and leaned against the backboard of her bed. "I saw Moore." Her heart hurt at the mention of his name. Damn it. "His son looks like him."

Alice's shoulders slumped, and she came to sit next to her, kicking off her slippers and getting under the blankets also. How she loved her sisters and their ability to push aside whatever they were doing to comfort those in need. Alice was no different, and probably the most caring of all her siblings. Not just for them, but for the general populace, too.

"Where did you see him?"

"In Hyde Park. He was giving his son, William, a riding lesson. He's a father." She paused. "Did you know that?"

Alice took her hand, clasping it tight. "I know it must be hard to see him with a child he adores. And William is such a dear boy. Too bad about his mother." Her sister paused. "We didn't tell you about Miss Hart's pregnancy because we thought it would only hurt you more."

The knowledge did hurt. If Isolde could remove her heart and throw it away she would, if only to never feel the constant pain of separation she endured every day she was away from Merrick. "You should have told me, although I can understand why none of you did." She sighed, thinking about Merrick and all the pain his name wrought on her body. "And be sure not to speak so basely of Her Grace; it'll not win you any favors in the ton."

"I shall say whatever I wish about the duchess," Alice said, catching her eye. "Miss Hart, Letty, your best friend, is not the woman you once knew, or any of us thought we knew. She's the talk of the ton, and probably the demimonde as well. I have no doubt Merrick doesn't know half of what his wife gets up to. And I can't help but think that's a good thing."

"He's not Merrick to us anymore. You must call him His Grace or Moore."

Alice played with the bedding, pulling at a loose thread. "I have an array of words I'd like to call him, and none of them are those." She sighed. "Just before Elizabeth was married, we spotted him about Town. Whenever he'd see us at parties or musicales, he always looked to see which of us were present. We could not help but think he was looking for you. I believe he still loves you."

Isolde bit her lip, unable to imagine such a thing. He had broken her heart, and for her to move on, she needed it to heal, become complete once more. "Although I believe

Merrick may harbor some regret in the way his marriage came about, I believe he is happy. He has a son, an heir whom he seems to adore. The duke and duchess obviously love each other enough to sleep together to create a child."

"His Grace, you mean?" Alice grinned.

Isolde rolled her eyes. "Yes, His Grace." Although he would always be Merrick to her, not a lofty title or a man who wielded power and influence. Just a man who'd captured her heart and then crushed it in the palm of his hand.

"And don't be fooled that they have a sexual relationship. They do not. William is the child created from the night of your intended wedding. I've had it from my maid, who's friends with one of Her Grace's maids, that they do not share a room, nor are ever together. Leonora has a lover, you know."

Isolde met Alice's gaze, shocked to hear such a tale. "How do you know such things? And I'm not even going to ask how you know about sexual relationships. Have you been reading books from the library again that are not for you?"

Her sister shrugged. "Those books are most interesting. And I'm telling you only what is common knowledge. In fact, they're hardly ever seen on amicable terms about Town. I know, just from my own observations, that they look less than pleased when out together at balls and parties." Alice frowned, thinking for a moment. "The duke and duchess often appear as if they've eaten something sour and wish to spit it out."

"You shouldn't gossip." Isolde jumped out of the bed, walking to the window and looking over the back gardens of their London home, watched the gardener cut pink roses and place them in a basket. Merrick was unhappy in his marriage? It was not something she'd ever wondered about. They were married now, with a child, and no matter what the rumors about Town were, it didn't change the fact that he'd married another and had carried on with his life. Not like Isolde; she had placed herself firmly on the shelf, content to stay there to repine for all time.

"I think it's time that I married and got on with my life. I've spent enough hours mourning the loss of the duke. More than he deserved."

"What!" Alice was beside her in a moment. "What has brought this on? I just assumed that you would never marry."

Despite herself, Isolde laughed. "I've decided to find a husband this Season. I want a child of my own, a family that's all mine. I'll no longer let myself rot in the wilds of Scotland, pining for a life that never came to be. I think," she said, swallowing the lump in her throat, "that I'm a little lonely."

Alice dragged her into a tight hug. "You're never alone, as we're always here for you. And you don't know how glad I am to hear this news. You're too beautiful, inside and out, not to be loved and adored. Any gentleman would be mad not to fall in love with you. And you're the kindest of us all. In fact, I should strive to be more like you."

Isolde didn't feel very kind or charitable at the moment, and the sister Alice described had withered away under jealousy and despondent emotions that served no one. She no longer resembled the carefree, happy woman she'd once been. All thanks to Leonora's perfidy that had ruined all her hopes. How she wished her life had, in fact, played out just as she and Merrick had wished—she would be happily married and even possibly a mother right at this moment.

Alice clasped her hand. "I declare, before the end of the Season, that we'll find someone most suitable and handsome for you to marry. A gentleman who'll adore and care for you like you've never known before."

"I'm not concerned about his features, so long as he's kind and secure. Not someone who'll say one thing while doing something else." She read the understanding in her sister's eyes and shrugged. "I want to be happy and content, not necessarily in love." Love was for fools and an emotion that caused only heartbreak when given to the wrong man.

"We want you to be happy, too." Alice studied the gardens for a moment, a contemplative look on her face. "With His Grace in Town, do you think you'll be well enough to withstand his presence? I know it must be difficult."

A knot formed in her stomach at the thought of seeing Merrick at most of the events they were to attend. The same sphere of friends suddenly seemed very small and select. "I will have to bear it as best I can. Our first meeting is over, and we're unlikely to be friends, but I shall not cause a scene, if that is what you're worried about." She grinned, although inside she wanted to scream at the top of her lungs at the unfairness of it all. "I will try to limit our interactions as much as possible."

"Do you still feel hurt by his marriage?"

Isolde sighed, not wanting to declare just what a severing to her soul he'd administered. How much they'd both hurt her. "I think back to how we had been and what happened that night, and it just doesn't make sense to me. I trusted him, wholeheartedly, and he broke that trust in the worst way imaginable. Watching him marry Miss Hart almost killed me. The day before, we'd been celebrating our forthcoming nuptials, and the next day I witnessed him marrying someone else." How could she put into voice that each word Merrick and Leonora had spoken in front of the priest had been like a stab through her heart? To see someone else promise herself to the man who'd made up all that she'd ever wished for had been a slow, painful death. It was what nightmares were made of.

Alice pulled her into another embrace, and she went willingly to her sister's comforting welcome. "I'm so sorry, Isolde. You did not deserve what they did to you."

"I know you are, and so am I. The mistakes we made that night are not only Merrick's. I must admit, I should have listened to him, believed him over Leonora. Father, too, for that matter. Had we, maybe my life would be far different than it is now."

"Did His Grace try to explain?"

She sighed, furious at herself for not listening, as she should have. "He did, but I was of half an ear and not thinking clearly. Papa and Josh weren't interested in his excuses, and Merrick was forced to marry Leonora. But I have wondered how I could've dismissed him so, not believed him over Leonora when he had been, in fact, my best friend. The man I loved and trusted beyond anyone. I was not fair, and I sometimes think that the hell we live is because I could not swallow my pride or tell my father to keep his at bay. I lost him. I allowed him to marry someone else."

Isolde sat before the unlit hearth, a chill running through her veins. "He stated he did not know it was Miss Hart who snuck into his room, said that she'd tricked him."

"And if she did," Alice said, joining her, "I would certainly not put it past Miss Hart. She was always jealous of you."

"Father refused me leave to speak to Merrick alone to get to the bottom of what happened. I think, should he have convinced me of his innocence, I would've run away to make him my husband. But that is not how it played out, and so we must move on and live as our lives dictate."

"That is very sad, Isolde and I'm sorry for you."

Isolde smiled, rallying her spirits. "Don't be, for I'm determined to make this Season fun and perhaps end with a happily-ever-after of my own."

Alice sat on a chair across from her, grinning. "I'm going to make it my Season's duty to ensure that's exactly what will occur. Now." Alice stood, walking to Isolde's armoire. "We need to find you the most scandalous, delectable gown you own for tomorrow night's soiree. Heads shall turn. I'll not have it any other way."

Isolde laughed, excitement thrumming through her veins. "Perhaps the red silk net gown with the embroidered chenille thread? It looks beautiful on."

Alice lifted out the gown and nodded enthusiastically. "Yes, this will do nicely. And perhaps Mama will loan you her rose garnets?"

"She's already said she would." Isolde grinned.

"La! What a shame the soiree isn't tonight. Tomorrow seems too many hours away."

Isolde smiled at her younger sister but didn't reply. Tomorrow night was soon enough, and hopefully, the scandal of her broken engagement was something that the ton had long forgotten.

CHAPTER 5

*T*he following evening, as her maid applied the last pins to her hair that was swept up in an abundance of curls with a string of garnets woven throughout, Isolde looked at what she would present to the ton.

The transparent red silk net gown sat perfectly over the ivory dress beneath, and her skin looked flawless. The cut was a little risqué for an unmarried woman, but she was no blushing debutante. Some considered her a woman practically on the shelf.

The tight corset pushed up her breasts but Isolde decided against using a fichu. She wasn't doing anything wrong by what she wore. What if some of the older matrons looked at her with disapproval? Never again would she hide from their censure. From tonight forward, she would hold her head high and let them talk, should they be shallow enough to gossip over something as trivial as a dress.

She grinned, nodding at her reflection. "I think I'm ready." Surely she could catch a husband while in Town. If her own merits as a duke's daughter were not warrant enough, perhaps her ample dowry would sway the reserved fellows. Barring that, her breasts really did show to advantage in this dress.

The ride to Viscount Chudley's was short due to its close proximity to their home. Carriages lined the road and waited for passengers to disembark for their first of many outings this night. By the time Isolde had reached the ballroom doors, the room was filled to its capacity.

They made their addresses to their host and hostess before slowly progressing into the throng. She recognized scores of acquaintances and paused to speak with many of them. It had been so long since she'd experienced Society, the rush of delight at seeing so many people only reaffirmed that her choice to return to town was the right one.

Her sisters stood sedately beside her, yet their faces were animated and glowing with expectation. She spotted Lord Kinruth waltzing with Anne and smiled when her dear friend waved across the floor.

"Your friend Lady Kinruth seems an affable woman." Isolde nodded in agreement. "She has such a sweet temperament. I do adore her."

"So does Lord Kinruth, it seems," Alice said, watching the pair and smiling.

Isolde couldn't agree more. She turned to study her younger sisters, their modest jewelry, their gowns—the height of fashion—were beautiful but plain, not that either one needed accessories to heighten their beauty. Both would have suitors coming from every corner of the ball.

"Mama, are there any suitors who I must meet and form an opinion of? Only the best for my siblings." Alice laughed at Isolde's words, but Victoria, annoyed at being at a ball and not a hunt out in the middle of the country, merely turned up her nose in distaste.

"Very much so, but the poor dear fellows are too scared to do anything about it. To court a duke's daughter takes courage, especially a Worthingham who has a protective brother."

Isolde nodded, understanding only too well how Josh could be toward his own sex, especially when it came to his sisters. And they loved him all the more for it. "In any case, that's not good enough. It is one thing for me to be on the shelf, but I cannot allow Alice or Victoria to suffer the same fate." Across the room, she spotted a gaggle of young debutantes surrounded by a bevy of beaus. "Alice and Victoria, go mingle and be merry. Perhaps if you're not standing beside Mother and me, someone will ask you to dance."

Her mother grinned, and, with a tinge of jealousy, Isolde watched her sisters move off toward their friends. How nice it would be to have no other cares but to fall in love and be loved. Not trying to forget a pain that, despite her valiant efforts, would not release her heart.

Isolde sighed. Have I made the right choice in coming back to Society? The possibility of seeing Merrick at every event maddened her, yet exhilarated her as well. And it should not. He deserved no mulling over whatsoever.

For all her talk of marriage, even if one of convenience only, it was another thing to go through with it. To say the vows that would bind her to another forever was not something to take lightly. Merrick had been the only man she'd ever loved. Adored, if she was being honest. How could she sleep with another, trust someone enough to give him her hand, after just one Season?

"What is the matter, dear? Please tell me."

Isolde turned to her mama and took her arm, hugging it to her side. "Nothing, Mama, truly. All will end well. You'll see."

"Isolde, look at me."

At her parent's steely tone, Isolde met her gaze.

"You must move on. I know we've never spoken of the

night before your wedding, but there is nothing for you there now. His Grace is married with a child, no matter how they came to be in such a situation. It is what it is."

That was certainly the truth, but it still didn't make it any easier. "I know it's over. But I thought coming back to London would be easy. Yet I'm surrounded by my friends, all of whom are now married and have children of their own, while I'm standing beside my mother at a ball, still looking like some desperate debutante." Her insecurities raised their pointy daggers. She felt sorry for herself. She hated that. It was not who she wanted to be. A vibrant, outgoing woman who turned heads was who she wanted to be. Not a woman others pitied.

"No daughter of a duke is ever desperate."

At her mama's words, she laughed, loving that her mother always spoke straight to the point. "No, I suppose you're right."

"I am, dearest, and I think it's time you started to enjoy what a little age will allow. Enjoy this Season. Take risks. Not scandalous risks, mind, but see where you end up. You may surprise even yourself."

Tears pooled in her eyes. She had not realized her mother had seen the struggles she faced. As one of the oldest girls, she'd always been the sister who set an example, on her best behavior, with impeccable manners at all times.

She'd failed them, and her years in Scotland hadn't helped her siblings in the least. "Do you really mean that?"

"I mean everything I say." Her mother threw her a pointed stare before turning back to the throng. "I see your sisters are about to partake in a quadrille."

Isolde turned to watch and was so amused by the dancers she didn't notice the couple who came up beside them.

"Oh, it is. It really is her."

At the high-pitched squeal, a chill sliced down her spine.

It was a very familiar voice that Isolde had fought hard to forget. She turned, shocked to find Merrick and his duchess, who all but hung off his shoulder like a cloak, staring at her. "Your Grace," Isolde said, nodding in welcome.

"My darling told me you were back in town, but I simply couldn't believe it until I saw you for myself. Oh, how lovely. How I have missed you." Although Leonora looked happy enough, her eyes were cold and devoid of any emotion other than annoyance.

Isolde's mama stepped forward, putting herself a little in front of her. "Your social calendar has kept you active, Your Grace. I doubt very much you've thought of my daughter at all, being so busy thinking only of yourself these past five years."

Isolde's eyes widened at her mama's cutting words before warmth bloomed in her heart. Her family was a core of strength for which she'd be forever grateful.

Leonora ignored her mother's words and pulled Isolde into a most unwelcome embrace. Heat rose on Isolde's cheeks, and she pushed the duchess away without causing a scene. "It has been a long time, Your Grace."

Not long enough.

Triumph glistened in Leonora's eyes, and Isolde's narrowed. "I'm all the better for seeing you again, my dearest friend. How we've missed not seeing you about London. To not have you a part of our life has been like losing a limb. And we have a son now. William is his name. He's the dearest little boy and will be a wonderful duke one day."

How had Isolde never noticed how false Leonora was? Without heart or feelings, she must be. Anyone with half a brain would realize that this little reunion was not easy for Isolde, and yet here Leonora was, pushing herself onto Isolde, as if they were still the best of friends. The woman was mad.

"You were always such a good friend to me and His Grace. Please tell us what is new with you."

Isolde kept her opinion from spilling out on what she thought of her friendship with Leonora. Her mother's words, "live a little," spiked a pinch of feistiness into her soul, and she pulled her emotions into check. "I hope you've not been pining for me all these years, for I certainly have not been pining for you. I've enjoyed my time away from this world." Isolde bit out the lie with a smile, not willing to let either of them see how much they'd hurt her.

"Weren't you in Scotland? Dreary, cold clime if ever there was one." Her Grace ran her hand down Merrick's arm, and Isolde noted the duke cringed a little under his wife's touch.

"Yes, I was in the north, but we frequented Edinburgh and traveled a lot. I was not without distraction." What Isolde said was mostly true. She'd traveled with Anne and her husband, and had had fun with them when they'd attended balls and parties, but there'd always been the constant pain that came with being made a fool in front of all your friends.

Her gaze flicked to Merrick, and she caught him watching her, his eyes a wealth of emotions she no longer had the right to, although she'd learned to read him years ago. Isolde turned back to Her Grace and fought to keep acting the daughter of a duke, not a woman who wanted to scratch her old friend's eyes out.

"We would've visited, but we've been so busy here in Town. I simply had no time to spare you. And then we had William, and there is hardly a moment left for a social life, you understand."

"As I said, Isolde, the duchess is much occupied," her mama said, taking her arm.

"Of course," Isolde said, indifferently, "that is to be expected."

Her Grace let out a loud guffaw, clasping her chest with

drama that Isolde hadn't seen since attending the theater last. "But you don't understand, do you? A woman of your age, still unmarried and without a babe, wouldn't know the pressures of Town life and what it is like to raise a child." Leonora clasped Isolde's hand, frowning with a falseness that was worth a prize. "Oh, my dearest, how I pity you. You must be desperate to have all that I do."

Isolde's blood drained from her face. She looked around the room, sure everyone was listening to the spiteful truth of Her Grace's words. But instead of fleeing, which she longed to do, Isolde ripped her hand out of Leonora's clasp and straightened her spine. "As a woman of independent means, I'll marry when the time is right. Which I suppose is something you do not understand, as you had to marry money or you would've had none."

Her mother covered her laugh with a cough, and Isolde smiled a little. "This Season is going to be so much fun, for me at least." Isolde refused to meet Merrick's gaze, which seared her skin. Love may never again be a point she'd look for in a marriage, but trust was paramount. All she required was a pleasant, stable gentleman who'd give her a future and children. She did indeed long for a child of her own. It would certainly make all the past hurts disappear. And she would cherish any man who could make such a dream come true.

Leonora glared at Isolde, her mouth pulling into a thin line of anger. "Of course," Her Grace said, turning to her husband. "Alas, my husband promised me the waltz, and I do believe it is next."

Isolde watched them join in with the other couples, sighing when the dance commenced. Her mother watched them also, her visage one of distaste. "Oh my dearest, I'm so sorry you had to go through that. If I had any idea that Her Grace would seek you out, I would've tried to keep you from her. What nerve she has."

Isolde waved away her mother's concerns. "I'm quite all right, I assure you. I was bound to run into her eventually." It was done now, and she was stronger for it.

"Ah, I see your brother has arrived."

Isolde smiled at Josh as he bowed to their hostess, noted their presence, and excused himself to join them. What a dashing brother she had, in his gold waistcoat and shining Hessians. "Good evening, Your Grace," Isolde said, dipping into a deep curtsy.

He threw her a dubious look. "Josh or brother will do, if you please. I welcome such respect from other peers of the realm, but you, dear sister, need not adhere to those silly strictures of Society."

Isolde laughed. "Well, thank the good Lord for that. We would hate to stand on ceremony."

Josh looked her up and down, nodding in approval. "I say, you look very beautiful this evening. Care to accompany me on the floor? There is still time to join the waltz."

Isolde placed her hand on his arm, only too willing to dance and take her mind off another duke and his wife who occupied the same ballroom. "Thank you for being my knight in shining armor. I thought I'd have to stand by and watch everyone else dance all night."

He twirled her into position, taking her into his arms with authoritative ease. "I noticed who sought you out, and I couldn't allow them to leave such a sullen look on your face." He preened, and a few young ladies behind her sighed and tittered. "And I find dancing always improves one's countenance...among other things," he said, looking past her and no doubt at the young ladies behind, throwing them a smolder that would only increase their chatter.

"Stop it," she hissed.

"What?" His surprised, innocent visage didn't fool her in the least.

"You're flirting."

He scoffed. "Dukes do not flirt."

The dance continued, and Isolde laughed beyond measure at Josh's antics. He was trying to make her feel better, and it was working. When the dance came to an unfortunate end, he took her arm and led her toward their mother. "You do realize that we're being watched."

"We are?" Isolde looked about, and although she spotted a few members of their set watching them, it was nothing out of the ordinary. "I think you're fibbing."

"Mama told me you're looking to be married by the end of the Season. Is this true?"

Isolde nodded to an acquaintance and answered her brother, "I am."

"Don't let the spiteful words from the Duchess of Moore make you act irrationally." He sighed. "I fear Leonora's marriage is not a happy one, for either of them, and she may say some things to you that might steer you away from the marriage state. Do not listen to her, if she does. She's poison, Isolde."

Isolde caught a glimpse into the gaming room where she spied the Duke of Moore at one of the tables, his brandy glass empty, his cravat untied and sitting loose about his neck. He looks disheveled and devilishly handsome. Damn him. "I've heard similar, but I cannot feel pity for either of them. They made their choice, and now they must live with it."

Josh pulled her to a stop. "You've grown a backbone. Bravo, Sister."

"I have, and it's here to stay." Yet the thought of Merrick being unhappy in his marriage made her uneasy. They had a child, after all. And no child wanted to grow up in a home where one's parents did not respect or care for each other.

Her brother gained them both a glass of champagne,

handing her one. "I must tell you something, if only to spare you the humiliation of finding out when you're not properly prepared."

Isolde took a sip, not liking the worry etched on her brother's face. "What is it?"

His lips pursed. "Did you notice Her Grace was favoring her stomach when speaking to you?" He paused, and Isolde wondered what was so dreadful that her brother would struggle to find the words. "She's pregnant with her second child," he blurted.

Isolde's stomach knotted at the thought of Merrick making love with her once best friend. It had tormented her for years, imagining the kisses, the sweet touches that had once been only for her. She shook the thought aside, needing to forget the past and all the hurt, for if she did not, she may as well pack her trunk and go back to Scotland, never to find happiness of her own.

"How lovely for them." Suffering coated her every word. Her brother steered her toward a window seat, partly secluded with ferns. "It's not the duke's."

"What!" Isolde clamped a hand over her mouth. People turned to look at them, and she laughed as if her brother had said something amusing. The child isn't his? "How do you know this?"

"I have my sources, and I know, without doubt, it's not Moore's."

The thought of such a thing, of Leonora having a child with someone other than Merrick, was absurd. How could she do that to her husband? Especially when she'd seduced the duke right under Isolde's nose. Why would the duchess seek comfort elsewhere? "Are you certain?" she asked, unable to believe such a tale.

"I am." He nodded, a serious look on his face. "That black-guard deserves all he gets with the spiteful wench." Although

Isolde didn't like the harshness of Josh's words, she understood her brother's dislike of the couple.

"Let them be, and let us get on with our lives. I don't want to talk about them anymore."

Josh pulled her to stand, and, spying their mother, started in her direction. "You're right. Apologies, my dear. I'll not mention them again. Tonight is for enjoyment, not rehashing of past hurts."

"I heartily agree."

The night, Isolde was happy to say, passed quite pleasantly from that point on. Josh introduced her to an array of suitable gentlemen, enough to make her head swim. All of them bowed, danced attendance to her, complimented, and flirted as much as they could with her mother present.

It was most diverting, and Isolde enjoyed the night more than she thought she would. Just after supper, she stood to the side of the room, watching her mother speaking to Josh and a young woman Isolde hadn't seen before. She was a sweet, delicate little thing, yet her determined intelligent gaze spoke more than any words could. The girl had her sights on her brother, a duke, and no other gentleman would do. Isolde laughed when Josh came to the same conclusion. He looked like a trapped lion with its tail between its legs who wished to run away.

Taking a sip of champagne, she watched Alice expertly perform the steps of a quadrille with a handsome gentleman with dark, brooding features. Looking past her smiling sister, her gaze landed on Merrick, who was conversing with the hostess.

His body was slightly hunched to enable him to hear the short viscountess who was talking vigorously, waving her hands about with gusto. She took in the clean lines of his suit. The broad shoulders and a body that no longer belonged to a gangly youth, but to a man in his prime. He was so handsome, so attentive to the lady, that Isolde found herself smiling. How she longed to dance with him again, if only to feel the press of his body against hers. To have his large, capable hands upon her person, to make the breath in her lungs catch…

She forced herself to look away, locking away the crushing jealousy that plagued her. From the first moment she'd met Moore, so many years ago now, she'd known he was hers. He'd stolen her heart and soul that night, and she realized she'd never really received them back.

No matter how much she told herself and others that she had healed, she had not. She would have to remedy that and quickly, if she wanted to marry and move on with her life.

CHAPTER 6

*I*solde's days were filled with shopping, lunches, walks in the parks, and the occasional ride. Surprisingly, she found her friend Anne was an avid purchaser of all things pretty and expensive. The merchants on Bond Street would not forget them anytime soon. Being an admirer of shoes, Isolde fell in love with Harding, Howell & Co—an industrious store that catered to everything and any type of shoe a woman could want.

They'd almost bought out their supply of walking boots, riding footwear, and evening slippers. Her first week back in town was, in one word, delightful.

Today, Isolde spoiled herself a little by ordering a new riding ensemble and purchasing a fur coat. They finished off their shopping extravaganza in the perfumery shop where Isolde bought her custom perfume of roses.

The day out was one of the most fun and carefree Isolde could remember. And even their trip home had been amusing when they'd had to hire a hackney cab to follow their own carriage, just to fit all their parcels.

Her nights were filled with endless balls and parties.

Isolde watched as her sister Alice was courted by the flattering Marquess Clifford. It was no use. There was no spark in her sibling's gaze when she looked at the gentleman. Alice would not marry him, no matter how much he wished it.

It seemed her quiet word to her brother that he needed to allow the girls some freedom to form attachments had been heeded. It hadn't hurt that Isolde also mentioned that should he not stop being so overbearing, he'd have them all living with him in his dotage.

"Lady Isolde, may I say how utterly lovely it is to see you back in Town." The Marquess of Wardoor bent over her gloved hand, all elegant and refined. "It has been too long."

Isolde curtsied a little. "Lord Wardoor, it is good to be back and to see you as well."

He studied her a moment, smiling, and Isolde noted how changed he was since she'd seen him last. He had always been a tall man, only a year or so older than Merrick, and one of his closest confidantes, although she was no longer certain if that was still the case. His hair was cropped short and made his pronounced nose seem larger than it was.

"We've missed seeing you in Town. I do hope the rumors that are circulating are true, that you're here for the Season."

Isolde only just managed to hide the revulsion on her face that the ton were gossiping about her return, discussing her, perhaps even laughing at her inability to marry at the ripe old age of three and twenty years. "Yes, I intend to be in Town for some time, and will visit Dunsleigh before returning to Avonmore."

Lord Wardoor took a sip of his brandy, motioning a nearby footman for another. "Ah yes, I heard you were living in Scotland. I always thought it a shame that we lost such a jewel with your leaving." He threw her a consoling look, and she lifted her chin, not willing to be regarded as someone to be pitied.

"Tell me, my Lord," Isolde said, quickly changing the subject, "are you married? I'm afraid my own Town gossip is most lacking."

"Alas, no I'm not, but the Season is young." He winked, and her eyes widened before she laughed at his gumption. "And I find what I've seen so far of the Season is much to my liking. More so than any other year."

Was Lord Wardoor looking at her to fill such a position? Heat rose on her cheeks at the thought, having never looked at him in that way. "I wish you all the best with your quest." She studied him for a moment. He was handsome, even with his forthright nose, but there was no fluttering of her stomach when she looked at him. No tremble of fingers when he neared. Nothing at all. And yet, wasn't that suitable for her? She wasn't looking for love, after all. Friendship, trust, and respect were all she wanted.

"I thought Moore was lying when he told me you were back, but I'm thankful he was not. How providential that we're both looking to marry before Season's end."

Isolde almost choked on her sip of wine. "I don't believe I said I was after a husband, my Lord." She smiled to buffer the censure in her tone. Thoughts bombarded her mind as to how he'd come to such a conclusion. Had Anne or one of her sisters mentioned it in a passing conversation with their friends? Or was he just guessing her presence this year was solely to find a husband…

He grinned. Maddening man. "Ah, but we know 'tis what all ladies are searching for, and you're no different, even if you boast that you are."

"I look forward to proving you wrong." Isolde looked back to the throng and ignored the deep rumbling chuckle beside her and that she'd just blatantly lied to a gentleman's face. It was none of his concern, in any case.

"Come, my lady. I hope I have not offended you. I'm only teasing, I promise."

Isolde let him stand beside her for a little moment longer before she deigned to reply. "Perhaps you ought to make it up to me by partnering me with the next dance?"

He bent over her hand, grinning up at her. "Forward chit, are you not? Should I expect a proposal next?"

Isolde threaded her arm though his. "The dance will do just fine. Thank you, my lord." And Lord Wardoor did dance divinely, even if those elusive butterflies never eventuated.

---

*T*hree nights after Viscount Chudley's soiree, Merrick fought the coiling anger that ate at his very soul as he watched Lord Wardoor dance attendance on Isolde. What was she thinking, allowing such a libertine to court her? With age, the man had only grown worse in his escapades; the number of whores he bedded, and how much coin he lost at table every night, worsened each year.

Wardoor would never be faithful, and surely Isolde had come to that conclusion. Or perhaps she did not care.

Merrick wasn't sure which thought worried him more.

Again and again he watched as Isolde was pulled onto the dance floor by not only his closest friend, but others as well, all of the fiends clutching at her waist, ogling her breasts that her gown fought to cover. They gazed at her like some sweetmeat ready to be gobbled up.

Bastards.

He closed his eyes, no longer wanting to see such a travesty. Isolde was no longer his. He had to let her go, even if such a thought threatened to buckle his knees. His fists clenched at his side before a bitter laugh brought him out of his misery. "Oh, my dearest husband, does the sight of your

Isolde stepping out with others upset you? You look positively pathetic."

Merrick covered her hand that came to sit on his arm, a serene front they had perfected early in their marriage. The ton was never to know that their marriage was in name only, if solely to keep their place in the society which Leonora enjoyed so much. "I see jealousy is your forte tonight, my dear. How it must vex you to see your once closest friend back in Town, especially since you have no one to steal from her this time. Whatever will you do with yourself?"

Leonora laughed, clutching at his arm as if they were enjoying each other's company immensely. "La, you amuse me. I've already conquered Wardoor. Poor pathetic Isolde is no competition to me." She sighed. "Perhaps I'll take that sweet innocent Isolde and corrupt her. How fun that would be to see her become as wicked as me."

A cold hard ball knotted in Merrick's gut. The hell he would allow Leonora anywhere near Isolde, if he could help it. He caught sight of Wardoor, and his jaw clenched. Had the man really slept with his wife? It didn't matter that the marriage was a loveless one, to think his friend could do such a thing was the worst betrayal. But then, he deserved such folly. After all, it was no different to what he'd done to Isolde the night before their wedding—despite the fact that Leonora had tricked him.

Merrick flicked a glance at Leonora and frowned when he noted the sly lift to her lips. "You lie."

She shrugged, chuckling a little. "Oh, but he is a lovely specimen of a man, if not too much of a libertine, even for me."

Merrick took a sip of brandy, wondering how his life had come to this. A pointless, empty marriage that was worse than hell. Leonora may be the daughter of a vicar, but she was the spawn of the devil.

"All of London is aflutter that the elusive Lady Isolde is husband hunting." The amusement in her voice grated on his already frayed nerves. He didn't want to hear about Isolde possibly marrying another. He'd rather die than see such a day. How selfish he was. Isolde deserved happiness and companionship. He ought to hope she would marry for love, not wish that she'd become an unmarried matron of the ton. Old, alone, and sad.

"But I can understand why she would be looking. It's awful being her advanced age and still on the shelf. How mortifying." She laughed.

Merrick looked at her with loathing. "You would refuse her the smallest amount of happiness. How can you hate her so much?" And how could he deny Isolde such happiness? She deserved every pleasure after what he had put her through. But he did not look forward to living through her quest for a husband. Isolde had been everything to him, and losing her once had been bad enough. It would be nigh impossible to live through it again.

Leonora looked at him, her eyes widening at his question. "Because it amuses me to do so. Isolde was always the most loved by all our friends. So sweet, so meek, so perfect." The duchess made a repulsed face. "It made me sick to see you falling all over your Hessian boots to speak to her. I'm glad she's now so desperate for a husband she would consider even Wardoor to fill the position. It makes me happy to see her so unhappy."

Merrick cast his eye over Isolde and noted her laughing at something Wardoor had said. "She doesn't seem unhappy to me."

His wife smirked. "Oh, you're so amusing to watch. I say, I'm glad Isolde is back in Town, if only to see you mourn the loss of her all over again."

Merrick tightened his hold upon her hand, and Leonora

gasped. "Do not push me, wife, or damn the scandal, I'll divorce you quicker than you can catch a cab to the hells of London you love so much."

She paled, and her smile resembled a snarl more than anything else. "You wouldn't dare. For if you do, I'll let it be known that William isn't your son. It would ruin your heir and make you look like the biggest, most pathetic duke this country has ever seen."

"It would ruin you, too, do not forget. And William is mine, and I will meet anyone on a field of honor if they state otherwise. With the protection of my name, the children will be fine." Merrick pulled away, distancing himself from her, less he strangle the wench before the throng of guests, some of whom had taken an interest in their conversation.

Her mocking laugh this time sounded brittle even to his ears. "We will talk later dearest husband." She patted his chest and left.

"I sincerely look forward to it," Merrick absently answered, not meaning a word.

CHAPTER 7

A week later, the Worthinghams held their annual London ball. The night was everything Isolde's younger sisters abhorred and their mother adored.

Isolde watched as Alice and Victoria tried to smile and converse pleasantly with everyone who came within hearing distance of them, but the crush was exactly that, a stifling crush that intoxicated one with too many differing fragrances.

A pang of sympathy filled her as Victoria paled to a shade whiter than her silk gown. She started toward her sisters; the poor dears really loathed Society's rules and strictures—the what's-done-and-not-done before the ton. Not to mention, the gentlemen who were skulking about their skirts looked less than ideal…

She came to stand between them, took both their arms, and excused them from their set. "Come walk with me a moment." Isolde steered them in the direction she'd last seen their mother. "What's the matter, my dears? Are you not enjoying yourselves this evening?"

Alice made an unladylike face. "I hate having to go to balls all Season long, but having to suffer at a ball of ours and be the center of attention is the worst type of agony."

Victoria nodded in agreement. "It's absurd, Isolde. Really, I would much rather be home with my horses and my dogs."

They came to stand not far from their mama and turned to watch the throng of guests. "'Tis not so bad. Surely there are some eligible gentlemen who've captured your attention. If not the ones you were standing with."

Victoria scoffed. "No, there are not. They all bore me to tears. I was almost crying, if you hadn't noticed."

"I agree," Alice said. "I wish Mama had listened to us and not made us have this dreadful evening. What I wouldn't do to be back at Dunsleigh."

"You cannot catch a husband cocooned in Surrey." Isolde knew that better than anyone, and she certainly couldn't lead by example, as she'd lost her betrothed on the very night before her wedding.

"Elizabeth took the last good gentleman of the ton when she married Henry." Alice sighed. "When do you think we'll get to visit her? I do miss her terribly."

Isolde smiled, thinking of her elder sister who was very well situated in life and in love with dearest Henry. "I'll talk with Mama. Perchance we can visit after Season's end, but on one condition."

Both Alice and Victoria's eyes brightened at the prospect. "What condition?" they asked in unison.

"That you enjoy the Season as I have set out to do.

Mama deserves more happiness such as what Elizabeth has bestowed on her. It's time we, too, played our part."

"Very well," they agreed, although their tones were less than positive.

"Excellent," Isolde said, spying Anne beckoning her from across the room. "And now I must mingle and be merry." Her sisters' laughter faded behind her as she made her way across the parquetry floor. With the rooms adjacent to the ballroom open for the gambling inclined, the crowd had dispersed a little, which made it easier to move about.

Isolde clutched Anne's hands as she came to stand before her. "I'm so glad you came tonight. I do hope you're enjoying yourself."

"Your family has a beautiful home, Isolde. We're having the most splendid time, even if I am feeling a little poorly."

"Is all well? Is the baby..." Isolde couldn't finish the question lest the reply was too upsetting to bear.

"No," Anne said quickly, understanding dawning in her gaze. "The baby is fine; I've just been sick most days. Our doctor says it's quite normal and should pass, but as yet, it has not. I may have to put a halt to outings, unless they're entertainments that I cannot live without. Clayton has promised to dance the next waltz with me, and then I shall be going home. I hope you do not mind."

"Never would we mind. You must look after your welfare above anything else." Isolde looked about the room. "Where is Lord Kinruth? I have not seen him tonight." A frown line marred Anne's forehead, and unease rippled through Isolde. "Is there something else that troubles you?" she asked.

"He wanted to catch up with an old school friend, but I'm loath to tell you who it is, for I fear it may upset you."

Isolde frowned. "If you're worried about Moore and Lord Kinruth rekindling their friendship, don't be. They went to school together. They may be friends without offending me."

"I know, but..." Anne clasped Isolde's hand tighter. "Will it not be difficult? It will mean you may be thrown in each other's paths more often. I would not want to cause you undue pain."

Isolde shook her head. "Anne, you could never do that." There was nothing to be done. Merrick was friends with Lord Kinruth, and as unfortunate as that association was, it was no one's fault. She would have to guard herself more when out with Anne, in case Merrick was with them. As it was, she struggled to tamper her emotions whenever she saw him. The way he looked at her when no one was watching left her morals conflicted in the worst imaginable way. And the best, too, if she were honest.

"I'm so sorry, dearest." Anne looked close to tears, and Isolde took her hands.

"None of this coincidence of friendship is your fault. If I'm to be a part of this Society again, I must move on and accept that His Grace and I will cross paths. It is a necessary evil."

Anne sighed, her relief evident. "I'm so happy you said so. I was worried that it would cause trouble between you and me, and I class you as the best of friends. I would hate anything to come between us."

Isolde shook her head. "Nothing could come between us." At the spoken words, a shiver ran down her spine as she remembered saying something similar to Letty, now the Duchess of Moore, many years ago. They had been the best of friends, two girls who'd shared everything: their secrets, hopes, and dreams. A pang of loss coursed through her that she'd lost her oldest friend, as well as her future husband, at their betrayal. Life was cruel at times.

The deep rumbling laugh that she knew as well as her own sounded to the side, and Isolde looked about the room, catching the gaze of Merrick as he strolled toward them with Lord Kinruth. As always, since the very first moment he'd been introduced to her, a sizzling attraction coursed between them. Isolde had hoped that after all that had passed, she would no longer feel the need to reach out and pull him to her side, touch him, laugh with him. How could something so good have gone so wrong?

She turned to greet them, and the curious gazes of the

guests who watched the play between two people once betrothed were like tiny pinpricks up her neck. She bobbed a small curtsy. "Your Grace, Lord Kinruth."

The gentlemen bowed. Isolde noted Lord Kinruth took Anne's hand and pulled her toward the floor. "You owe me a dance, my dear."

Anne laughed and followed him without question. Isolde met Moore's gaze and wondered if this situation looked as awkward as it felt. "Are you enjoying yourself, Your Grace?" His inspection of her was reminiscent of the looks he'd once bestowed upon her when she'd been his and he was hers. Those looks should be saved for his wife, yet Isolde so wished they could be hers. All day and forever.

"I am now." He took her gloved hand in his and pulled her toward the floor. He should've placed her hand on his sleeve, and yet, he kept it firmly clasped in his. She fought to release his hold without success. Damn him.

"What are you doing?" she hissed, spotting Leonora's furious glare from across the room.

"I'm about to waltz with the most beautiful woman here."

He pulled her into his arms, and she fought not to fold herself into his embrace. Familiar hands clasped her waist, strong and sure, and time fell away. All that was wrong with them, the mess that made up their past, became nothing but a nightmare of long ago. If only it was as easy as a dance to forget. Isolde looked up at Merrick, and pain pricked her heart.

"You should dance with your wife."

He threw her a self-deprecating smile. "My wife doesn't wish to dance with me, I can assure you of that. For instance," he said, turning them so she could see Leonora. "Do you see the gentleman standing beside her?"

Isolde glanced over his shoulder. "Lord Barkley. Yes, I see him." She could also see the duchess leaning so close against the gentleman that her breasts were pressed against the man's arm. It was perhaps more scandalous than His Grace dancing with his ex-betrothed.

"Let me assure you, the duchess much prefers the company of others over her husband."

Isolde met his gaze and noted the troubled look in his eyes. "That doesn't give you leave to make another wrong. You should go to her, fight for her, even. As is your duty."

He pulled her into a tight turn, the skirt of her gown brushing his breeches. They had not been this close since… Isolde pulled her thoughts away from such musings. Reminiscing of all that she'd lost did no one any good. This Season was her chance for happiness.

Moore leaned down, his breath but a whisper against her ear. "I don't want to fight for her."

Isolde turned to meet his eyes. The action placed them close enough to kiss, just a slight lean toward him and they would touch. His attention dropped to her mouth, and she licked her lips, cursing herself for doing so when his attention turned smoldering. Lifting her chin, she pulled away, giving them both much needed space. "You need to stay away from me, Merrick. I'll not have you do this to me. You made your choice, and now you must live with it."

"There was no choice in what happened." He pulled back, his eyes narrowing. "And what if I said I no longer wish to live with it. What would you say to that?"

Isolde shook her head. How dare he act like the victim in what had occurred? It had been his choice. He didn't have the right to now play her a fool just because his choice hadn't turned out as well as he'd liked. "Oh no, there was a choice, and you made it perfectly clear. I watched you take your vows. In fact," she said, anger taking hold of her good sense, "the moment I found you naked in your room with my friend in your bed, your decision was perfectly clear."

"Had your family allowed me to explain what had occurred, that day could've turned out a lot differently than it did. After all that we shared, how could you think I wanted anyone other than you?"

She looked away, noting only a few people were looking at them, which surprised and relieved her. It always seemed as if all the world's eyes were boring down on her. This conversation was far from appropriate, and it wouldn't surprise her if the whole ton were leaning in, listening to their every word.

"I think you, of all people, can understand why they didn't think you deserved the honor of explaining how my best friend ended up in your bed the night before our wedding." He paled, but Isolde was past being sorry.

"Leonora was never our friend," he said, his gaze narrowing. "And do not think, no matter what she says, that she will ever be one to you again."

"I do not care to be the duchess's friend, now or ever. This conversation is over, Merrick." Isolde pulled out of his embrace, curtsied, and smiled delightfully. The less the ton suspected, the better. "I wish you very happy."

Moore kissed her gloved hand, pinning her with his heated stare. "You may wish all you like, Isolde, but I'll never be happy so long as we're apart."

She wrenched her hand free. "Then I'm very sorry for you, because that is something that no one can change. Good night." Isolde walked away and fought to keep her knees strong lest they give out and collapse beneath her.

Unaware of where she was heading, she stood beside a window and cursed the moment Leonora sidled up next to her and clasped her arm. "Did you enjoy your dance with my delightful husband?"

Isolde was sick of being kind and acting the perfect lady. It was obvious Leonora wished a war of words, and if that was what the harlot wanted, then that was what she would get. "Very much so. He's most adept."

Leonora's eyes narrowed. "If you want a dalliance with him, I'm willing to share. We've done it before, you see, had grand parties and well, all I will say is that Merrick is most accomplished even with more than one woman in his bed."

Isolde gasped at the vulgarity of such talk. To think such things was a notion she'd never contemplated. She shook her head, unsure if Leonora was playing her a fool or trying to shock her into the vapors. "Should you be placed beside the girl I knew as a child, I would not know you now. What happened to you, Letty?"

Her Grace glared, her fingers clawing into Isolde's arm. "I was never that girl, and that girl is thankfully dead. I love my life and the scandalous way in which I live. And if you think to include yourself in Merrick's life or to even become his mistress, you're sadly mistaken. I'll crush you, should you try."

Annoyance pricked her hard in the gut, and Isolde removed Leonora's hand with a punishing squeeze of her own. "Threatened, Letty? How droll of you. And if I wished to have Merrick, I would only have to click my fingers and he'd be mine." Isolde smiled sweetly and walked away, pleased that for the first time in what seemed eons, she'd rattled her old friend and now nemesis.

CHAPTER 8

*T*he following morning, instead of going for her early ride, Isolde was to meet Anne on Bond Street. With her maid in tow, she started toward the shopping precinct, wishing a good morning to those she passed along the way. Anne had stated that today she had woken without feeling ill and wanted to purchase a new hat before the sickness returned.

The day was without fault, not a cloud in the sky or a breeze dared to mar it, and the thought of more shopping with her dearest friend made her outing even more enjoyable. Over the last few weeks, she'd become more enamored of shopping than she'd ever thought possible. To indulge oneself was freeing, and it had been a long time since she'd wanted to pamper herself and just enjoy life.

The houses that ran around her square were a marvel in beauty, with large imposing doors and windows ornate with their architectural designs. Most of the houses were shuttered asleep, their occupants unaware the day had dawned a few hours ago. A few carriages rocked to a halt before homes, their occupants more than likely returning home after a night of revelry.

Just as she was about to turn down Brook Street, she stopped as Leonora stumbled from a carriage, turning back to lean into the equipage, laughing and seemingly kissing whoever it was inside. Isolde braced herself to see Merrick step out after Her Grace, but whomever traveled with the duchess did not follow, but merely moved off. After last night, Isolde could hazard a guess as to whom the gentleman was, if not Leonora's husband. Her Grace continued to stumble up the stone steps and disappeared inside.

Isolde continued on her way before a commotion behind her made her turn. Loud voices sounded from the ducal residence and, within moments, Merrick ran down the front steps just as his carriage came barreling around the corner from his mews.

As he was giving directions to his driver, he caught sight of her staring at him. Such a faux pas would normally embarrass her to the brightest red, but the panicked fear she could read on his face gave her pause, and she hurried to his side. "Your Grace, has something happened?"

"Isolde," he said, forgetting to address her correctly. "William is gone. I stupidly allowed Leonora to take him this morning for a walk, and she's returned just now without him. You know how small he is, and he's alone, and God knows where. I don't know what I was thinking. What she was thinking!"

Isolde took his hand and noted it shook. She clasped it tighter. "Did the duchess say where she'd been?"

"She remembers going to the park in the square and then being picked up in a carriage that headed toward the east end, but from there she says her memory of the outing becomes hazy. I cannot begin to know why."

The sarcasm of his words was evident, and Isolde didn't

know what to say in return. To think of a little boy lost in that part of London wasn't worth imagining.

"I should never have trusted her."

Isolde frowned, wondering why Leonora couldn't remember, not to mention how on earth someone could forget her own child. "Did she visit anyone? Perhaps she's left him in a shop or at the markets."

"I must go and find him." He hesitated at the carriage door. "Would you help me?"

His plea was something she could not deny. She would never deny anyone in such a state of panic. "Very well." She motioned for her maid to join her before alighting into the carriage. She sank onto the leather squabs, her maid beside her, before the coachman flicked his whip and the horses started forward.

Merrick gazed out the window, his brow furrowed. "I don't know what I'll do if I can't find him. What if he's befallen some misbegotten git?"

Isolde leaned over and touched his hand. "We'll find him." She took a calming breath, her stomach roiling in fear that, should they not, what horrors could become of the sweet little boy. "Do you know of any places that Her Grace visits? I must admit, I know nothing of that part of London."

"*T*here are two places that we'll start with. After that I'm at a loss as to where he could be." The moment Isolde let go of his hand and sat back, he missed her comforting support, her concern for his child. His wife, most likely passed out on her bed, didn't care an ounce for her son. Had never cared for him, if he were being brutally honest.

The carriage rolled through London, the greater homes of Mayfair giving way to the dwellings of the less fortunate of the city. They crossed London Bridge and turned east toward the wharves. The streets in this part of town were less kept, rubbish stacked beside the road, the children, without supervision, ran about in ragged clothes that wouldn't be fit for cleaning cloths.

Isolde frowned. "This degradation of people is not right. It makes me wonder what the lords running Parliament are doing to allow people to live in such squalor."

Merrick nodded. "I suppose you include me in that decree?"

She raised her brow but didn't reply.

He sighed. "I agree. Something must be done about it, and I promise at the next sitting of Parliament I shall bring up my concerns."

Isolde nodded before she said, "How long since Her Grace took Lord William?"

The question pulled him from his thoughts. "Just over two hours. She promised to play with him in the park, and there was no stopping his excitement. It's not often that his mother takes an interest, and so he gobbles it up whenever she does."

Merrick read the question in her gaze, and he didn't want to answer it, didn't want to face what his wife had become in the five years since they'd married.

Isolde's hands fidgeted in her lap. "I still don't understand how Lord William was left behind. Had the duchess given any indication as to why it occurred?"

"There was no point in asking her much. She doesn't know of what she speaks." And had he known Leonora would've left the safety of the park and visited such a place with their child, he would never have allowed such an outing. And he would hunt down anyone who was associated with this travesty should anything happen to his boy.

Isolde made an unladylike sound, and he met her gaze.

"Stop telling me only tidbits of the story, Merrick. What is going on with Leonora?"

He cringed, wanting to hear his name on her lips, but not in a situation such as this. Damn his wife to Hades. "After we married, the duchess grew quite fond of Town life, spent most of her time here alone, while I remained in the country with William. There are certain locations she's fonder of than others in the city."

Isolde grabbed his cane and rapped on the roof. They rocked to a halt, and Isolde turned to her maid, speaking quickly to the young woman, before the woman alighted from the carriage and strode toward the hackney cab beside the curb. Isolde watched as her maid spoke to the driver and climbed up into the carriage before it started forward. Isolde shut the door with a snap and settled back into the squabs. "Now tell me the truth. All of it."

*M*errick rubbed his jaw as their own equipage moved on, wondering where he ought to start. The tale was not one he even liked to think about, nevertheless speak of. "Her Grace is addicted to laudanum and opium. Whatever one she can obtain access to, she'll partake in."

Isolde's eyes flew wide, and her silence was crushing. Shame washed over him that his wife had fallen so low. No matter what he thought of Leonora, he should never have allowed her to succumb to such depths. He should've stopped her when he first suspected her of the addiction. He was a disgrace of a husband.

"I'm so very sorry. I had no idea..."

Her apology only made him feel more wretched. "Don't be sorry, anything but that. I certainly do not need your sympathy. It's of my own doing that she's become the woman she has."

"Why do you say that?" Isolde clasped the seat as they rounded a corner faster than they ought.

"Because it's true." He ran a hand over his jaw and then realized in his haste to find William, he'd only half finished his dressing. His shirt hung open and the lapse of a cravat only made it look worse. At least he'd grabbed his jacket from the back of his desk chair before hightailing it out the door. "We've not had the marriage she hoped for. I pushed her away, and she sought entertainment and friendships elsewhere."

"You weren't to know that she would leave Lord William anywhere. For all that has passed between you and the duchess, I'm certain that there must be some other explanation for what's occurred. Leonora was never so careless."

He scoffed, knowing how mistaken Isolde was. "You would be wrong. You only have to see her to know she's not competent enough to walk straight, nevertheless look after a child. I should never have trusted her."

"If you cannot trust the mother of your child, whom can you trust?"

The carriage turned again, and they rode along the embankment for a short duration before rocking to a halt in front of an alehouse, gin-laden drunks slumped against its walls.

Merrick didn't bother waiting for his tiger, but jumped down and started toward the door to the inn, Isolde right behind him. He paused at the threshold. "You cannot come in. It's not fit for human occupancy, never mind a duke's daughter."

Isolde crossed her arms. "I'm more than capable of looking after myself."

"All the same," he said, trying to placate her, and by her

raised brows it was a battle he was losing. "I would prefer you stay here. I'm going to ask if anyone's seen William or the duchess earlier this morning." When Isolde didn't make a move to do as he asked, he did what any sensible gentleman would do—he begged. "Please, Isolde. I don't need anything to happen to you as well as my son."

At his words she sighed and stepped back. "Very well, I'll wait in the carriage, but if you're too long, I'm coming in after you."

He nodded and went into the inn. The moment he crossed the threshold a cloud of gray smoke, mixed with the sickly flowery scent, met his senses. Opium. Merrick headed for the bar and caught the eye of the barman, a burly man with arms the size of Merrick's legs. The man gave a nod of greeting and slowly made his way over to him, serving his customers as he went. The time ticked by agonizingly slow, and Merrick had the overwhelming urge to shout at the man to hurry the blasted up, but the thought of William and that this man may know what Leonora had done with him, made him hold his tongue.

"Bruce," he said finally when the man poured him a brandy and slid it across the bar.

"Your Grace, whatever have we done to have the honor of your presence?"

Merrick slid a gold coin across the bar. "Has the duchess been in earlier today? She's left my son somewhere this side of London."

The barman's eyes flared before he frowned. "Aye, she was in, but came in with that gentleman friend of hers she's always about with. Can't say I saw a boy with her, though."

"Did you happen to serve her? Maybe you heard where she'd been?"

The man grinned. "That'll cost ye another pretty coin."

Merrick handed one over without delay. "Where?"

"It's walking distance from here. You'll not get a carriage down the laneway. Turn left when ye leave here and make another left at the first opportunity to do so. A few doors down may be the premises you're looking for."

Merrick left his drink and headed toward the door, wondering if he'd ever see his son again. Down in this part of town, there were no rules. Children went missing all the time, never to be found again. He couldn't allow his son to be one of them.

"I'll keep an ear to the ground about ye boy, Your Grace."

Merrick turned, surprised by the gesture. "Thank you." He threw open the door and strode toward the carriage. He wrenched the door open to tell Isolde of his next move, only to find it empty. He slammed it shut, turning about and looking to see if he could spy her anywhere. He cursed, not seeing one dark strand of her pretty hair. He'd not thought the day could get any worse, and yet it just had.

---

*I*solde watched a steady stream of misbegotten drunkards walk farther along the docks and turn down the alley. Laughter sounded, along with the banging of a creaky wooden door. She looked down at her lavender gown and cringed. She didn't meld into the location at all and instead stuck out like the woman of wealth she was.

Reaching into the carriage, she opened the compartment beneath the seat and pulled out a plaid blanket, draping it over her head and shoulders. It masked her in some way, not a lot, but it would have to do.

She walked toward the alley, ignoring the command from the driver to stop and wait for His Grace. Standing at the corner, she noted the worn stairs that led down into a darkened street. Taking a fortifying breath, she climbed down quickly and passed door after door, some with men asleep on their thresholds, others with women and children, sitting, waiting, for what, Isolde could only imagine.

She gave some coins to the children who asked, looking about for the one boy who was lost among them. A man stumbled onto the street before her, and she stopped, watching as he turned in her direction, his eyes unfocused and red-rimmed.

"Aye, you're a pretty one. I have some coin aye, and a wall ready and willing to support ye while I have me way with ye, pretty lass."

Isolde stared, unable to speak as the drunkard's words made her stomach churn. She needed to think, and fast. "Right at this moment there is a gun being pointed at you by my companion. Don't bother to look, you're too far out of your wits to see him in the shadows," Isolde said, when he cast a look toward the alley. "But I would suggest, if you do not desire your brains to be splattered against the wall at your back, to let me pass."

The man grinned, stumbling a little. "Ah, come on now. I'll not take too long."

"Step any closer toward me and you're dead." He stopped at the steely tone of her words, his eyes narrowing in consideration.

A movement behind him caught her eye, but she didn't react. Her only defense was bluffing, and if he thought for a moment that what she said was untrue...well she didn't want to venture what that would mean for her.

The blaggard grinned. "Aww well, mayhap I'll see ye again to have me fun with ye."

Isolde glared, wishing she really did have a gun to remove such a vile creature from the earth. He walked past her and headed back the way she had come. Isolde watched him until he was out of sight, and then turned to see what had moved farther along the alley.

Almost luncheon, the sun was finally overhead, which helped in lighting the alleyway a little. But with washing hanging over her head, all the makeshift structures, and general chaos, it was still hard to see anything. A pile of rubbish beside the door that the man had exited moved again, and she peered closer, only to see a small boy huddled beneath the mess.

"William?"

He looked up with tear-stained eyes, his face marred from the grimy street. Without thought for herself, Isolde pushed the broken bits of crates, material, and food scraps away and pulled out the frightened child.

He threw himself against her, clutching desperately to her neck. "Shush, all is well. We've found you. Come, your papa is searching for you desperately."

"Mama left me." His little body shivered, and he started to sob in earnest. Isolde rubbed his back, feeling the chill of his skin through his coat. She wrapped the blanket about him as best she could and turned toward where the carriage was stationed.

"Shush darling. You're going home now." Isolde started up the stairs, coming to the top of the street just as Merrick ran down the alley.

"William!" The duke threw his arms around them both, kissing the boy's cheeks and murmuring apologies all the while.

"We should go, Your Grace," she said, when his tight grip enabled her.

The use of his title seemed to pull him from his relieved daze. He stepped back, taking William into his own arms. "I apologize, my lady. I was overcome."

Isolde smiled, turning him toward the carriage. "It's

perfectly fine, but I think we should get Lord William home and seen to by a doctor. He's awfully cold."

Merrick nodded. "You're right. Let's go."

They bundled into the carriage, their driver pulling away quickly, and it wasn't long before they were crossing London Bridge once more. The tension, the fear of having lost William, was now replaced with a simmering anger Isolde could read as clearly as a book on Merrick's face.

She looked at William and realized the little boy had fallen asleep, his head on Merrick's leg, his father's hand idly stroking the small child's hair. He looked so sweet and innocent and so much like Merrick with his dark locks that had just the slightest curl to them. The little boy wiggled a little to make himself more comfortable. A pang of jealousy shot through her that she did not have the one thing she longed for most, a baby of her own. How lucky Merrick was to have a son. At least she'd been able to help reunite them safely and without incident. A huge relief for everyone involved.

"What will you do about what happened today?" she asked, worried that Merrick looked ready to murder someone over this morning's events.

"There is not much to be done other than to keep William from any more outings with his mama." He sighed, the strain of the situation written all over him. His eyes looked haunted, dark shadows stark against his skin, his clothing even more rumpled and now dirty from holding his son who looked like a poor street child. "I'm not sure how to carry on, in all truth."

"Talk to her, Merrick. Help her. I think she may be in need of it, if what you say is true."

He looked away and back to William. "I will try, but I cannot promise any more than that. Leonora stopped listening to me years ago, if she ever did."

Isolde watched as he, too, shut his eyes. A longing to go to him, to allow him to enfold her in his arms once more near broke her resolve. He was a man with everything anyone would ever dream of: a title, money, lands and estates all over England. He was married, with a child and one on the way, but right at this moment, she pitied him and his gilded life. For all he had, there was one thing it seemed he did not. Happiness. And without that, life was no life at all.

CHAPTER 9

Over the next few days, Isolde didn't see Moore or Her Grace at any of the events she attended. She hoped Merrick was able to help the duchess in some way, make their life more congenial and, above all else, safe for William and the child who was on the way. For, after what Leonora had done to William, there was nothing anyone could say about the duchess that would sway Isolde in what she now thought of the woman—that she was of unsound mind and required help.

Tonight she was to attend Vauxhall Gardens and sample all its delights. Ever since she'd been on the crux of adulthood she'd wanted to attend a ball in the Gardens, and now, finally, she was going to. The outing was just what she needed.

Her mother had refused to allow her to go prior to her betrothal to Moore, but now, as a woman well past her first blush, and with the assurance that Lord Kinruth and Anne would chaperone her, the duchess had finally relented.

She'd purchased a crimson gown of sheer cotton mull, embroidered with heavy red cotton thread in satin stitches and French knots, and a black domino for warmth that she fully intended taking off as soon as they arrived.

When the Kinruths arrived to accompany her, she was surprised to see Lord Wardoor sitting in the open carriage, the seat beside him empty, her name all but imprinted on the red velvet cushion.

Isolde tried not to see the reoccurring theme that had sprung up between the four of them. To the ton, it looked as if Lord Wardoor was courting her, and she was agreeable to the situation, but something about the man gave her pause. He was affable enough, but from what she understood of his life, it was dissolute, at best. He was certainly a man who would have to earn her trust.

The journey was short, and soon they were turning into the park, traveling toward the Temple of Comus, which she could just make out through the trees.

"We have a pavilion that's close to the Italian Walk this evening. It should be grand, Isolde."

Lord Kinruth laughed at his wife's words, patting his stomach. "Are you trying to tell us that after the meal, we should walk off all the wonderful food and wine?"

Anne threw him an innocent glance. "Never. That's what the dancing is for."

Lord Wardoor nodded in agreement, keeping his direct gaze locked on Isolde. "I agree. Dancing tonight will be a must."

They rocked to a halt, and she smiled her thanks as Lord Kinruth helped her down. The pavilion had a long, rectangular table within it, covered in a white linen tablecloth and an array of flowers and seasonal fruit. The tableware sparkled in the candlelight and gave the small room an air of elegance not normally found outdoors.

Music punctuated the still night as other groups of revelers headed toward their own destinations for the evening. Isolde took her seat and looked about, noting that the class distinctions were quite noticeable here. The pavilions held the wealthy, the upper ten thousand of London, while the people gathering around the orchestra, waiting for the dancing to commence, their gowns less ornate, their hair without adornments, were of the lower class. And some, by their antics, their cloying of the opposite sex, plied their trade each night within the pleasure gardens of Vauxhall.

At least the location was suitably named.

A liveried footman poured her champagne and she took a sip, seeing that not all the chairs were occupied within their little room. "Are there more guests to arrive?" The question died on her lips when Moore and Her Grace, accompanied by another couple Isolde didn't recognize, joined them. She fought not to wince at Lord Barkley, who stumbled into their dinner with reddened eyes and a disheveled cravat, taking a seat beside the duchess, as if by right.

Lord Wardoor leaned toward her. "Don't let Lord Barkley alarm you, my dear. He's drunk, to be sure, but you're among friends. No reason to pale. Your skin is fair enough already."

"The northern climes are a more accurate assumption on my skin tone, my lord." Isolde smiled and bid the new arrivals welcome while listening to Anne rattle on about the festivities she had planned for the night.

Isolde fought not to fidget as the intense gaze of Moore bore down on her from across the table. Taking a sip of champagne, her cheeks burned as she caught him staring. He was all casual elegance, leaning back against his chair without a care in the world, but beneath the facade was a man who was in no way shy of hiding what he was obviously thinking. His gaze flicked to her lips, and she inwardly swore. What on earth did he think he was doing! Was he as foxed as Lord Barkley?

She took another sip of champagne, hoping the fruity

drink would cool her discomfort. It did not. The Duchess of Moore barked out a loud laugh, and Isolde jumped, almost spilling the contents of her drink down her gown. And soundly inappropriate, Her Grace leaned over, pulled Moore toward her, and kissed him on the lips.

Lord Wardoor coughed, meeting her eyes quickly. Her friend Anne was less circumspect and gaped at the duchess with absolute shock.

Isolde took in Lord Barkley's reaction to such an open display of affection and read nothing but amusement in the gentleman's visage. For a man who was supposedly having an affair with the duchess, she would've thought the opposite reaction more likely.

That the pair were possibly making fun of Moore, showing him the fool they believed him to be, irked. Merrick didn't deserve such disrespect, and certainly not from his wife. All told, he was a good man, kind to his tenants and staff, and loved his child. He certainly took an interest in his offspring that many gentlemen never bothered doing. Many women had sought to capture his heart and become his duchess before he married, so why Leonora treated him thus, after she had tricked him into giving her his name, eluded Isolde. The duchess's disdain for her husband made no sense. She narrowed her eyes as Her Grace finished the kiss and turned back to face them all, grinning.

Thankfully, the first course of leek soup was placed before her, and Isolde turned her concentration to the dish, hoping the dinner would end soon and she could escape to dance. To be seated at table with two people with whom she didn't want to socialize was uncomfortable, at best.

And perhaps she was wrong in her assumption that Moore detested his wife. It was, after all, a rumor the ton had made up, due to their supposed loveless marriage. But Moore had allowed the kiss and so, perhaps, their marriage wasn't as bad as everyone thought it to be. It was possible everyone was wrong. It had been some days since the incident with William; maybe Merrick had taken her advice and was trying harder to save his marriage and help his wife through her affliction.

She stared down at the creamy green soup, and an overwhelming urge to cry consumed her. It was wrong to allow the past to hurt her still, and yet it did. After seeing the duchess these past weeks in town, Isolde concluded that Leonora was, in fact, wholly to blame for what happened on the eve of her wedding. She ate a spoonful of soup. The more she thought about it, the more it made sense. The letter she'd left, her amusement at being caught, and Merrick's horror… How even now she liked to crow that she'd acquired Moore's hand in marriage and Isolde had not. It fueled a long simmering anger to life, and Isolde took a deep calming breath. How dare she be so cruel? So selfish? So fake?

Lord Wardoor placed his napkin on his lap, pulling her from her thoughts. "You seem to like the soup. I'm so glad. I've taken great care with the menu tonight."

Isolde met his gaze, surprised by the fact. "Have you hired this pavilion tonight, my lord? I thought Lord Kinruth had secured it for us."

"Indeed it was I. No expense spared for people I hold above everyone else." His smile left her in no doubt he was courting her in earnest. It had been so long since she'd been the object of anyone's aim that it was a little unnerving.

"Thank you for allowing me to be invited. I've never been to Vauxhall before and have always wished to go."

He picked up her hand, running his fingers along her gloved arm as he kissed it. "You're very welcome. I'd do anything for a beautiful woman," he whispered, for only her to hear.

She pulled her hand from his, looking about and hoping

no one had noticed the kiss. The glower on Moore's face, his lips pressed into a thin line, said more than words that he had witnessed it.

The duchess tittered, waving her hand to gather everyone's attention. "I must announce my deepest thanks to my dearest friend, Lady Isolde, who helped out my husband with our son the other day. That you traveled with Moore, unaccompanied, mind, was probably not the best course of action for an unmarried spinster such as yourself, but these things happen, and I'm happy you were free to assist us."

All eyes turned toward Isolde and heat suffused her cheeks. Flustered, she spoke indignantly. "I beg your pardon, Your Grace."

The duchess raised her brow innocently. "I'm sure you do beg my pardon for taking advantage of such a situation with a duke. And even though I know you were only trying to be a help to my family, and I'm grateful, truly, but I really must scold you for your impertinent actions in traveling alone with my husband in a carriage. I so wish for you to find a husband of your own, my dear. To marry before you're too old to bear children." Her Grace drank down the last of her wine, before jiggling the glass beside her head for a refill. A footman filled it immediately.

"Leonora, remember yourself," Moore whispered, glaring at his wife and taking her wine away.

"Yes, remember yourself, Your Grace," Isolde said loud enough for everyone at table to hear. "And perhaps you ought to remember why we were together in the first place. If you can."

Lord Kinruth said, "Some dancing is in order, I think."

"My most humble apologies." Moore stood, pulling the duchess up to stand also, his hand firmly about her arm. "Excuse us a moment."

Isolde watched them go, glad she hadn't disgraced herself

by speaking of why she'd been alone with the duke in the first place. But she would not allow Leonora to shame her in Society when she'd done nothing wrong. Perhaps she'd acted improperly in going with Merrick, but what else could she have done in such a situation? A child's life had been in danger. No matter the cost, she could not have stood by and refused help at such a time.

"Were you really alone with Moore?" Anne asked, sitting beside her, her brow furrowed. "Why on earth would you do such a thing? It is plainly obvious the duchess dislikes you and looks to ruin you in Society. You must think of your reputation, Isolde."

Isolde sighed, not wanting to remember the dreadful day and the cloying fear of why they'd been together in the first place. "If I tell you something, you must promise to keep it to yourself. You're not even to tell Lord Kinruth. Can you do that?"

Anne nodded. "Certainly. You know you can trust me." Anne turned to her husband and Lord Wardoor, who stood at the entrance to the box. "Darling, would you be so kind as to leave us for a moment. I wish to have a quiet chat with Isolde."

Both gentlemen bowed. "I shall return soon to claim a dance."

Anne smiled. "Thank you, dearest."

When finally alone, Isolde told Anne of how she had happened across Moore on her way to Bond Street and the reasons behind his distress. Anne sat back, clearly at a loss for words. Her friend took in the throng of dancers outside and Her Grace, who was now partaking in a reel with Lord Barkley.

"How disgraceful of her," Anne said, her tone full of censure.

"Very much so, and that she placed her son in danger is

beyond forgiving. The woman she now portrays is nothing like the girl who was once my friend. She used to be so giving, loving, and now..." Isolde turned to watch the dancers, noting Leonora was already well on the way to being foxed or worse. "Now she's callous, mean, and selfish."

"And horrid toward you, most of all." Anne clasped her hand. "Do not let Her Grace ruin your Season in town. Lord Wardoor is making it as clear as the air we breathe that he likes you above anyone else. He's one of the most sought after gentlemen in Town, you know. You should make use of him."

Isolde raised her brow. "Anne, what on earth are you talking about?"

"You should let him perhaps kiss you every now and again, allow him to show you there is more to this life than memories of a certain duke who left you standing at the altar."

"He didn't leave me standing at the altar. And Lord Wardoor is one of Moore's closest friends. Wardoor was the one who introduced me to Merrick. Do you not think it would be odd to allow him to court me?"

Anne took a sip of her drink, grinning. "I'm merely stating he's eligible and taken with you."

To flirt with Wardoor seemed innocent enough, and yet something told her it would be similar to poking a lion with a stick that had a piece of meat on the end of it. "He's also a rogue."

"Even better."

"Anne!" Her friend laughed and Isolde did the same, unable to stay shocked for long. "I cannot do that; I've always seen him as more of a friend than anything else."

"May I ask you something? It is quite personal, so you may refuse if you like."

"By all means." Her friend looked around to ensure their privacy, and Isolde's interest was piqued. "What is it, Anne?"

"Do you still love the duke?"

The blood drained from Isolde's face, and she quickly took a sip of wine. "No." The answer almost choked her. How could she still harbor feelings for a man whom she could not have and had married, not some unknown stranger, but her closest friend? A woman whom Isolde had seen almost as a sister. She could not love him. Not at all.

"Isolde, you may try to lie to yourself, but you cannot lie to me. You always bite your lip when you're trying to keep something from me. Remember my birthday last year when Lord Kinruth hid the puppy he was to give me at your house? You were biting your lip every time I came around to visit."

"How is dearest Poppet? I have not seen him for months," Isolde asked, wanting to discuss anything but her feelings for Merrick.

Anne tapped her with her fan. "Do not try to distract me onto the subject of my dog. Now, tell me the truth. Do you still love Moore?"

Isolde spied Merrick standing alone beneath a copse of trees, his brow furrowed and his attention seemingly focused on the ground. Once upon a time she would've gone up to him, clasped his hand, and asked what was wrong. Once she would've kissed his concerns away. Once upon a time. What a terrible fairy tale that had turned out to be. "I don't know what I feel for him," she said. "He broke my heart into a million pieces, and yet, to be around him again is bringing forth emotions I hadn't thought to concern myself with ever again. I shouldn't care for him at all. He's married to another, and no matter how abhorrent and loveless their marriage supposedly is, I cannot help but yearn to be near him. It's an affliction that I cannot cure myself of, no matter how much I wish I could."

"Oh, Isolde…"

"I know I'm a fool, and I should know better, but whenever we're together I want what I lost. I want to pluck that day five years ago out of history's page and throw it in the fire. Locking myself away in the Scottish Highlands may have removed him from my sight, but being thrown into the same social sphere has only made me realize I'm far from over my youthful engagement."

Anne threw her a pensive look. "Do you think he still feels the same? Has he given you any indication that your feelings toward him may be returned?"

A shiver stole through her at the thought of some of the heated gazes Merrick had bestowed on her since returning to Town. Of how he sometimes looked as wretched and lost. "He may still care for me, but it doesn't signify, as he's married."

"Yes, he's married, but that doesn't stop some gentlemen from claiming what they want. Perhaps Moore wishes to make you his chère-amie?"

Isolde didn't even want to think such a thing or admit to herself that the thought was tempting. "No, he does not. He made his choice, but that doesn't mean I can look to Lord Wardoor, either. I hardly know his lordship anymore, and I must be certain of my choice before I make any promises to anyone involving my future."

Anne nodded. "You'd be wise to guard yourself with any of your gentlemen admirers, at least until you know them a little better."

Lord Kinruth started toward the pavilion, a man who'd seemingly had enough time without his wife. Isolde finished her champagne and stood. "We will talk later. I see your husband is coming back."

His lordship came into their pavilion and held out his

hand. "My dearest wife, come dance with me. The music is as lively as you'll find anywhere."

Anne took his hand, but not before leaning toward her to ensure privacy. "While I agree that you should tread with caution with Wardoor, it doesn't mean you cannot use his presence to make your Season one to remember. Even if you happen to marry a man who's more sedate and, need I say it, boring." No sooner had her friend said the words than she was whisked off into her husband's arms.

Isolde watched her go and thought over her friend's opinion. The man himself, as if sensing her musing of him, turned and started toward her. Lord Wardoor was handsome, with his short, well-kept hair and attire that was always perfectly starched. Isolde smiled back, for really, what gentleman hadn't sowed his oats about Town and enjoyed himself before marriage? Wardoor really was no different than any other. Maybe Anne was right. Perhaps it was time to have a little fun and enjoy the privileged life she'd been born into. This Season was to take risks and see where they led her. She may not trust Wardoor at present, but that didn't mean she wouldn't come to.

"Care to dance, my lady?" he asked, bowing over her hand.

"I would love to, my lord." Isolde placed her hand on his arm and followed him into the crowd. They danced the Allemande, which gave them plenty of opportunity to converse. While Isolde never experienced the butterflies that took flight in her belly every time she was around Merrick, she had to admit that being in Wardoor's arms wasn't unpleasant. In fact, with his lively discussion on the night and the ton in general, Isolde found herself laughing and enjoying herself more than she thought possible.

Some hours later, the night had degraded into a scene that, should Isolde's mother ever find out about, would've sent her home to Avonmore for a reeducation on proper decorum. Not that Isolde indulged in inappropriate behavior, but the scenes playing out before her, the light-skirts who plied their trade, and the gentlemen, some of whom she knew, who took up their offerings with gleefulness and pride, was a little shocking.

Lord Barkley and the Duchess of Moore seemed to have disappeared, and Isolde hadn't seen them in an age. Not that the absence of his wife seemed to bother Moore, and again she wondered if the rumors about their marriage were true. To her, Moore was enjoying the night and seemed relaxed and happy. It was only when his wife was about that he took on an annoyed stoic character with a dash of fear, as if he was uncertain of what would come out of her mouth. It seemed, with Leonora, anything was possible.

"What is your meaning behind courting Lady Isolde? Do you mean to marry her?" Merrick met Wardoor's eye and ignored the mocking laugher he read in them. They stood watching the orchestra and the array of dancing couples from all levels of Society who were out enjoying the music.

"I don't know what you mean." Wardoor took a sip of his wine. "And if I did presume to know what you meant, I wonder at your question, since you're nothing to the lady. You're not her brother."

"We've been friends since we were in short coats. Why would you court a woman I once harbored feelings for? Whom I was going to marry?" Merrick clenched his jaw, hating the fact that his jealousy had made him have this conversation at all. He should not care a fig what Isolde or Wardoor did in their personal lives, but he did, blast it.

"Once had feelings? Are you sure you do not wish to make the delectable Isolde your own? Admit it, man, you're jealous."

Merrick ran a hand through his hair, wishing he could erase the last five years of his life and not be living this nightmare playing out before him. "You are not the marrying kind. If you hurt her…"

"Like you did?" Wardoor scoffed. "Please."

"Because we're friends, I'll let your comment pass, but be warned, if you hurt one hair on Isolde's head, I'll kill you." Merrick watched as Lord Kinruth took Isolde out for a dance, her face alight with pleasure. She was so very beautiful, long dark locks that were artfully up in an array of curls and partly hidden by her domino hood. An ache formed near the vicinity of his heart, and he rubbed his chest.

Wardoor sighed. "If I ask Lady Isolde to be my wife, she'll know how I mean to go on, married or no. I'm not one to marry and bed only one woman for the rest of my life, and I will be honest with her in relation to this. It'll be her choice, should she choose to saddle herself with me."

"She deserves better than that, and you know it." Not that he had bestowed any better on her. When did I become such a hypocrite?

Wardoor shrugged. "As I said, it'll be her choice. And I must marry sometime. Isolde is pleasant and very beautiful. I'll not struggle when it comes to bedding the chit to ensure my future heirs."

Merrick clenched his fists, wanting to haul his friend up against a tree and land a good solid blow to his gut. The thought of Wardoor caressing Isolde, kissing her sweet mouth, having children with his former betrothed made him see crimson. "Do not speak of her in that way! She's a duke's daughter, and you'll show the proper respect she's entitled to. Don't push me on this, friend."

"Who the hell do you think you are? You may have been betrothed to the chit five years ago, but you no longer have the authority to chastise me on how I speak or choose to live my life." Wardoor glared, and Merrick fought to control his rising temper.

"You will not marry her," Merrick said, his voice brooking no argument.

Wardoor swore. "You lost the right to dictate her life when you married her best friend."

"And you know the circumstances surrounding that night. The truth, I might add, and still you seek the one woman, above all else, who should not be sought after by you. If you court her, we are no longer friends." Moore pushed him away, his body thrumming for a fight to release the pent-up anger over every disappointment he'd endured being married to the wrong woman.

"I'm sorry you feel that way, but you cannot stop Isolde from marrying. She will marry one day. It may not be me, but it will be someone. And if the reports around London are correct, she is looking for a husband."

"Damn you to hell." Merrick left Wardoor, grabbed a half-filled bottle of whisky from the pavilion, and started toward the Italian Walk. He found a secluded grassy spot within the trees. The sweet-smelling scent floating on the breeze did little to lesson his ire.

Merrick clung to the tree branch above his head and fought not to snap it off, imagining it as Wardoor's neck. He flung back a good portion of the whisky and welcomed the burn to his throat. How could his closest friend do this to him?

The thought of Isolde welcoming his attentions was like a physical blow.

Damn them. Damn him.

"Moore!"

It had always boded trouble when Isolde called him by his title. He turned, wanting and yet not wanting her here right at this moment. "My lady."

She came up to him, standing but a few feet from his person, close enough to reach out and touch, to pull close and take what he desperately sought. And wished for.

"What do you think you're doing, running off Wardoor from courting me?"

"He told you?" Merrick made a note to choke the bastard to death the next time he was in range to do so.

"Yes, he told me. After seeing you two trying to kill each other, in front of everyone, I might add, I asked him what you were about. Demanded to know, in fact." She placed her hands on her hips, her perfect brow marred with a slight frown. Hell, she was beautiful. More beautiful than when he had met her at Cranleigh. "Now answer the question."

"He's my friend."

She stood staring at him a while, before she slouched, as if gauging his meaning. "Merrick, you keep forgetting you married someone else. You have to let me go, if this is your struggle."

It was his struggle. A constant gnawing on his soul that would never leave. "What if I do not want to?" And he didn't. Never had. He'd loved this woman from the first moment he'd laid eyes on her, and it had never faded. No matter how many years they'd been apart. "I should never have married Leonora."

Isolde sighed, stepping closer and taking his hand. "Don't say that. It's unkind, and there is nothing anyone can do to change what's come to be."

"It's the truth." He slurred the last word and took a sobering breath when he spotted the near-empty whisky bottle at his feet. He was a disgrace. What was he doing here? Trying to seduce an innocent woman into being with him by using his pitiful existence as an excuse? Merrick ran a hand over his jaw lest he act on the impulse to taste her once more and be damned forever.

"You must think of William, Merrick. Your son and heir. He's one precious soul you cannot regret."

Merrick nodded. It went without saying how much he loved his son, more than life itself. Even if his lad had been fathered with a woman he loathed. "He's the only saving grace in my marriage."

Isolde walked to stand beneath a large elm and looked up at the sky. "What really happened that night, Merrick?"

He came and stood next to her, looking up to the heavens also, hoping to God that he could find the right words. "I'd had too much to drink with your father and brother. More than I should have imbibed the night before our wedding. It was quite late; even the servants were abed when I went upstairs. I had given my valet the night off, since I was to celebrate our forthcoming nuptials with your family and didn't want the old retainer up all night."

He met her gaze, but she didn't venture to speak. Merrick fought the urge to reach out and touch her cheek, to touch her, however fleetingly. He fisted his hands at his side.

"I fell to sleep quickly and woke to someone crawling over me. It was dark, the fire having long burned down to coal. I couldn't see much past my own nose. Leonora had your perfume on and her hair down, so it was of similar length to yours. I know I asked if it was you, and she shushed me, but stated, 'yes.'" He cringed at the memory, hating to relive something that caused so much pain. "I never noticed the voice belonged to someone else."

"But surely when you kissed her…it was different."

Even in the moonlight Merrick could see the hurt reflected in her eyes, and he hated himself for being the cause of it. "I should have. I had wanted you in my bed for so long that I thought myself dreaming. Please know, I did not do it intentionally, Isolde. We were not having an affair. I was not playing you false, in any way. No matter what Leonora said otherwise, I swear on William's life, I was faithful to you in all ways up to that point. I loved you. From the first moment we met, I wanted to marry you. Please say you believe me. Please forgive me."

*I*solde wanted to believe him. Had wanted to hear for years that Merrick had not broken her heart with intention, but even so, knowing what she now did, a restless fury ate at her, pricked her pride.

"We had been kissing for some time, Merrick. You should have known it wasn't me in your bed, dream state or not." Had the roles been reversed, not that Isolde would ever find herself in such a position, surely she would've noticed the difference.

The difference of lips. The difference of touch, taste, and smell. Merrick had always smelt of fresh laundered linen with a soft fragrance of lavender. She loathed the smell of that little purple plant now.

"It's the one mistake I'll regret for the rest of my life." Moore clasped her hand, and she pulled away, placing some distance between them.

She didn't like how her body reacted when they were close, all shivery and achy in places she didn't want to admit. She glowered at him instead and fought to sound stern with what she had to say next. "It's time I married, Merrick, and for me to do that, you must allow others to form attachments to me. You cannot be involved with my suitors, in any way, from this night on."

"Wardoor? He's admitted himself that he'll not be faithful. Is that truly the type of husband you wish for?"

She shrugged, having gathered that much herself from the reputation that preceded the gentleman. "That may be so, but I'm not looking for a love match. I'm looking for a husband who'll give me a home, children, a future that's not under the same roof as my brother."

"You have Avonmore. There is no need for you to marry."

She laughed, the tone condescending, even to her own ears. "How dare you. Who do you think you are? I am not allowed to marry because you cannot have me? You're married with a child. Why should I not have the same?

"You, above anyone, knew how much I longed for children. To have a child of my own, to love and dote on? Am I not entitled to such happiness?" Anger thrummed through her; she needed him to see sense.

"I cannot watch you marry another." His voice sounded hoarse and thick. There had been a time that, if she heard him speak so, she would've rushed to offer comfort, to ensure he was well. That she could not any longer, hurt more than she wanted to admit.

She glanced at him. "You have no choice." Scant inches apart, she said, "You will watch me, Merrick, as I promise myself to another, marry someone who is not you, just as I had to." He flinched. She was being cruel, but she could not help herself. Years of anger and frustration wanted to lash out and vent and, with Moore's confession, he'd given her a port to do that. Her vision of him blurred, and she blinked away the tears, her heart and mind warring with each other. One wanted blood, to hurt and seize revenge, while the other wanted comfort, to forgive and be loved.

"That night was the only night I've ever been unfaithful to you." His eyes beseeched her to believe him. And maybe Isolde did, not that it changed their situation.

"This," she said, gesturing between them, "is no more. You must accept it."

"I cannot," he said, his gaze as glassy as her own.

"Leonora is pregnant, Merrick. You should not be here with me while your wife is carrying your second child." She should leave, get as far away from this man as possible. Around Merrick she could not trust herself.

"The child is not mine. It's impossible, as I have not touched Leonora since the night you caught us in my room."

For a moment, Isolde was speechless, unable to comprehend that Merrick had not lain with Leonora in all this time. Then another dissembling thought occurred. The duchess was increasing with someone else's child. How could she have such little regard to her station? "If what you say is true, and Leonora tricked us both the night before our wedding, why would she do such a thing? She broke my heart, the friendship we had, to marry you. To give her affections elsewhere makes no sense."

"Leonora ruined all my hopes and was only ever after the title of duchess, Isolde. I have never forgiven her for that, and we do not have a marriage in any way. We share a roof, and that is all. I do not care how she lives her life or vice versa."

"You should care," she said, frowning. "You may never be able to forgive the duchess, but you must forget the past. Look to the future, enjoy your children, and make the situation you now find yourself in as best as it can be. You said you would try to help her curb her lifestyle. She is your wife, Merrick. You have to at least try."

"I still love you."

The words dropped between them like a cannonball, and Isolde gasped. "You cannot. I will not allow you to say such things." She cleared her voice, hating that it sounded thick and uneven or that she longed to hear more of the same from him. That he'd always loved her. That he would shift heaven and earth to make her his again.

If only...

"There is nothing you can do about it," he replied, running a finger along her arm all the way to where her glove sat at her elbow. Isolde shut her eyes, missing the touch of the one man who made her burn. "I love you as much today as the last day we were together at Mountshaw. Had your father and brother allowed me to know of your location, I would've followed you to Scotland. I would've begged your forgiveness and lived in sin with you, if it meant I could be with you."

Isolde shook her head, swallowing the lump wedged in her throat. "Stop saying such things, Merrick. They help no one." Not the least her, who had stupidly looked out from her bedroom window at Avonmore, willing his ducal carriage to appear on the hills beyond her estate.

"They help me. For years, I've carried this burden. That you did not know the truth. That you thought I would do such a heinous crime against you willingly. I would not. I could not."

He stepped closer still, the hem of her gown sweeping across his Hessian boots. She should move away, run away from emotions she no longer had the right to feel, but she did not. Instead she stood still and started only the slightest when he ran a finger along her cheek before lifting her chin. "Merrick." Isolde wasn't sure if she was imploring or warning him.

"Please…" he begged, his eyes darkening with intent. Her eyes closed at the sound of his need, raw and consuming, and then, God save her sinning soul, she watched as he dipped his head as if to kiss her.

With a will born out of sheer desperation, Isolde pushed him away. "No, Merrick."

He looked wretched. "Tell me you do not care. Look at me and declare that you do not want this as much as I."

She hugged her domino about her like a shield, yet it did little to protect her from the man before her. Nothing could. Nothing ever had. "I will always care for you, Merrick. How could I not? We had planned and dreamed of a life together, one we both were desperate to start. But damn it," she said, stomping her foot a little. "What do you want from me? You're married, and I will not be your whore, no matter who is wrong or right in this putrid triangle in which we find ourselves."

"I want to leave Leonora, but she's threatened to spread a rumor that William is not mine."

Isolde gasped. "Well then, you cannot. Think of your son and what it will do to your name. A family would never recover their good standing if such information got out. Even a duke's."

He growled, running a hand through his hair and leaving it on end. "I'm being selfish, I know. Certain members of the ton will think I'm a bastard, but the majority know the truth of the situation." He took a step toward her, and she stepped back. "Being a duke will also help, to a certain degree, not to mention Leonora has a reputation as a liar among our peers. And I want you. It's as simple as that."

"Nothing is simple, and you cannot have me. Now or ever. Divorce is not an option, and you cannot risk placing a shadow of doubt on William's parentage. He's not to blame for what passed." The truth of the words was like razors in her throat. They cut and hurt. "We shouldn't even be here in such a private locale. This nocturne rendezvous is as wrong as what the duchess did to me to gain your hand, if what you say is true."

"You think after how much I adored you, how much I wanted to marry you, that I would lie about how we were torn apart? It killed me to see you standing in my room, witnessing my shame, and unable to comfort you, as I wanted. Listening as lie after lie spewed from Leonora lips. Isolde, please..." he begged.

She pinched the bridge of her nose, tiredness swamping her. "Very well, I admit it, Merrick, we were wronged, and in the worst imaginable way, but the papers were signed and vows were spoken. We both must make the best of a situation that is not to our liking."

"And so you will marry."

The words sounded as dead as the prospect seemed, considering she would never marry the man before her. "Yes, I will marry. Is that what you want me to say? To torment you with?" She adjusted her tone, fearful others may hear. Tears blurred her vision, and she wrenched away when Merrick went to hold her. If he were to touch her now, she'd never have the strength to pull back, to walk from a man who should be hers. "Be happy for me, please." Isolde turned to leave, her feet as heavy as stone. "You mustn't seek me out again, Merrick. I have a life to live, as you do, and you must allow me to live it, just as I have you." She swiped at a tear and fumbled for her handkerchief, hating every word she spoke, and Leonora more for placing them in the situation in the first place.

"It's not over between us, Isolde," Merrick said, the words a low growl in the darkened gardens.

"Do as I ask, I beg you." Isolde left quickly, thankful when the row of pavilions came into view, and Anne, who stood before them, but the pensive look on her face gave her pause.

Isolde checked that Merrick wasn't following her as she exited the entrance to the Italian Walk. What had she been thinking pursuing him into the park? They could not be anything to each other than passing acquaintances.

Nothing more could come of it. If she was to have any

chance of forming a future with anyone else, she needed to forget what it was like being back in Merrick's arms. Of longing to be back there again, if only for a moment. Once married, she would never look to anyone else, no matter what the marriage bed was like. A duke's daughter did not cuckold her husband. She had almost kissed Merrick while he was married to another woman. A stab of shame shot through her heart. That was not who she was, and never again would she allow such a slip.

She had acted no better than the loose women plying their trades here this evening.

Lord Wardoor joined Anne and looked about. Spotting her, he smiled in welcome. "I'm glad you're back. I was about to come find you. We were getting a little worried."

Isolde laughed, ignoring the nervous edge to it. "I went for a little stroll. I'm sorry I did not tell you."

Lord Wardoor's attention snapped to where she'd walked from, and Isolde didn't need to turn to know who had appeared; the narrowing of his eyes and thoughtful expression was proof enough.

"Well, you are back now, which is all that matters," Wardoor drawled.

Anne smiled at her. "I believe Lord Kinruth wishes to leave. Are you ready, my dear?"

"Whenever you are," she said, placing her hand on Wardoor's arm. "I'm at your disposal."

They walked toward the carriages, discussing the night and the remainder of the Season, which was starting to pick up in gaiety, before Moore stepped before them, halting their progress.

Heat bloomed on her chest and rose up her neck. She took a calming breath and met Merrick's intense, frustrated gaze head on.

"Good night, my lady." Moore bowed before her, holding her gaze longer than he ought.

Wardoor cleared his throat. "Moore."

"Wardoor." The name sounded like an insult and Isolde moved quickly to the carriage. She tampered down the conflicting emotions zipping around her insides, determined to forget this night and look only to the future. "Good night, Your Grace," she replied, taking her seat. "Please give my regards to the duchess."

Merrick nodded before walking away, not bothering to acknowledge Lord Wardoor's farewells.

Isolde noted Wardoor's attention didn't leave Moore until he was out of sight. That she was coming between friends left a sour taste in her mouth, but for all Wardoor's rakish tendencies, he was suitable for her, as Anne had said. If only she could have some of the attraction that she'd always had for Moore when it came to Wardoor. It would certainly make marrying the man a lot easier to allow.

He was one of Moore's closest friends. How fiendish could Wardoor be? No more than any other who were a part of their set. Others had married for lesser qualities and been happy with their choice. Had lived long, contented lives that eventuated with children. A happy thought, if ever there was one. There was no reason she could not also.

CHAPTER 10

*T*he following morning, Isolde washed away the late evening of the night before and gathered her wits to attend her mother's picnic lunch that was being held on the grounds of their London home.

Isolde padded to the window and pulled back the drapes to see what sort of weather they had for the day. Not a cloud marred the sky, and no tree swayed with any wind. She smiled, happy her mother's planned daytime outing looked to be a success.

Sometime later, she joined Victoria, who stood in conversation with some friends and their hovering mamas. Raucous laughter caught her attention, and she watched as a few gentlemen partook in a game of lawn bowls, some younger debutantes watching with feigned awe.

Taking a sip of orange and raspberry shrub their delightful cook Mrs. Arthur had made especially for the day, Isolde almost purred with delight at having the citrusy drink once more. How she'd missed it during the summer months when living in Scotland. For some reason, her cook had never been able to reproduce the exact taste Mrs. Arthur could.

Alice came to stand beside her, all beautiful elegance in her pink muslin gown. "There you are. I don't like to see you standing here alone, not speaking to anyone, so I thought to rectify the deficit."

She laughed. "You didn't have to come over here and save me. I'm quite content just listening to everyone, I assure you." A footman passed with a plate of syllabub, and she took one. "Are you enjoying yourself? I saw you talking to Lady Harsam. Isn't she a distant relative of our neighbor Lord Arndel?" Alice's cheeks turned a delightful shade of rouge. "I see the gentleman is also here today."

Alice shrugged. "I hadn't noticed."

Isolde didn't believe that for a moment. "Well, he's talking to Mama right now. I'm surprised that you have not...and that he keeps looking in your direction, certainly tells me he knows you're here."

Alice laughed, but her attention didn't stray from Isolde, and she realized her little sister had grown up while she was away. Had matured and in no way resembled a ridiculous simpering debutante who so often graced their entertainments.

"Lord Arndel, I'm sure, is well enough, but he's so quiet and secretive, I'm never able to make out his character."

"Maybe he's just shy." And very handsome, Isolde conceded.

"Perhaps," Alice said, shrugging. "But I'm not expected to marry before you, so I'm not in a hurry to choose with whom I want to spend the rest of my life."

"Have you told Mama that?" Isolde grinned, spooning another delicious mouthful of dessert into her mouth.

"Well no, but I'm sure she would be in agreement." Alice

turned to watch their parent who was now all but gushing over Lord Arndel. "I wonder what they're discussing."

"Why don't you go and find out," Isolde said, trying hard not to smile at her sister, who wished to appear disinterested while clearly the opposite.

Alice checked her gown, and Isolde had a niggling thought that her sister's marriage wouldn't be so very far away. Probably was, in fact, closer than any of them thought.

---

*M*errick arrived a little later than was deemed appropriate, and stood for a moment hidden in the library, watching the garden party and wishing he were anywhere but here. He hated to attend events where the invitation had come out of polite courtesy to his standing in Society, and not because they wanted the pleasure of his company.

His wife stood with a group of ladies, tittering over nonsense, no doubt, and blushing over the men who played bowls on the lawns. He gnashed his teeth at his wife's falseness. Never in his life had he come across someone so callous and fake. Leonora seemed to embody everything that was wicked.

A familiar voice caught his attention, and he spotted Wardoor in discussion with Lord Barkley on the terrace beyond. Merrick frowned, not aware that the two gentlemen were good enough acquaintances to have such a private tête-à-tête. He stood there, debating whether to walk toward the partially open window and listen in on the conversation.

Lord Barkley shook his head, condescension masking his features. "Enough with the benign talk, we have more serious matters to discuss," his lordship said, cutting off Wardoor's verbal estimation of the picnic.

Merrick stepped through the doors and joined them. Looking at Wardoor's all but pulsating tension, he was sure something disastrous was about to take place.

"Gentlemen," he said. "I hope I'm not interrupting anything?"

Wardoor's eyes flared at his intrusion. "We were just discussing the congenial weather and lovely company."

"Your friend lies, Your Grace. There are many things I wish to discuss, not that Wardoor is interested in doing so." Merrick noted Wardoor's fisted hand, and his interest was piqued. His once friend had never been one to condone violence, but if Barkley didn't take a care, a bloody nose certainly could come his way.

"Such as?" Wardoor took a sip of his drink, his brow glowing with a sheen of sweat.

Lord Barkley leaned against the balustrade, all cool aloofness, and yet cold calculation swam in his gaze. "Such as, how your finances are coming. My pockets are overflowing with all the IOUs you've placed there."

Merrick noted Wardoor's ashen face. His lordship's family was flush with coin, so to owe Barkley money, a lecherous cur on Society, was not a welcome realization. "Why do you owe Barkley anything?"

"I never tolerate vulgarity at garden parties, and your talk of money is surely that, hence—" Wardoor said, taking a step toward the guests on the lawn. "I shall leave you now." Lord Barkley wrenched Wardoor to a halt. "I need that money, Wardoor. And I need it today...with interest, you understand."

Wardoor faced them, his eyes wide with humiliation. "What do you mean with interest? That wasn't part of the deal."

"There are always variables with gambling, and you

played with the wrong type of people, my lord." Barkley tsk-tsked Wardoor. "It is time to pay the piper."

"I cannot pay today." Wardoor looked at Moore as if the duke could save him from himself. "At least give me to the end of next week. I'll have it by then."

Barkley smiled. "Very good, my lord, for I'd hate for the lovely, delectable, and let's not forget, innocent, Lady Isolde Worthingham to find out where you laid your head last night."

"Do not involve Lady Isolde in this," Merrick warned, pinning Barkley with a hard stare.

Wardoor pointed his finger at Barkley. "You cannot prove anything. Nor do I believe you even know. You're not one to remember your own whereabouts on any given night, never mind any others around you."

"Oh, I know." Barkley paused. "And does anyone in this Society have to prove anything? Just saying the words to a select few can create a beast that not even a marquess could tame. I would hate to ruin your reputation and your chances of marriage over a pitiful amount of coin."

"You wouldn't dare." Wardoor glared.

Barkley laughed "Aye, I would. And if you do not pay, you can kiss a marriage to the rich wallflower good-bye."

Moore ground his teeth at the reference to Isolde as a wallflower and that she'd be willing to marry Wardoor. Over his dead body. From the first moment he'd known her, she had been a beacon of purity, of kindness, that he'd always strived to replicate. He'd failed miserably, but she had not. Even after all that had happened between them, she was courteous, cool, and amiable around him. It was more than he deserved.

"If you're so sure of what I do, please enlighten me," Wardoor demanded, his voice tinged with sarcasm.

Barkley snarled with triumph, and Merrick knew he wouldn't like what the chap had to say.

"That you're adventurous behind closed doors. That your taste isn't limited to the fairer sex. Do you understand me now?"

"I have never..." Wardoor blustered, turning a deep shade of red.

Barkley winked at him, and Merrick's gut twisted in disgust. Was Barkley right in his assumptions? Wardoor was wild and had a tendency to overindulge in sex and alcohol, but this, his sexuality being brought into question, was not what he'd expected.

"Women, my friend, are not to be trusted, and when blunt is offered, will spread more than their legs when paid handsomely." Barkley shrugged. "Who knows what story I shall spread about Town if you do not pay up? But know I will ruin you, should you continue to fob me off. I will call in your debts and destroy you both financially and emotionally. No one will want you after I've finished with you, my lord." Wardoor studied the gardens, silent for a moment. "You'll get your money and soon," he said, pushing past Merrick and the laughing Barkley.

Merrick pinned Barkley with a hard stare. "How much does he owe?"

"What, are you going to save him, yet again? Even your pockets are not that deep. Wardoor needs a dowry, and he has his hopes set on your past fiancée. After he pays me, he'll need to marry someone of immense fortune."

"How much?" he ground out, sick of Barkley's games. "A thousand pounds, give or take a few pence."

Hell, Merrick swore to himself. He hadn't thought it would be so much. He searched for Wardoor in the crowd and spotted him talking to Isolde. Anger thrummed through him that his friend would use her in such a way, after all

Merrick had put her through. Damn it, she deserved so much better than this. "You'll have the money by tomorrow eve. My man of business will meet you at my London home, where you'll produce and hand over every IOU you have of his lordship's. Do you understand?"

Barkley nodded. "We have an agreement."

Merrick watched him leave and was glad of the reprieve. Should Wardoor continue down this road he would ruin himself and his family. As for the assumption that his friend liked more than women to warm his bed, he'd leave that be for now. What the man did in his own time was his own concern, but should it impact on Isolde, he'd make it his, and that was not acceptable.

He walked toward the lawns and fetched a glass of champagne from a passing footman, needing the alcoholic beverage more than ever, before he had it out with Wardoor and got to the bottom of just what the hell the man was about.

He cornered him standing beside the rose garden, small pink blooms still bursting with color. It should've been a serene place, yet Wardoor paced along the garden beds, not seeing any of the beauty before him.

"Wardoor," Merrick said as he came to stand beside him. "What have you got yourself into? What is going on with Barkley?"

Wardoor shook his head with a self-deprecating laugh. "It's none of your business, and you should have buggered off the moment you knew the conversation was private."

"Damn it, man. What are you about losing a thousand pounds to such a fellow? He's as bad as they come, and you must have known he would threaten you when you could not pay."

"I was drunk." He sighed. "I made a mistake."

Merrick turned toward the gathered guests and spotted

Isolde picking out her lunch at the tables decorated with white linens and colorful fruit. "You will not marry Isolde for her money. She deserves better than that."

Wardoor met his gaze. "And you're the judge as to what's best for her? I'm sorry, but when did you become her protector? Was it before you fucked her best friend or after?"

Hot rage flared through him, and Merrick fought not to knock Wardoor on his ass. "This isn't about me. This is about you courting a woman I care for, to secure your future." Merrick shook his head, at a loss as to what to say. "And what was Barkley insinuating about your sexuality? Is what he says true?"

"I'm selling Benner House and all the land surrounding the small estate. You do not need to bail me out, so forget about buying those IOUs."

"Your mother resides there. Where are you going to place her? With you?" Merrick didn't think any wife would welcome Wardoor's mother as a permanent houseguest. Cold and with a severing tongue, the woman was a known harridan. "That will not work for a new wife."

"The property is not entailed, and Mama will have to be content with the dowager house on the family's main estate or the London townhouse. There is nothing for it. The sale will be finalized by Wednesday next." Wardoor swallowed. "As to what else you ask, it's none of your business."

Merrick narrowed his eyes. "If you do not desire a woman to warm your bed, I would advise you to never marry and allow the estate to go into your cousin's hand. Although I do not understand the troubles you live with, I do not wish your lifestyle to impact on an innocent woman." The thought of Isolde being unhappy in her marriage, of sickening with disease because Wardoor couldn't keep his cock out of whatever took his fancy, made him ill.

"If Isolde agrees to my terms of marriage, there is nothing

you can do. Although her money will be welcome, once I sell Benner, her dowry will not be so desperate."

"You're right. If Isolde chooses you then there is nothing to be done, but if you've told her only half-truths, I will ensure she knows full well who she's agreed to marry and what type of man you are."

"Some friend."

Merrick cringed. He was being no friend at all, but he could not allow Isolde to be unhappy in her future. He'd caused her so much pain, he couldn't permit any more to trample on her fragile soul. "Yes, I'm married and cannot fight for her as I would wish, and therefore I must step aside. But I will not see her hurt. Not even by the man whom I once viewed as close as a brother."

He left and headed toward a footman, in need of sustenance of the liquid kind. He caught sight of Isolde laughing at something her sister Lady Alice was saying, her long locks falling out of their style and curling about her lovely neck, her cheeks rosy from the consumption of too much champagne. He took in her beauty, feeling pleasure and loss at the same time. If only he could stroll up to her, take her in his arms, and kiss her senseless. Lose himself in the feel of her warmth, her welcoming embrace, and kisses that used to send his pulse racing.

Shaking his head, he wondered how it was that their lives had turned out the way they had. How, by a series of events not of their doing, a future had been destroyed that should've been happy and full of love. Instead, he was stuck in a bad marriage to a woman who loathed him as much as he loathed her, and now, to top it off, he would have to watch the woman he loved marry another. Possibly his best friend.

It wasn't to be borne.

CHAPTER 11

*I*solde looked up at the sky and shut her eyes, enjoying the warmth on her face. Her friend Anne lay on the chair next to her. She, too, enjoying the beautiful weather the London Season had gifted them. They had opted to seat themselves on the terrace of Lord Kinruth's townhouse, where the sunlight dappled through the wisteria hanging above them.

"Did you receive your invitation to Lord Wardoor's estate? I understand he's just recently returned from the country, some business transaction he had to take care of last week. I shouldn't think he'd leave the capital for any other reason." Anne threw her a pointed stare, grinning.

Isolde ignored her goading. "We received ours with the morning post. I have not decided if I should go. The Season has only just started to be fun. I'm not sure if I want to leave to attend a fortnight-long party in the country."

"You're not accepting his hand in marriage, if you decide to go, if that is your concern." Anne rubbed her swelling belly, and a pang of envy shot through Isolde at the thought of her friend soon becoming a mother. "Please tell me why you're so unsure of him."

Isolde sighed, biting into another lavender tea cake to give her more time to answer. Why was she so unsure of Wardoor? Or, was she sure of him, but just didn't really want him and was coming up with all the excuses in the world? "I'm sure I'll end up going. Mama wouldn't allow me to stay in Town, in any case. And do not forget, Anne, Wardoor is yet to even ask for my hand, and he may not, when all is told."

"Oh, he'll ask you. Of that I'm sure. But will you say yes, I'm less likely to give an opinion on."

Isolde nodded. How well her friend knew her, but then, a closeness was only natural after so much time in Scotland together. "You will be attending, I hope?"

"Indeed. It'll be nice to have some rest away from the capital. I'm not sure how much longer I'll be able to attend the parties in Town with my stomach being so unsettled and growing at such a rate."

Isolde laughed. "But what a beautiful stomach it is. I'm so happy for you."

Anne rubbed it anew. "When your time comes, you'll be a wonderful mother, as well. And you will have your turn. I promise you this, as your friend."

Tears pricked Isolde's eyes. "I almost kissed him." The words blurted from her lips, and she couldn't meet her friend's eyes, which just by her peripheral vision were as wide as tea plates. The following silence sounded as loud as a death knell.

"Wardoor?" Anne asked, sitting up. "Tell me everything."

If only it was Wardoor, the guilt spiraling through Isolde would be nonexistent. "No, not Wardoor. Moore."

Again silence ensued, and she finally looked at Anne who was now gaping at her like a fish. "Please say something.

Anything. Even if it is only to say what a fool I almost was. How I'm an awful person who should be banished from England."

"I wondered seeing you both reappear at Vauxhall, but as you said nothing, I didn't want to venture as to what you spoke about." Anne sat up, turning to face her. "What happened?"

If only Isolde could answer such a question. Why had she followed him, trying to talk sense into a man who refused to let her go? "I confronted him about his conduct toward me, and we argued. Somewhere along the way he told me his version of the night before our wedding. He still loves me, Anne, and it was just after his declaration that I almost allowed him favors he should never have."

Anne stood, pacing before her. "I must declare that I'm relieved you did not kiss the duke. That is one complication you do not need. Not that the Duchess of Moore would be too vexed if her husband did stray. Her Grace has no shame when it comes to men she takes to her bed." Anne stopped, turning to look at her. "That Moore tried to kiss you does not shock me. He's so indifferent to his wife. Why, I've never known a man so emotionally removed from his spouse. What a sorry state of a marriage to be in."

Isolde agreed Moore's relationship with the duchess was a disaster. But that did not give her the right to come between them. Society expected her to make a suitable, if not grand, match, and she would. No scandal would shadow her again. "I need to keep away from him. Even though I believe that he did not know it was Leonora in his bed that night, he is married. No matter how much I may want him, I cannot change his circumstances to suit my feelings."

"It does not excuse what happened, Isolde. They still slept together and had a child, need I remind you."

"I know that," she bit out more severely than she'd meant.

"I'm sorry, Anne. I didn't mean to be short with you. I'm just so confused." And she was. Terribly so.

Anne sat on Isolde's chair. "You're not conflicted. You still love him."

She looked out over the lawns, the roses and wisteria above them. It was so beautiful here, so peaceful and without the complications of Town life when they relaxed in such a way. "A part of me always will, I fear."

"Oh, Isolde…" Her friend threw her a consoling look. "He's not for you, my dear."

She sighed, knowing only too well how true that declaration was. "Should I have my time again, I would've fought for him, at least listened to his excuse for what had happened that night. My father never gave him the chance, and I think that was a mistake. Leonora's treatment of me is proof enough it was her scheming that gained her a ducal coronet. I was such a fool." Tears pooled in her eyes, and she blinked them away, hating the fact that after all these years Merrick could still bring her to tears. But this time, not tears of pain, but regret.

"And if a gentleman asks you to be his bride, will you accept, knowing you still have these strong feelings for Moore?"

Anne's bulging stomach caught her attention, the perfect, plump little lump that housed life. A little baby, a son or daughter that she herself longed to have most in the world. To finally have a child, a family, a home of her own was what a husband could give her. Moore, on the other hand, could not.

He was lost to her, and she must accept it; no matter how hard such a realization was, she must move on with her life and start living it, before it was too late. "Yes, I will accept a proposal, if one arises, and be forever faithful to my vows."

Anne took her hand, squeezing it slightly. "I know this

choice is not easy, and I wish I could turn back the hands of time for you so you could have all that your heart desires."

Isolde let out a self-deprecating laugh. "I wish you could, too, dearest, but we must endure as best we can, and make the most of what is offered to us. I will find a kind, trustworthy husband, free of scandal and suitable for a duke's daughter. I may never love him, but we will have children and a future. That is all I wish, for now."

The fortnight before the house party at Lord Wardoor's country estate was filled with balls and parties, shopping trips, and nights at the theater. Lord Wardoor accompanied her at most outings. He was attentive and kind, and as much as Isolde tried to like him more than she did already, she could not see him as anything other than a friend.

As expected, Isolde came across Moore at the many events about town, but after their near kiss at Vauxhall, he seemed to be avoiding her. Not even when the opportunities had arisen for them to converse had he sought her out, if only to apologize for what they'd almost done. Not that she wanted him to speak to her. She was in London to marry a suitable, trustworthy gentleman. It was unfortunate that Moore encompassed everything she'd ever wanted in a husband, a lover. No matter how much she wished circumstances were different, they were not. He was married, and that was the end of it.

Isolde sighed. The thought of the near kiss left a fluttering in her stomach that had no right to be there. She ought to be ashamed of herself. He was married, for heaven's sake, but it still did not stop her from thinking of him late at night when she was alone in her bed. Imagining the feel of his hands sliding over her flesh, of what his kisses used to do to her, the delectable, heart-stopping embraces for her only.

Tonight they were to attend Lord Kinruth and Anne's home for a small dinner party of their closest friends, before those who were invited to Lord Wardoor's Surrey estate left Town.

It didn't take long for her carriage to arrive at her friend's home, and with the chaperonage of Anne and Lord Kinruth, her mama had allowed her to attend on her own. Isolde found the freedom liberating, but it also reminded her that should she marry, she could attend most outings this way, if she liked. No longer would she have to ask for permission to go anywhere or do anything.

All her life, even now on the cusp of being on the shelf, she'd had to ask to do anything. The thought that it could change in the foreseeable future was exciting.

Dinner was pleasant and seated beside Anne, it was over before she wanted it to be. The men, as customary, partook in their after-dinner drinks, while the ladies headed toward the withdrawing room, situated on the bottom floor.

A small fire burned in the grate to take out the slight chill that had settled in the night air, and the women gathered in groups around the room to talk. Isolde sat on a golden settee and watched the ladies as they laughed and gossiped. She sighed, pining at the notable absence of Merrick. Friends with Lord Kinruth, Isolde had thought he would be here tonight. Certainly Wardoor was, but maybe Merrick had had a previous engagement.

The door to the room opened, and Isolde turned, expecting it to be the men joining the party, but instead Moore and Leonora entered the gathering. Much to her horror, a tremble of expectation shot through her, and she cursed herself as a silly fool for yearning for someone who was no longer, nor ever would be, hers.

Anne greeted the late guests warmly and the duchess, with a spark of insolence in her eye, looked Anne up and down. "Oh, would you look at our increasing waistlines, my dear. How vulgar of us to be out in Society with such ghastly bodies." The words were spoken loud enough for everyone present to hear, and Isolde noted Anne's embarrassed blush. Thankfully, Lord Kinruth walked into the room at that moment and greeted the duke warmly, before passing Merrick a tumbler of brandy.

Moore looked about, taking in the guests, and Isolde drank in the sight of him. His black unruly hair matched his dark hooded eyes that sent her stomach to tumble each time they met. Now that Merrick had told her the truth of what had happened all those years ago, Isolde found it hard to be indifferent to him. Her attention snapped to his lips, and she swallowed, realizing how much she wanted to kiss him.

Wanted to feel the longing and desire that coursed through her body at his every touch.

As if sensing her interest, he turned, his gaze raking her form with a hungry intensity that left her breathless and ashamed. The look on his face reminded her of how he used to gaze upon her person, how much he had doted on her. He nodded in welcome, and she smiled a little in return, before trying to turn her mind back to the conversation going on around her.

"I am looking forward to your company at my country estate, Lady Isolde. I hope you'll find my home to your liking."

Isolde didn't need to decipher Lord Wardoor's statement or what he meant by the words, and as much as she was sure she would like his home, as much as any other, it was not likely to capture her heart, just as the man beside her would not.

"I'm sure it'll be beautiful, my lord. And I'm looking forward to seeing it very much."

Wardoor started gushing about his estate and the improvements he would make should he marry, and Isolde stopped listening at the mention of his abundant lawns.

Watching the guests mingle about them, she noted Merrick didn't seek out Wardoor to speak to him, but instead moved to the opposite side of the room with Lord Kinruth. She plucked a glass of champagne from a passing footman, hating that disappointment coursed through her each time he didn't seek her out. He shouldn't seek her out. Instead, he ought to concentrate on his marriage and how to amend Leonora's ways.

"Will the Duke and Duchess of Moore be attending your house party? I know what close friends you are, after all." Wardoor frowned, looking in Moore's direction but didn't deign to speak. So it was true, she had come between the two of them.

Isolde sighed, hating the fact. However, she could do little since Wardoor had taken it upon himself to look at her as a suitable wife. He was kind and pleasant looking, and was ready, from his own admission, to start a family. She would be a simpleton indeed, if she walked away from such an alliance. Her attention sought out Anne, and she watched a moment as her friend rubbed her belly, and longing overwhelmed her. Yes, as hard and painful as moving on would be, it was time she sought what she wanted most. A child.

"They are not attending. Another engagement elsewhere, or so the duke informed me." Wardoor's smile was brittle. "I know you have a past with the duke, but I do hope you're willing to grasp a future when one's offered to you with a gentleman you like, if not love."

Heat bloomed on her cheeks, having not thought Wardoor would be so forward with his words. Hearing him state her struggles aloud and his willingness to be patient soothed her unease over the match. "You are right that I have a past with Moore, but that was many years ago, and he's married now. And should I find a suitable husband and was offered marriage, I would seriously consider the proposal."

The words were so clinical, so different from when Merrick had asked her to be his bride. Isolde hated them, so cold and without heart. She indeed had not moved on from Moore, would forever yearn for him in some way, but

Wardoor need not know that. Nor was she looking for a love match. If she tried hard enough, the marriage could work.

Wardoor nodded. "And would you consider me, should I ask for your hand in marriage?"

Isolde studied him a moment. "You have not asked me yet, so I do not know." Was she ready for him? A moment of panic assaulted her at the thought that he would ask her here, now, tonight.

He laughed, raising his glass in salute. "Well then, I may have to remedy that."

Relief poured through her, and Isolde smiled in earnest. Thankful he'd not asked, after all. "Maybe you should," Isolde said, clicking her own glass against his.

---

*M*errick stood as far away from Isolde as was possible. The sight of her tore his heart in two. It was beyond absurd the emotional turmoil going on inside his body each and every time he observed her around Town. Something had to be done about it, and that thing unfortunately was to cut her off. Leave her to live her life as she'd asked and make the best of his life with his son. Whether he liked it or not, he was married to Leonora. Had

138

he not been so cold and unforgiving toward her, would she have turned to others for comfort? Probably not. Not only had he let Isolde down all those years ago, but he'd let down his wife, as well. He'd failed as a husband, and he was the worst of men for doing so.

"I see Lord Barkley isn't here this evening. My wife will be sorely disappointed." Even to his own ears the disdain and venom in his words was evident. He ought to stop, and yet he couldn't. It was so ingrained in him, almost like breathing, natural and automatic.

Lord Kinruth grimaced. "I pay no heed to gossip." Merrick scoffed. "You should, for in this case it's true."

He paused, knowing his own hand had played his wife into the lifestyle she now lived. "I'm glad we're here tonight. I wanted to pay my regards before I head back to Mountshaw estate."

"You're leaving Town?" Kinruth's eyes widened. "The Season's only halfway through. What takes you from us so early?"

"William, first and foremost. I want him to start schooling with a tutor I've hired. And there are some pressing estate matters that I should attend to." Not to mention he needed to distance himself from Isolde, and quickly. If he stayed, he would fail at doing so. And no matter how much he wanted her, had almost stolen a kiss at Vauxhall, he would not break the vows of his marriage. Even after all Leonora had done to him, how she loved to make his life a living hell, he would not become what, so sadly, she had.

"But your steward can handle the estate, and a letter to your boy's tutor asking him to come to London instead of Mountshaw will suffice. Surely there is no other reason for you to hightail it back to the country."

Merrick stole a look at Isolde. "It's for the best. I believe we're soon to hear of a betrothal, and I think for my own self-preservation that I shouldn't be here when that occurs." Merrick ground his teeth as Isolde smiled at Wardoor. Whatever were they talking about that was so amusing? The blood in his veins chilled, and shame washed over him that he couldn't be happy for one of his oldest friends at finally finding someone whom he could marry. And damn him to hell, that Merrick wanted her, too, married or not. "I cannot stay."

Kinruth clapped him on the shoulder, understanding dawning in his eyes. "I comprehend what you're saying. And I'm sorry, my friend. For whatever it's worth, I do think Lady Isolde believes your side of events on the night before your wedding and forgives you for them. In time, we shall all look back on these days and laugh at how inane it all was."

Merrick nodded, doubting that would ever occur, and it still did not change his circumstances. He drank down the last of his brandy and welcomed the burn to his gut. At least he had William, the most important thing in his life. "The duchess will stay on in Town, but from tomorrow, I will be away. You know how to contact me should you need to."

"We look forward to your return."

The time away from Town would be just what he needed. To move on he must rid himself of the melancholy that had plagued him ever since Isolde's return. He was no good to his boy or estates the way he was, and with Isolde leaving for Wardoor's country home, he could take the time to regroup. "As do I," he lied, smiling for good measure. With any luck, estate business would keep him away indefinitely, and he'd never have to return. That prospect was something to look forward to, but something told Merrick it was a dream that would not come to fruition.

CHAPTER 12

*L*ord Wardoor's home was an Elizabethan designed manor, rectangular in shape with two circular Corinthian pillars that stood on either side of the entrance and reached all the way to the roofline. The family's coat of arms was engraved on the stonework and stated a date of 1577.

The estate house sat on a flat piece of land with rolling hills surrounding it. It was a very pretty residence and, as the carriage rolled to a stop before the front door, she contemplated it as her possible home, where she would raise her children and watch them grow up and prepare for Seasons of their own. Three footmen came out and waited for the carriage.

"We're here."

Anne's excited declaration pulled her from her thoughts, and she clasped the squabs as they rocked to a halt. Stepping down, she took the chance to further inspect the gardens, and noted a vast amount of lawn surrounded by native plants and bushes. At least it explained why Wardoor had discussed his lawns at length the other evening. The gardens were not manicured or perfectly set out like the gardens at Dunsleigh. Here, the plantings had a cottage feel to them and yet, she wasn't disappointed. In fact, it suited the home and made it feel warm and welcoming.

Lord Wardoor came out to greet them, his Hessian boots clicking on the stone steps. "Lord and Lady Kinruth, Lady Isolde, welcome to my home. I hope your journey was pleasant."

Isolde dipped a small curtsy. "It was very pleasant, thank you."

Anne agreed as he ushered them inside. A footman dressed in green livery took their gloves and coats before they walked into the front drawing room, a pleasant, yellow painted space with light wooden furniture that made it seem larger than it was.

She smiled at Wardoor. "Your home is truly lovely, my lord. I'm surprised you do not stay here more often." Isolde sat down next to Anne who was busy pouring tea for them all. "Papa spoke of your estate before he passed away, and he said your stream has some of the best fishing he'd ever known."

Wardoor chuckled. "It does, and if you fish, my lady, I'd be glad to take you down to the river's edge, or we could take out the small wooden boat I dock at the boathouse."

"I would like that very much," she said, taking a sip of tea and welcoming the warm beverage. "We were raised in a home full of adventure. Not the most conventional for a duke's residence, I suppose, but those days were fabulous and perfect for children."

"Just as it should be." He sat across from her and regarded her with benign appreciation. Well, it was certainly what she believed it to be, even though it was nothing like how Merrick often watched her, his gaze all but burning with pleasure.

The realization made her wonder just what married life would be like with Wardoor, a friend for whom she had no romantic feelings. Would they come to have those feelings over time, or would they eventually regret their choice, start seeing the other as a hindrance they never should've saddled themselves with?

While others who made up the party trickled in from their journey from Town, they spoke of inconsequential things. Then Lord Wardoor had them shown to their rooms and Isolde, too, took the opportunity to rest before dinner.

Her room was comfortable, if lacking in finery, but the house was of a different style to what she was accustomed, and one had to make allowances when making a marriage match. The walls were paneled and painted blue with paintings of people and landscapes. The bed was covered in a cream duvet that matched the material on the headboard. Her windows overlooked the lawn and rolling hills beyond, all of which she could see while lying down. She supposed it had a very French feel to its design, and the room was probably the best he had for his guests.

That evening, Isolde dressed in a chiffon mint-green gown with gold beading on the small shoulder cuffs. She stood before the full-length mirror and studied how the gown suited her dark hair and pale skin, but as much as she was happy with how she appeared, even she could see her eyes lacked vitality or excitement.

She was bored and it was only her first day...

With a sigh, she headed downstairs and found most people already seated for dinner. Lord Wardoor sat at the head of the table, and he gestured to a seat to his right. Her sister Alice, seated on the opposite side of the table, caught her eye and winked, grinning as she took a sip of wine. Isolde looked to see if Wardoor had caught her sibling's action and was relieved he had not, but startled to find him watching her instead. She smiled and also took a sip of wine, hoping the feeling that she was doing something wrong would pass.

Lord Clifford, the Marquess of Nottingham, sat to her right and was very pleasant, if not a little older than the congregation. Isolde noted his attention toward her mama and liked hearing her parent laugh, her cheeks rosy with flattery. It had been a long time since she'd seen her so lively. "I do hope you find my home suitable, Isolde. I would so like to have your approval of it."

"From what I have seen so far, I do believe there would be very few indeed who would not approve. You have a lovely home, truly." Even if she wasn't quite certain that the home was for her. Could she really marry without any deeper feeling than congeniality for her husband? A vexing thought told her that after all she'd been through, she could.

He smiled easily at her praise. "Thank you. I've worked hard to keep it from falling down around my ears, and I know it needs some improvements, but they will come in time. Would you care to walk the gardens after dinner? I have lamps scattered throughout the grounds, and my gardener ensures they're lit every night when I'm in residence."

Isolde noted Alice watching her, knowing her sister would've heard Wardoor's request. Did she wish to walk with him, in the twilight, alone? The thought left her a little uneasy, and she took another sip of wine. She met his expectant, if not a little excited, gaze and nodded. "That would be lovely, thank you." Isolde sat back as a course of turtle soup was placed before her. "But should we go outdoors? I would surely be taking you from your guests, and I wouldn't wish to do so."

Wardoor waved away her concern, spooning a healthy amount of soup into his mouth before stating, "You would not be. We will go outdoors for only a few minutes, and there will be others about, I'm sure. None of my guests will feel slighted, I assure you."

She cleared her throat. "I look forward to it then." Isolde ate the soup, which tasted more like chicken broth than turtle and did her best not to think about why Wardoor wished to walk with her...alone. But in reality, she knew why. His courting would naturally lead up to them being alone.

She'd known Wardoor for years, but now that the time had arrived that he could possibly propose, nerves assailed her. If she said yes, she would be doing so without any deeper feelings for the man than friendship. Isolde studied him a moment as he laughed and conversed with Lady Sewell to his right. He wasn't vicious, had always been congenial with her. She supposed they could have a happy match. Initially, they might muddle along, but maybe in time, real affection would grow. It wasn't an impossible dream.

With such a thought, Isolde shook any doubts aside. With marriage came children, and that, above all else, was what she wished for, and Wardoor promised both children and security. An alliance with him was better than pining for things she could not have.

"I should imagine the next fortnight will be very busy for you. What activities do you have planned for us all?" she asked, wanting to distract herself from her thoughts of the walk.

"Many, all of which I hope you'll enjoy. I've set up a room for the women to paint, if they wish, and I've had a harp brought from London as I believe your friend Anne likes to play. There are horses, of course, for both the men and woman to ride, and I have game on my property, if any of the gentlemen wish to partake in that pursuit."

The thought of going for a ride was welcome, and Isolde put it on her to-do list for tomorrow. "I'll admit, I'm not as accomplished a rider as Victoria, but I'd like to go out some-time while I'm here. I prefer to be outdoors over being secluded inside."

He nodded, his smile warm, giving her hope that maybe affection could grow. Someday... "I thought as much, and we could invite the others to join us.

"I think that sounds like a wonderful idea. Perhaps a picnic?"

He smiled fully then. "I do hope we're able to become more acquainted during this time, Isolde. It is what I had planned when I had the idea of a house party."

Isolde could understand why. But the continuing war that was waging inside her body—her mind screamed to move on with her life, clasp what was offered and make the best of a situation. Her heart however, the beating little beast, refused to feel anything for the gentleman before her. Refused to even try to form some emotional tie to Wardoor. He was firmly locked in the friendship box, and there he was bound to stay. "I'm sure we will, and since we're going to stroll the gardens after dinner, we're making a good start." He smiled but didn't reply, and she was thankful for the silence that descended between them as they finished their meal.

A little after dinner, when everyone was settled in the downstairs drawing room, partaking in card games and music, Wardoor walked her onto the terrace. It was a warm night, and the air held the soft scent of flowers and freshly cut lawn. They headed toward the stairs that led to a grav-eled path, walking, if her memory served correctly, in the direction of the lake.

He took her hand and placed it on his sleeve. "I wanted to talk to you in private and thought, instead of leaving you all week to wonder when I would gather my courage, I would speak my desire on the first night of the house party." Isolde swallowed, keeping her gaze fixed on the path ahead, trying and failing miserably to not get too carried away at his words and what they could mean. "What did you wish to speak to me about, my lord?"

Please don't propose. Please don't propose.

"You may be aware of my rakish reputation in London and what that would mean for my wife, should I ever acquire one."

They continued to walk, and Isolde glanced at him. He seemed pensive but determined. "I have heard of your reputation. I doubt there are many who have not." She chuckled to quell any concerns he may have. Men did have lives before marriage, more freeing than women did, but it was nothing Isolde wasn't aware of and she was secure enough not to worry.

He smiled down at her and seemed to relax further. "I wanted there to be no secrets, no misunderstandings, should we become betrothed. There are certain aspects of my life that I do not wish to be parted from, as I'm sure you do as well."

"And they are?" Isolde asked, curious now.

"Should we marry, I would desire us to start a family immediately, and that would entail me coming to you at least four times a week, if you're in agreement. We would have separate bedrooms, of course, joined by a shared dressing room. You would have a generous allowance and freedom to attend or do whatever pleased you. I would spend some nights at my club and…"

Even in the moonlight Isolde spotted the high color that marked Wardoor's cheeks. "And what?"

He cleared his throat, his smile a little pained. "I want to be honest, Isolde, but I fear what I will say next may result in me losing you, and I do not want that."

"Tell me. I value honesty above anything else."

"I have a mistress and should I marry, that is not something I wish to change." He pulled her to a stop. "What are your thoughts on this?"

For a moment Isolde was lost for words, but she checked her emotions, looked for jealousy, anger, or resentment, and nothing happened. The man before her was offering her a home, children, and asking for only one thing in return, to keep a mistress. Had she loved him to the very core of her being, Isolde would never allow such to occur, but she didn't love him. If anything, Wardoor was a friend and nothing more. "Do not tax yourself, Wardoor. If you wish to live your life after marriage in the same way in which you do now, I shall not stop you. I trust that should we marry you will ensure my health, happiness, and wellbeing, and should I wish for you to end your association that you will, without complaint."

He frowned. "Could you see yourself asking me such a thing?"

She shrugged. "You have been honest, brutally so, in fact, and so will I in return. I do not love you, and therefore your lifestyle as a rakehell will not affect my happiness. If I should ask you to quit such lifestyle, it will be only because I've grown to love you and would not wish to share you with anyone. If I promise not to impinge on your life, can you promise to honor my request should you ever receive it?" The balance of their union hung on what he said next. Isolde held her breath, curious to see what he would say.

"I can promise you that wholeheartedly." Wardoor took her hand and kissed it.

Isolde pulled him into another stroll, not quite ready to go back inside. "Tell me of your home and lands. What are your plans for it?"

Wardoor gestured quite a lot as he discussed his wishes and plans for the estate in the future years. The conversation only grew in enjoyment, and coming back to the house and joining the party, Isolde was more at ease with Wardoor than she ever had been before. He was a libertine, and the tales about London of his conquests were as wild as his gardens, but that did not mean he wouldn't make a good husband. His honesty and outlay of their life together calmed Isolde's unease over the union, and hope bloomed in her chest that what she longed for above all else—children—was close to coming true.

The two weeks at the house party flew by, and Isolde came to feel genuine affection for his lordship. Not love—that emotion she doubted she could ever feel again—but certainly her ease and friendship with his lordship was a good base for a marriage, if he proposed.

On the final night of the house party, Isolde found herself once more walking with Wardoor after dinner. A ritual they'd continued from the first night.

He pulled them to a stop beside the lake and turned to face her. A sheen of sweat beaded on his forehead and glistened in the moonlight. Never before had he looked so pensive and scared, and Isolde braced herself for the proposal that would come. "I believe you know that I would like, above all else, to marry you, Isolde. To make you the Marchioness of Wardoor. The house party, bringing a small portion of Society to my estate, was all an effort to get you away, to have you to myself and out of London, so I could ask you a question that has been burning within me for some time now."

She stood still, unsure how to respond. This question was what she'd prepared to hear from Wardoor. The chance to move on, to clasp a future with a marriage and children shimmered before her—if only she could take a leap of faith and hope for the best. "I…"

"You're unsure?" He frowned, and she could see the hurt her pause in answering him inflicted.

Isolde shook herself from the thoughts that always plagued her mind. If she said yes, in only a year, God willing, she too could be pregnant with their first child. Living life in the country, her beloved England again, secure and happy as best she could be under the circumstances.

"I'm of an age, Isolde, when it's time for me to marry. I must have an heir, and I wish for my children to have you as their mother. I want us to build a life together out of mutual respect and necessity, if you would accept me, that is." He clasped her hands, and she noted they were shaking. "I have had a wild past as you well know, and you're aware of how that lifestyle may impact on you, should you say yes," he said, shrugging. "Will you marry me knowing who I am and how I wish to carry on? Will you be my wife?"

"Would you think me a silly fool for not knowing what to say?" she said, a little lost for words. He pulled her farther into the gardens that bordered the lake, where no lights from the path could intrude on their seclusion.

"Let me kiss you. Let me show you what I may offer you as a husband. I can make you happy, I'm certain of it. I will strive to make each and every day of our marriage a pleasurable one, even enjoyable, if only you would allow me to try."

She bit her lip. "I...um..." She cursed her stupidity for thinking of Merrick at the mention of the word pleasure. Could she kiss another man? The only gentleman she'd ever allowed such privileges had been Merrick, and oddly, it seemed a betrayal to want to try such an embrace with another. An absurd thought she squashed the moment she considered it. "Yes, you may kiss me."

Wardoor didn't shy away from taking her in his arms and doing exactly what he'd asked for. He dipped his head slowly and delicately swiped his lips against hers, urging her to respond to his teasing. She shut her eyes to lessen the nerves that wracked her body. She didn't want to think about the fact that when her eyes were closed she couldn't see who was, in fact, kissing her, and she could just enjoy being the center of someone's intent and purpose.

Wardoor's hands cradled her face as he deepened the kiss. She opened for him, allowing him to persuade her to be his, to allow the man who was sweet, and trying desperately to woo her, to win her hand. Isolde went through all the motions that made a kiss wonderful, fulfilling, and coaxing, but her body refused to react in the way it always had with Merrick. But then, one could not always have everything one wished for, and what Wardoor offered was a very good option for her. It was identical to most ton marriages she knew, with the exception of Anne's and her sister Elizabeth's. "Marry me, Isolde. I will take care of you, I promise," he whispered against her lips, kissing them softly.

His words resonated with sincerity, and she let go of all the worries that had held back her answer to his question. "I will marry you, my lord."

He kissed her again, a quick brush of lips, before escorting her back to the house. "I will speak to your mother directly and ask for your brother's consent when we return to Town. Are you in agreement?"

"Yes, that sounds suitable." She followed him, not certain what her feelings were about the whole situation. It was all so different to the last time she'd been betrothed. The happiness she'd had with Merrick, the sureness of what she was doing, had been beyond any doubt. But Wardoor had been honest; she was entering the union with her eyes wide open. Once she was married and increasing with their first child, all her concerns would be nothing but a silly memory to dismiss.

"I will have the banns read and send word to London tonight for the announcement to be made public. We can marry a month from now, if you're happy to do so. I, myself, do not see any reason why we should delay."

Isolde ignored her tumbling stomach. "I agree. We should marry as soon as it's arranged. I'm sure Mama will help us, and a Town wedding during the Season should enable all our friends to attend."

Wardoor pulled her through the terrace doors, and Isolde noted her mama watching her entrance with calculated interest. He clasped two glasses of champagne from a passing footman and called the room to attention. Her sister Alice's eyes widened and darted between her and Wardoor, and panic seized her, realizing he'd forgotten to address her mother first before making the announcement public. Isolde took a large sip of wine and mouthed "sorry" to her mama, who composed herself with an affable, knowing smile.

"Thank you everyone for taking your time away from Town and joining me here on my country estate. And now, with not a little amount of pleasure, I can announce that Lady Isolde Worthingham has agreed to be my wife, and we will be married before the Season's out." He lifted his crystal glass and urged her to do so. "To us, my lady. May I always honor our vows and our life be nothing but bliss and prosperity."

"To us," Isolde mimicked, raising her glass and then smiling, laughing, as everyone present came up to congratulate them. Alice came up to her last of all and, making an excuse to Wardoor that she wished to discuss wedding details, pulled her aside.

The moment they were out of her betrothed's hearing, she hissed, "You said yes!"

Isolde wasn't sure if it was a statement or a question or even an outraged declaration. She nodded, remembering that the future she wished to have could start the moment she said, I do. "I have, and it's for the best. Please don't try to persuade me otherwise. He'll give me a good home, the opportunity to have children of my own. You know I wish that above anything else."

Alice slumped and then pulled her into a fierce hug. "I was going to try to make you see reason, to perhaps look to the past for your future, but I see your mind is made up, and I'll not change it for you. And I truly do hope that your dream of being a mother will come, and your heart will finally be full again."

Isolde understood exactly what her sister meant by her words, and she was thankful for her honesty. "I hope you're right, and I'm willing to do my best to ensure we have a happy marriage."

"I know you will." Alice hugged her again, and Isolde fought the prickling behind her eyelids. Wardoor was a good choice—secure and honest. All would be well. She was sure of it.

*M*errick spent a week with William on his estate in Wiltshire before his man of business summoned him back to Town. The missive was precise and to the point. His wife, and her nightly pursuits into the bowels of London, were becoming extreme and more dangerous to herself and the baby she carried. It had to stop and, by God, he'd stop it, if at all possible.

He stared down at the cartoon image of the duchess in the morning paper, fighting not to cast up his accounts. The drawing showed Leonora with a bulging stomach, awkwardly seated upon a man, no doubt Lord Barkley, a drink in one hand and cigar in the other. It was a disgrace. And not only to herself, but her family, his family, and all that they stood for. She was a vicar's daughter, for the love of God. How could she fall so low as this?

A voice in his head murmured that it was his doing and no one else's. That Merrick had made her become who she was today—a cold, calculating woman who lived without the love and support of her husband.

A ruckus out in his foyer caught his attention, and he stood, striding from the room to see what the servants were blustering about. A maid dashed upstairs with linens, another with a pail of steaming water.

"Has something happened?" he asked, catching the head housekeeper who followed the maids up the stairs.

"Your Grace." She bobbed a quick curtsy. "The duchess's time has come. You should have a new son or daughter within a few hours."

Merrick nodded, shame washing over him that hearing such news brought forth nothing but ire and disdain. He'd only ever thought of Leonora as a friend, prior to her deceit on the night before his wedding to Isolde. Afterward, he'd hated her more than he ever thought to hate anyone.

And now, with a child coming that wasn't his—a child he would bestow his name upon, feed, and clothe—his loathing of his wife was even more profound. What she'd done to him was unforgivable, and no matter how wrong such thoughts were, he could not bring himself to care what happened to the woman above stairs.

Screams and yelling punctuated the quiet of the house, followed by other women and their commands. Merrick walked into his library and shut the door, only looking up from the day's paper at the mumbling sounds of the doctor being greeted in the foyer before he, too, headed upstairs.

Merrick continued to read the paper; having been out of Town, he'd missed what had happened in London. The business section and political news were mostly unchanged, but the notice of a forthcoming nuptial, an occasion foretold as the event of the Season, caught his attention with sickening force.

A cold chill ran down his spine as the words of an engagement between the Lady Isolde Worthingham, daughter to the late Duke of Penworth and Blake Marlborough, Marquess of Wardoor, were printed in black and white before him.

It could not be true… Taking a deep breath, he sat back in his chair, running a hand through his hair before picking up the paper and reading it once again, lest there was a mistake. But no, there, in little mocking letters, were printed the words that had the power to stop the heart that beat too fast in his chest.

Merrick stood and poured himself a large glass of brandy, downing it in one swallow. How dare Wardoor, a supposed friend, even if their relationship had been strained of late, do such a thing to him? But then, why would he not, when Lady Isolde, pure and kind, sweet-tempered woman that she was, could possibly be his wife? It also helped that they were both unmarried, of a similar age, and circulated in the same sphere of friends.

And now that Wardoor had sold one of his estates, he was no longer in debt to Lord Barkley, or so his steward had informed him. With a more secure footing on which to start a future with Isolde, and with his wife's dowry—which was a very large sum indeed—they would be comfortable, to say the least, as would any children they were blessed with in the future.

At the thought of Wardoor getting Isolde with a child, his stomach turned and he stood, walking to the window and throwing up the sash. He didn't want her to marry another. Selfish bastard that he was, he wanted her to remain a spinster, someone he could admire from afar and know that no matter what others thought, he was hers and she was his. Always.

A light knock sounded on the door, and he turned, answering more sharply than he ought. "Yes."

His butler entered, a slight smile lifting his lips. "Your Grace, I have joyous news."

Merrick shut the window and leaned against the seal. He fought to show some emotion other than indifference to what he was about to be told. "What is it?" he asked, smiling a little at his old retainer.

"The duchess has given birth to a healthy daughter. She is in the nursery with the wet nurse now, if you wish to visit her. The duchess is in good health and recovering. She's asked for peace and quiet."

"Thank you," he said, watching as his butler bowed and left, shutting the door with hardly a noise. Merrick stared at the dark wood, his mind conflicted as to what to do. Do I want to see the child? No, in all honesty, he couldn't give a damn about the babe, but morbid curiosity got the better of him and, within minutes, he found himself climbing the stairs and going to see the daughter who would bear his name, if not his blood.

The wet nurse stood beside the small cot, rocking it slowly as a small figure slept under the white blankets. She greeted him warmly, stepping aside as he went to inspect the child. He thought he would see Lord Barkley staring back at him—a horrible image and one that was wont to give anyone nightmares—and yet it was not what he found.

Instead, a small delicate little girl, with a button nose and perfect lips, lay sleeping, a little dried milk on her bottom lip. Her small perfect hands clutched at the woolen blankets as if she'd never let go, and her ears, the tiniest things he'd ever seen, were covered slightly by dark curls.

Shame washed over him that he could ever be indifferent

to this child. He rubbed his jaw, reaching down instinctively and, without thought, picked her up, popping her onto his shoulder. Merrick rubbed her back just as he used to do with William when he had a stomachache.

She made sweet gurgling sounds, and he walked to the nearby chair, sitting and holding her in front of him to take a better look. She was the most adorable little thing he'd ever seen in his life, and he kissed her sweet cheeks and nose until she made it clear such actions were not appreciated.

"You're as pretty as a flower. I think we'll call you Lily. Lady Lily will suit you very well." He counted her fingers and toes and marveled at their miniscule size. "You're my daughter, and I promise from this day forward that nothing will ever come to harm you. You will have everything your heart desires and more." Lily fussed in his arms, and he smiled, looking up to the wet nurse. "Under no circumstance is the duchess to take this child outdoors or be left alone with her. Do you understand?"

The wet nurse's eyes widened, but she nodded. "Yes, Your Grace. Whatever you say."

"Her name is to be Lily, and I wish for her to be brought down to my study whenever she's not sleeping so I may visit with her. I will, naturally, check on her here throughout the day, as well. If there is anything you need, or are worried about, do not hesitate to come to me. I will assist you, without question."

"Thank you, sir. I assure you I will."

Merrick stood, giving Lily another little kiss before handing her to the wet nurse. "I think I may have woken her a little. She may be in need of another feed before she settles."

The wet nurse smiled. "I think you may be right." She took the child, and Merrick watched her for a moment before leaving the woman alone with his daughter.

He strode to Leonora's room, knocked once, and entered.

She lay on the bed, facing the windows. Striding to that side of the room, he sat and faced her. "I wish to call the child Lily. What are your thoughts on this?"

"Do what you like with the child." She sighed. "I'm tired, please leave." She rolled onto her back and stared at the ceiling.

"You're not to take the child out like you did William. In your condition, you're not to be trusted. Do you understand?" He was being harsh, and this was probably not the best time to have an argument with his wife. Certainly not after she'd given birth. But now that he'd seen his daughter, an overwhelming urge to protect his children against the woman before him overrode all other cares.

She glared at him, her face distorted with so much hate he hardly recognized her. "My condition? Pray tell what you mean by such a statement."

"That you're addicted to opium and laudanum. That you have a tendency to take our children out and leave them in the bowels of London, for who-knows-what to happen to them."

"I forgot William once, and he survived. Do not be such a bore, Merrick. You've been fun only once, and I had to spike your drink with opium to get the result I wished."

"When did you tamper with my drink?" he asked, knowing what her answer would be. Had suspected it for years.

"On the night I seduced you at Mountshaw. I knew to have you sleep with me, and not guess who entered your bed, something a little stronger than spirits was needed. What a triumph that my plan worked." She grinned. "But you are very tedious to put up with; maybe I should've allowed you to marry your boring Isolde, after all. You're more suited to her than you and I." Leonora laughed, the sound maniacal.

It was a question he had asked himself often. Why had

Leonora wanted to marry him? From the first moment after taking their vows, she'd made it clear that she didn't care for him or his thoughts. It had taken him only a few weeks to realize that she'd wanted the title of duchess and the triumph over Isolde more than anything else. Even if she'd had to threaten them all to realize such a win. "Your supposed friends do you an injustice thinking that such behavior is an acceptable and healthy way to live. I'm embarrassed to call you my wife."

"Well then," she said, still laughing, "what a shame it is that there is nothing for you to do about it." She met his gaze, no emotion behind her black orbs. "Now leave. I want to be well again so I may have some fun without you, and your presence halts my progress."

He ignored her. "I have purchased a house for you, where right at this moment your maids are packing up your things to move you there. I will no longer live under the same roof as a woman, who, frankly, repulses me. I will not let the underbelly of this Society grace this home. The children shall be protected from your seedy dealings, and if that means you must live elsewhere, then that is a price I'm willing to pay."

"Your children? Only William is yours." She snickered. "What a lark laying with you when you were so foxed. 'The duped duke,' I should call you. La, what a triumph! Poor Isolde, still pining for you, all these years later."

Merrick ground his teeth, hating that part of what she said was true. He had been duped and a damn fool to not know when he was being deceived, even now. "The children are mine, and I'll not have anyone slander their name, not even their mother. Heed the warning, Leonora. It's in your best interest."

"Do you want to know who the father is of your precious Lily? You'll never guess."

Merrick stood, not willing to hear any more. She was as

vicious as a snake just out of hibernation, wanting to strike and injure any who were about. "As soon as you're well enough, you will be leaving. We cannot divorce, and you'll have an allowance, but should you exceed it, do not think to ask for any more funds, as I will not grant them."

"How dare you, you bastard. How dare you dictate to me. Your wife."

"Very easily, and I should've tightened the reins on you years ago. I'm ashamed of myself that I did not." Merrick stood, striding toward the door. Leonora threw back the blankets and shuffled out of the bed, following him.

"I hate you. You're as pompous as that sniveling fool, Isolde. Always right, always kind to those in need. You make me sick." She came up hard against him and slapped his face. Merrick narrowed his eyes against the sting and walked out, calling a footman over who hovered in the passageway. "The duchess requires rest. She is neither to leave nor receive visitors."

The footman's eyes widened, but he nodded, going to stand beside the duchess's door.

Leonora leaned out into the passage, grinning like a woman without wits. "The girl's father is Wardoor. How do you think Isolde will take such news?"

Merrick halted.

"It's quite a funny story, and one I'm sure you want to hear, so I'll tell you." She walked out into the passage, running a hand across the footman's chest, the lad blushing furiously. "I found your closest friend, passed out in the opium den where you found William that day. Quite naked, I might add. Well…" she paused, smirking, "from the chest up, in any case. I was curious if an unconscious man could still perform as I like them to, and so you can imagine my pleasure when I found out he could. Lord Barkley enjoyed the show as well, and we've had many a good laugh about it since then."

Merrick stared at her a moment, not wanting to listen or commence another argument. He met his butler at the top of the stairs as he started down them. The more distance between him and his wife, the better. She was beyond help. No woman with any self-respect could do such a thing to another human being, or gloat about it afterward, as if it were as common as cake and tea. "Please have the duchess helped back to bed. I fear she's not herself."

His butler nodded, walking toward Leonora who followed Merrick, leaning over the balustrade.

"He has a lovely large cock, Merrick. Thick and long. Isolde will be well pleased when she beds him, now that they're to be married." She started down the stairs, her laughter echoing through the house. "I know you are aware of it. The news is almost front page in the morning's paper."

Merrick turned and met his wife's wild gaze. "Go back to your room, Leonora. I think it's fair to say we have nothing further to say to each other, now or ever. In fact," he continued, "if you're so well to be out of bed, I'm sure I can have you moved from here sooner than I thought."

She huffed. "Oh, you'd like that, wouldn't you? But I'm not going anywhere, dearest husband. I intend on being your lovely wife for a long time to come." Leonora ran down the stairs, her eyes feral with anger. "You always thought—"

Merrick took a step toward her when he noted her misstep. A piercing scream rent the air and horrified, he watched as Leonora tripped over her own shift, toppling forward and hitting the marble stairs with a sickening crack.

He ran to her as she lay at the bottom of the stairs, her lifeless eyes staring at the ceiling, her body at an awkward angle to her head. With shaking fingers, Merrick reached to feel her neck, and the protruding bone told him it was broken. Leaning down, he listened for a heartbeat, but no comforting sound resonated in her chest. His stomach roiled. What had just happened? This could not be. Not this. No matter how much he hated Leonora, he never wanted her dead. The butler kneeled beside Leonora, his eyes wide with shock.

"Your Grace?"

Merrick slumped onto the floor, feeling, more than seeing, the ducal staff surrounding them. "Send for the doctor." When his servant didn't move, he yelled, "Now, man!"

The butler sent two footmen to do his bidding. Not sure if he should move Leonora, he stood and walked into his library and collected a blanket. Coming back into the foyer he placed it over her and sat down, closing her eyes, as if in sleep.

He stayed there until the doctor arrived, and confirming his own supposition that she'd died during the fall, the doctor helped the servants organize for Leonora to be placed back in her room. Merrick summoned his man of business who would prepare the funeral.

Merrick dropped into his leather desk chair, the last words between him and Leonora loud and tormenting in his mind. He cringed, standing and pouring himself a large glass of brandy, hoping the amber liquid would drown the horrible situation in which he now found himself. Downing the beverage quickly, he refilled the crystal glass, walking to the settee before the fire, staring at the flames but feeling no heat.

How could he have been so cruel? How could he have said such words to his wife? He stared at the orange flames licking the wood, wishing he could take back the last two hours of his life and knowing with sickening dread that he could not.

The thought of laying Leonora, such a young woman, to rest, was not something he wished to contemplate. Nor the fact that he would have to tell William that his mama had died, and so tragically, as well.

A light knock sounded against the door.

"Enter," he said, not looking to see who intruded.

"Your Grace," the doctor said, coming over to where he sat and taking a seat himself, even though Merrick didn't offer him one. The rotund man placed his bag on the floor, steepling his fingers before his chin. "I believe it would be best, under the circumstances, for you to say the duchess passed away during childbirth. I've just spent the past hour with an inconsolable maid who told me of your purchasing a house for your wife and having her move there, instead of living with you."

Merrick frowned, looking up at the doctor. "What of it? It was no secret that our marriage was not a love match, and I'm sure you're aware that the child born only hours ago is not mine. The whole ton knows of our disastrous union, but I fail to see why I should lie about her death."

"Can you not?" The doctor leaned back in his chair, and Merrick wondered how he could seem so calm at such a time. His own blood pumped fast in his veins, and no matter how many glasses of brandy he consumed, something told Merrick they would not help him in the least.

"No. I cannot."

The doctor sighed. "Some may think it not an accident. And before you state otherwise, I know there were witnesses to what occurred, but it wouldn't be the first time a man of influence has paid off his servants to keep quiet."

"I didn't kill my wife." Merrick leaned forward in his chair, slamming his glass upon the mahogany table before them. "Is that what you're implying?"

"I know you did not kill Her Grace, but to keep your

name from any more tarnish, it would be best if you stated she died of complications during the birth of your daughter. Society does not need to know everything."

Merrick stood, walking to the mantle and leaning against it when he swayed. "I would know."

"Think on it." The doctor stood, picking up his bag. "I'm very sorry for your loss, Your Grace. May the duchess rest in peace."

"Thank you," he replied, tugging the bellpull. Within moments of the doctor leaving, a footman entered. "Have the carriage readied. I'm leaving for Mountshaw on the morn. And please notify the wet nurse in charge of Lady Lily to prepare the child for travel also."

"Yes, Your Grace." The butler bowed, fleeing as fast as he'd come.

Merrick scribbled a note to his man of business, telling him of the circumstances that had befallen them all and ordering him to hire the best funeral furnishers he could find to have Leonora brought to Mountshaw for burial as soon as possible.

And after he'd said his final good-byes to his wife, Merrick would close up the London home and leave for Mountshaw where he would stay indefinitely. London and its detrimental pressures and temptations could go hang.

CHAPTER 13

*I*solde was numb as she traveled with her family to Merrick's country home, Mountshaw Estate, for Her Grace's funeral. She had never wanted to see the place again, and to be going back for the burial of a woman who'd been her childhood friend and adult enemy wasn't something to which she looked forward.

The crunch of the wheels on the graveled drive was loud as they made the turn through the gates. No one spoke. Her sisters Victoria and Alice were quiet with their own thoughts, their mother idly looking out at the gray, drizzly weather.

"Oh, this is a sad day," her mother said at last, breaking the silence. "To think Leonora will not get to see her sweet children grow up. Oh, it's sad indeed."

Isolde patted her hand, consoling her as best she could. Not a lot of information had been forthcoming over Leonora's death, other than she'd passed after the new babe was born. It was almost impossible to fathom that the duchess was gone. No matter how much Isolde and Leonora had despised each other, death was not something Isolde would ever have wished upon the woman.

"I would like to know how it happened. The rumors going about London are tragic and scandalous at the same time." Alice met her gaze. "Some even say she had packed a small valise and was leaving the duke!"

"Don't be absurd. She tripped down the stairs, lost her footing in some way or another, and fell. After birthing a child I should imagine you're not as stable on your feet as you are normally. I won't have you partaking in these rumors about the duchess. You're better than that." Isolde stared down her sibling before looking back out at the familiar drive. The last time they had traveled down this very road, her heart had been broken in two, and now she was to pay her last respects to the woman who had been the cause of her ruined dreams.

"Since we're to attend the placing of the duchess in the mausoleum, the duke has offered for us to stay, and I have agreed."

"Mama." Isolde gaped at her. "Why would you do such a thing? You know it is awkward between His Grace and me and, with him mourning his wife, this will make it even more so. Others in attendance will think I'm trying to force my way back into his affections." Isolde crossed her arms. "I'll not do it. We're staying at the local inn."

"We will not. Your brother will be here also, and no impropriety will be thought of during such a time. Do be serious, Isolde."

She gritted her teeth. "I am being serious. I don't want to stay here, Mama." She paused, wondering how else she could persuade her parent to leave. "How did you manage to get Josh to attend? He hasn't been pleasant to the duke since the night we caught Moore with Leonora."

"Josh has agreed, for duty's sake, to hold his opinions of

His Grace and his actions toward you at bay, until he's returned to London. Just as he should as the head of this family."

"With us staying, tongues will start to flap. I don't like the situation at all."

Her mother sighed, facing her, her features brooking no argument. "We are not the only families staying, due to the distance his estate is from London. You will act civilly and like the lady you were raised to be. Now, I do believe we're nearly there."

Looking out the window, Isolde watched the large oaks that lined the drive pass by before the house came into view. Being back here brought forth all the emotions she'd bottled up and packed away. She wasn't ready to see it again, a home she'd adored, along with the man, knowing they could never be.

As the carriage pulled to a halt, it was only the liveried footmen that came out to greet them, their welcome warm but tone very somber. Isolde followed her mama into the house, once more in awe at its grand size, beautiful furnishings, and spacious light rooms that had always reminded her of Dunsleigh and were so different from her future home at Wardoor's.

Merrick strode from the library; dark circles lined his eyes and a haunted look was set across his features. Isolde studied him a moment and, even knowing the marriage between him and Leonora was not a happy union, she could tell he was emotionally spent. That there was a cloud of suspicion about the way Her Grace had died also didn't help. "Your Grace." She curtsied, and his attention snapped to her, but his eyes remained guarded.

"Lady Isolde." He bowed and greeted her family in turn before summoning the waiting staff to show them to their rooms. "When you're settled, we have a light repast set out in the drawing room."

The moment the invitation was offered he turned on his heel and walked back to the library, shutting the door firmly in their faces.

"Come, my dears. Let us get settled and venture down for a cup of tea. I'm in desperate need of one."

The room allocated to her was thankfully different to the one she'd had the last time she'd stayed here. This room faced the front of the house, and she watched the guests who arrived to pay their respects. Black carriage after black carriage rolled to a stop. She recognized most of them, people she'd been introduced to but not socialized with much, due to her time away in Scotland.

She looked up toward the hill where the mausoleum stood and thought about her childhood friend. To think that Leonora would be laid to rest tomorrow evening in the cold stone structure left an ache in her chest she'd not thought would occur. It was all such a waste. Life could be so cruel. To take someone so young, well before their time, was wrong.

The dinner bell rang out below, and she quickly changed before heading downstairs. Dinner that night was a morose affair, talk was muted, and His Grace bid them all a happy evening but didn't partake in the meal itself, instead opting to lock himself away in the library again.

Thankfully, the dinner service was short. After the many hours of travel, she was looking to rest and to remove herself from her current companions, as their talk was depressing, at its best. And tomorrow would be worse. And it was.

The sight of little William, holding his father's hand as tears streamed down his chubby cheeks, brought tears to her own eyes. Isolde looked at the coffin as it was carried into the vault and forgave Leonora and prayed for forgiveness herself after their many hurtful words over the past few weeks.

She swiped at a tear, surprised at how emotional she was toward a woman who had been so unkind to her. She looked up to the sky, remembering the fun they'd had together as girls. The mischief of their games, the seriousness when having their maids do their hair like the ladies who graced the ton—even if they'd still been in pigtails.

The Leonora from only days ago was not the girl she'd loved and would forever remember. Opium had taken that girl from them, and Isolde was ashamed that she hadn't done anything to help her overcome her addiction. She should've stepped in and made her see sense. Should have pushed their past differences aside and been her friend.

"Come dearest, it's over."

She started at her mother's words and turned for the carriage. She noted Merrick placing William in his carriage before he walked back toward the mausoleum. He stood alone, rain marking his overcoat as he watched the doors close and lock.

"Funerals are so sad, makes you not want to attend even your own," Alice said, stepping into the carriage and sitting beside Isolde.

Isolde frowned, wondering at times if Alice had any sense. "That is something none of us can escape, I'm afraid," she said.

"I don't want to be entombed in a wall or buried. I hate confined spaces. I want to be free as a galloping horse, to blow in the wind, and feel the rain on my face." Victoria climbed up into the carriage. "That is what I would wish for."

"Unfortunately, a corpse lying out in a garden wouldn't be the done thing." Isolde placed the carriage blanket over her and Alice's legs.

"If you burned me, it would be."

"That is enough talk of death and what you want done with your bodies." Their mother sighed. "Sometimes I'm at a loss with you girls." Victoria patted their mother's hand, not saying anything further on the subject.

"May I be excused from dinner tonight, Mama? I would prefer a plate in my room," Isolde asked, not wanting to attend another meal like the night before. Tomorrow they would leave, and the terrible churning in her stomach at being so close to Merrick and not being able to give comfort would cease. She looked out the window, swaying a little as the carriage rocked toward Mountshaw. With time, Merrick would be well again, not this devastated shell of a man he seemed to resemble. It was not her duty to worry over him. She had her own future to carry on with. Especially now, as she was to wed Wardoor in a few weeks.

"Of course. In fact, any of you may cry off dinner. I doubt we'll be missed, and no one wishes to socialize, in any case."

By the time they arrived back at the estate it was dusk. Isolde made her way to her room and ordered water to wash. With soup for dinner and a little bread, her bed beckoned, and yet, no matter how much she tried, how many times she adjusted her pillow, nothing would allow her to sleep.

Wrapping a shawl across her shoulders, she left her room, made her way downstairs, and toward the library. The house was eerily quiet and dark; only a lamp beside the front door burned low on a turned-down wick.

The library door was slightly ajar, and she walked into the room, lighting a lamp just inside the door with the small candle she carried. Blowing out her candle, she picked up the lamp and held it toward the bookcases. A shadow appeared near the fire surround, and she stifled a scream.

Merrick stood before the darkened hearth, his foot idly kicking at the charred bits of coal. His shoulders were hunched, and had she not entered the room, he would've been standing there in full dark.

"I'm sorry, Your Grace. I didn't know you were still up." He didn't turn and greet her. In fact, he didn't react in any way at all. Isolde walked into the room a little, unsure if she should stay or go. "Are you happy for me to find a book to take up and read? I find that I cannot sleep."

"A fatigue we both suffer from, it would seem." With one last kick at the coals, he walked to the nearby chaise lounge and sat, resting his head against the back of the chair. "You may take whatever book pleases you."

"Thank you." She walked to the shelf directly before her and grabbed the first novel she found, not caring what it was about. Turning to leave, the pallor of his skin and the empty decanter of brandy on the sideboard caught her eye. Isolde frowned and, striding toward the lounge, sat next to him. "When did you eat last, Merrick?"

He shrugged. "Yesterday." He paused. "I think." Standing, she rang the bell before sitting back down. "What are you doing?" Merrick sat up, looking at her for the first time. Bloodshot eyes with an unfocused stare gazed back at her. "When I ask when you ate something, I don't mean of a liquid kind. You cannot survive on brandy." The butler entered the room, the collar of his jacket at an odd angle, and Isolde could see he'd failed to pull on a waistcoat in his haste to attend them at this late hour. The servant bowed. "You called, Your Grace."

"No," Merrick said, sagging back onto the seat. "I did not."

"I did," Isolde said. "Please prepare some food for His Grace. He has not had his dinner this evening." The butler smiled a little, his shoulders slumping in relief, before leaving quickly to do as she bid. They didn't speak as they waited for the late repast, and in no time at all, a plate of sandwiches was set before them with a fresh pot of steaming black coffee that smelled divine and strong.

Isolde prepared a plate and placed it on his knee. "Now eat and do not argue with me."

"When did you become so authoritative?" He nibbled one corner of the sandwich, his face turning up in disgust.

"I grew up, I suppose, and with age comes bossiness." She smiled at him and poured them both a cup of the sobering liquid. Not sure what to say, she ate a sandwich, too, if only to give her something to do. "You must go on, for your children's sake, at the very least. Leonora would've wanted that for you."

Deep frown lines marked his brow, and he placed his plate on the side of the lounge. "Should they one day learn the truth, they'll never forgive me." He sat forward, staring absently into the fire. "Hell, I don't forgive myself."

The despair in his tone tore at her heart, and she hated seeing him so despondent. "Tell me what happened, Merrick." He didn't speak for a long moment, just continued to stare at his cup of coffee.

He ran a hand across his jaw, and the sudden action startled her before he said, "And you're wrong. Leonora wouldn't care a kipper what we thought or how we reacted to such a tragedy." He shook his head, disdain crossing his features. "Hell, she would think it a lark and be offended that not more people are here to pay their respects and not enough tears were shed."

Isolde could understand what he meant, but he was wrong. "You're talking of the Leonora we all know now, but had she been thinking clearly, she would mourn the loss of her young family. Just as much as you shall mourn the loss of her from your life. You must believe that."

He cringed. "I killed her, Isolde. Though I may not have physically harmed her, emotionally, I did." Merrick swiped at a tear, and Isolde remained silent, sensing he needed to gather his thoughts. "If you must know what happened, it started after I had seen our new daughter to ensure all was right with her care. I visited Leonora soon afterward, and we argued. I said things I will forever regret."

"What did you say?" Isolde placed down her coffee, folding her hands in her lap.

"I told her of the house I had purchased for her use and that as soon as she was able, I would have her removed to live there permanently. I notified her that her time with the children would be limited going forward."

Isolde couldn't fault him in regard to the children, but being told she was no longer wanted, so soon after giving birth... "I gather she didn't take your news well."

"You think I was too harsh?" He looked at her then, and a slither of unease coursed through her at his wretchedness. Merrick seemed ragged and worn and nothing like the cultured duke he normally was. "She threw at my head the fact that only William was mine and laughed that Lily was not. I warned her not to try to slander their names or she'd feel my wrath tenfold."

So it was true. Leonora had been having an affair, and the child she'd just birthed was not Merrick's. Relief poured through her, followed closely by guilt at even thinking such a thing and at such a time. "You said yourself that Leonora wasn't in a right state of mind. You must try to remember that when these dark thoughts attempt to sway you. And given time, I'm sure Leonora would've grown accustomed to living separately from you."

She certainly had.

He let out a self-deprecating laugh. "Yes, it was no secret that our marriage was a disaster, that she was addicted to opium, and preferred the bowels of London to her family.

173

But she refused to leave and said as much before the accident."

"What happened that made her fall, Merrick? Please tell me."

"Our argument continued, before all the staff, most of who were watching, albeit surreptitiously. I was standing in the foyer, Leonora on the first floor landing, when she started down the stairs. Her foot caught the hem of her shift, and she tripped. I was too far away and couldn't catch her."

Tears welled in Merrick's eyes, and Isolde wanted nothing more than to comfort him, to help him in any way she could, but she refrained. "It was an unfortunate tragic accident, Merrick. Please tell me you don't blame yourself."

"I was dismissive and cruel and my final words...hell, I will not even say them aloud. Everything I touch I hurt." He met her gaze, his eyes haunted and bloodshot. "I've hurt you, Leonora, my children... All of you, I've injured beyond redemption."

"Oh no." Isolde would hear no more of that, and taking his hands, she started to rub the chill out of them. "While I have no doubt things were said by both of you that are regretful, things that were cruel and edged with a pointed dagger, neither of you were to know what was going to happen. I will not let you blame yourself for this, Merrick. I will not."

He slumped back onto the settee, weariness covering him like a cloak. "I should have helped her as you suggested. I should have done it years ago. Instead, I scorned her, ridiculed her, and turned my back without a thought of what I was doing. Leonora was the woman who ruined my life, and not one day since we wed had I allowed her to forget it. Had I done right by my wife, none of this would've happened, and she would be alive today."

"You are not responsible for her actions, Merrick. And

this was an accident, no matter what was said." Isolde grappled for words, but what could one say to someone who was determined to see no point other than his own. And perhaps, today of all days, Merrick needed to loathe himself, hit the lowest point a person can hit before picking himself up and moving on with his life. "I believe Leonora's trickery on the night before our wedding did stem from her love of you. I didn't see it at the time, and perhaps I didn't want to admit to myself that my friend had feelings for you, but I can see it now, looking back. Everyone makes choices in life, and they're not always what we wish them to be, but that's life. Leonora chose to live as she did, and while I will admit that part of the blame is yours, she, too, is responsible."

"I've acted contemptibly," he said, his voice hoarse. "I don't deserve happiness because of how I treated Leonora. If I had any sense, I'd lock myself here at Mountshaw and never return to Town."

They sat, both lost in thought. Isolde had never seen Merrick so low before and, in all truth, she didn't really know how to help him. Other than to listen. "Did Leonora say who the father of your daughter was? Do you know the man?"

Merrick pulled away and, without meeting her gaze, leaned forward to rest his head in his hands. "I've never met the gentleman."

His answer was curt, and something in his tone told Isolde he didn't want to talk any further on the subject. She stood, pulling him to stand. "Come, you must get some rest. I have no doubt you've been greeting the dawn these past few days and not with a clear mind."

He conceded and followed her to the door. "Perhaps you're right. Maybe some sleep will be of help."

"I'm sure it will." Isolde reached for the door and Merrick

held it closed, pinning her somewhat between him and freedom.

"Is it true that you are betrothed to Wardoor?"

The breath of his question shivered down her neck, and with it came the smell of alcohol and coffee. She turned to meet his hooded gaze that burned with so much pain that her own eyes welled.

"Yes. We're to be married after the banns have been called." She took a calming breath that in no way reassured her shot nerves. "I have not asked, but I wondered why Wardoor was not here. He is one of your oldest friends, Merrick. I had thought to see him present."

"He had other business matters to attend. No doubt organizing the banns." Sarcasm laced his words.

Isolde frowned. "I'm sure that's it." Not her, and that Wardoor's courting of her had severed a rift between the two friends, so much so that her betrothed hadn't attended his closest friend's wife's funeral.

"It would seem congratulations are in order."

Her grip on the handle increased as he swayed closer than he ought. "I'm sure he'll make me very happy," she said, hating that she, too, was adding to Merrick's pain.

"Will he?" The question dropped between them, shattering her calm.

She swallowed, reminding herself that Merrick wasn't thinking clearly. He was mourning and upset. "I believe so." He didn't reply, just watched her for a long moment, the air in the room crackling with a tension that left her heart pounding and her legs like jelly. "Get some rest, Merrick. I promise you tomorrow will not be so dark if you do."

"You're leaving tomorrow, are you not?" he said quickly, halting her departure yet again.

"We are." She nodded, turning the handle. "There is much to do in Town."

His attention flicked away from her for a moment before returning with an intensity that scared her. "I wish you so very much happiness, Isolde. You are the best person I know, and I hope you're always content."

A lump formed in her throat, not only at his good-bye, but the day in general. It was a day she longed to escape from. Too much sadness. Too much heartache. "I know you do." She leaned up and kissed his cheek, lingering too close to him, feeling the prickling of his stubble against her lips, the smell of sandalwood on his skin, and the warmth of his body. All that she loved and everything that she'd lost.

Longing tore through her hot and wild. What she wouldn't give to throw herself at him, to have him kiss her, if only once more in her life. To feel the passion and feed the desire that so often overran her body and soul but was never quenched.

His hand clasped her hip, and their eyes met. Moments ticked by as neither of them moved, neither one of them sure of what to do next, although they both knew what they wanted...

"Merrick..." His name floated from between her lips, pleading for him to do the right thing.

He stepped back, bowing. "Good night, Isolde."

She left without a further word. Her gaze blurred with unshed tears as she raced to her room. On such a day as this, how could she long for Merrick to kiss her? A widower of less than a week and she, too, newly engaged. She ought to know better and, from this night on, she would be a better person. The woman her father brought her up to be—a duke's daughter who acted with grace and decorum and was always above reproach or scandal.

*M*errick stood in the quiet room, demanding his feet not to move one inch. He wanted to go to Isolde, to lose himself in her comfort, her kind words, and truthful wisdom. Now, more than ever, he wanted to take back what was rightfully his. What had been ripped from his future five years ago.

But he could not.

He clenched his fists at his side, commanding himself to get hold of his emotions. She was marrying his lifelong friend. Not that Wardoor was so much of a friend now. Certainly, not after finding out that he was possibly the father of his daughter. But what he'd said to Isolde was true. He did not deserve love. He'd been the worst of husbands, had pushed his wife to the life she'd lived, and now she was dead. It was beyond forgivable.

He was the worst of men.

Merrick walked to the settee and slumped into the cushioned seat. He would, however, talk to Wardoor about the accusation Leonora had laid at his friend's feet. Not that he could do much about the fact, nor did he wish to. Lily was his and would be raised as a duke's daughter. But it didn't mean he wouldn't seek retribution as to Wardoor's conduct toward his wife. Nor would he allow the fiend to marry Isolde under such circumstances. Isolde deserved better than both of them and, devil take it, he would make sure she got her happy ever after.

CHAPTER 14

The next few weeks in Town were filled with dress fittings for the wedding and planning for the nuptials. Isolde's siblings threw themselves into the arrangements, ordering the most beautiful flowers, talking to tradesmen about pavilions and placements around the London townhouse's lawns. How large the wedding breakfast would be and how many invitations had been agreed to.

They were to travel abroad and visit Paris after the wedding. It was all so delightful for those about her, and Isolde allowed them to pull her into their excited expectations of great things to come, but, after each day was done, and Isolde lay abed at night, her heart ached for someone else.

Images of Merrick at Mountshaw the last time they were alone together haunted her every waking hour and even her sleeping ones, too. This severing from Merrick was made worse by the fact that Wardoor hadn't been helping at all in relation to the planning of the wedding. Yes, they had signed contracts and he'd had the banns called. A license was procured, but he was distant, uninterested, almost a different man to the one who had courted her only weeks ago.

Isolde wondered at his change of character as she stared out at the garden square before their London home. Their marriage was not a love match, they had both agreed to that, but surely he should've been a little interested in the day's planning, at least with input on how many and who would attend.

And tonight she was determined to find out exactly what was going on and if he was regretting his decision. A fact she silently hoped for, as she was certainly regretting her hasty answer to his marriage proposal.

The sound of her sisters coming down the stairs, and their mama calling out orders to the servants, brought her attention back to the ball they were to attend this evening. Isolde gathered her dance card and fan and went to meet them in the foyer.

"Are you well, my dear? You seem distracted," her mother asked, walking with her out to the carriage. Isolde stepped up into the equipage, her mother seating herself beside her.

"I'm concerned, Mama. Wardoor has been distant since the house party, and I'm not sure why."

"Do not concern yourself, my dear," her mother said, patting her leg. "Now that he has gained your hand, he's just celebrating his good fortune. I'm sure he's not being purposefully removed."

"Hmm," Isolde murmured, not totally convinced. "Even if he should celebrate, why stay away from me? And Anne said she ran into him on Bond Street a few days ago and said he seemed odd, even to her. Distant and nervous for reasons unknown. Do you think he's regretting his choice of bride?"

The duchess laughed, shaking her head. "Don't be absurd. Wardoor has courted you since your return from Scotland. I did hear his mother has come to town for the Season, so he may be a little distracted with her."

Isolde started, having not known that. "When did the marchioness arrive?"

"Two weeks past now," her mother said, checking the set of her hair.

Isolde frowned. "Then why hasn't he introduced me to her? As his betrothed you'd think it would be the first thing he'd want to do."

"He's a man, Isolde. Need we say any more?" Alice said, interjecting her opinion into their conversation.

"I agree," Victoria said, her voice droll. "Gentlemen of our set are nothing if not stupid and unaware of what is expected of them. It often makes me wonder if some of them have any common sense at all."

"Come girls," the duchess interjected. "You are being very harsh and unfair." She caught Isolde's hand. "I would suggest you speak to his lordship and ask him. Do not worry yourself sick that it's this or that, but find out for certain why he's shying away from you. As his betrothed you have every right to ask him such things."

Isolde nodded. "You're right, and I will do it tonight. Thank you, Mama."

The carriage ride was of short duration, but the line into the ball was long and arduous, and by the time they entered the ballroom, the event was already in full swing.

She looked about the room and spotted Wardoor at the opposite end, an assembly of men about him, and by the looks of their animated faces, the conversation was holding all their interest.

Alice threaded her arm through hers, and they strolled along the outside of the dancers. "You don't seem yourself, my dear. Are you worried about talking to Wardoor?"

Isolde blew out a frustrated breath, loving and hating that her little sister was so apt at reading her emotions. "I'm sure it'll turn out to be nothing, but his actions are bothering me, and have been for some weeks." But when she'd spoken to her family in the carriage, there was another point she hadn't told them, and Isolde wasn't sure if she should say anything now.

"What is it?" Alice pulled her beside a window and, looking about, lifted the pane a little to allow the night air inside. Isolde was glad of the cooling breeze as the room, full to its capacity, was stifling.

"It's something that Leonora said to me only a few days before she passed away," Isolde whispered, not wanting anyone to hear what they were talking about.

"What did she say?" Alice frowned. "Not that I really care as to what she had to say, for deceased or not, I cannot forgive her."

Isolde smiled, taking her sister's hand. She understood the hatred Alice held toward the duchess. Isolde had experienced it, too, for years, in fact. If only she could do over her time in Scotland, she would've gone to Town after her separation from Merrick and married straightaway. She would have had the children she'd longed for and Leonora and her trickery be damned. All those years wasted, when she could've been a mother instead.

But the duchess was gone now, and one shouldn't speak ill of the dead. "Leonora hinted that I didn't know Wardoor as well as I thought. When she said such things I assumed she was just being catty, wishing to hurt me in any way she could, but now I'm not so sure. I think she was trying to tell me something without stating it directly. And now, with his distance, I can't help but think her words had some basis to them."

"About Wardoor?" Alice looked across the room to where

her betrothed stood. "What's to know? He's a rogue, which you knew already, but, as this isn't a love match, that doesn't signify. His lordship is handsome, from a good family. He wants you, and no one else, as his wife. What else is there to know?"

As her sister pointed out all his attributes in such a callous way, Isolde inwardly cringed. That was certainly not how a woman should choose a husband, but it would seem she had. For when there was no love involved, only friendship or cordiality between a pair, what else was left to explain such unions?

"Leonora seemed to be laughing about a secret that I did not know, and now, well…" She paused, biting her lip. "You must agree that since the day I agreed to the marriage, Wardoor's been remote. He no longer calls and has not asked for any information regarding the wedding. It's so different as to how he'd been acting before I said yes."

Alice held up her hands to halt her words. "Leonora hated you and would do anything to place doubt in your mind. To me, Wardoor sounds like a normal, everyday lord who graces our Society. As I said in the carriage, one who lacks in smarts, like most of those surrounding us." She shrugged. "A boring, self-serving rogue. In fact, I'm surprised you're balking at him no longer paying court to you. You should probably get used to such goings-on, as it's pretty much what happens in a tonnish marriage."

Isolde slumped against the wall, heedless to those who noted a duke's daughter standing in such a way. "I must speak to him and see what the meaning is behind his behavior, or I'll never rest. For surely, even as friends, if you were betrothed, you would call, no?"

"Well, you would assume, but Wardoor may not. Do not forget, he's been living for years as a bachelor and, as mama said, now his parent is living with him. His life is probably upset." Her sister laughed. "Once he'd been able to act upon whatever took his fancy. Now that you've said yes, and he has the assurance that you will meet him at the end of the aisle come your wedding day, he probably believes the courtship dance between you is no longer necessary. He's starting the betrothal as he means to go on in your marriage."

Not that his courtship dance was required or wished for, but to have all contact severed when finally betrothed was odd. Isolde was not convinced. She was missing something, and before she said "I do" she would find out exactly what that was. "I think I shall still speak with him."

Alice took a glass of champagne from a passing footman and took a large sip of the sweet drink. "I think you shall find that Wardoor is merely distracted and likely to be acting the man he was born to be. A little dumb and forgetful of his obligations."

Isolde chuckled. "You are the most forward-speaking woman I know, and I love you for it. I knew you would speak the truth. Do not ever change, not for anyone."

Alice grinned. "I shall not."

Isolde looked toward Wardoor and noted the gentlemen he spoke with were dispersing, some going out to dance while others wandered off to other members of their set. "I think this is my chance. I will let you know how it goes."

Alice bade her good wishes, and Isolde persevered as patiently as she could as she worked her way through the crush toward Wardoor. Coming up to him, he threw her a dismissing glance, and the concern she'd been feeling these past days doubled. What is going on?

"Good evening, my lord." She smiled to temper her tone, which, even to her own ears, sounded annoyed. "I'm glad I've found you through this crush. I have not seen you in quite some time."

Wardoor's attention took in her face, her gown, before

lazily coming to meet her gaze. His eyes were unfocused and glassy, as if he'd partaken in too much wine or spirits. "I've been much busy elsewhere, but I should imagine you are, too. What with our wedding to organize."

"Hmm, yes, I've been busy." She looked out toward the dancers, her temper simmering to a boil at his bored tone. "I thought I would've seen you at the Duchess of Moore's funeral. Your non-attendance was quite a shock."

"My friendship with Moore is at an end, as you can well understand, considering our understanding. And as for paying my respects to the late duchess, well, I cannot bring myself to care much for her departure from this world."

Isolde raised her brow at His Lordship's words. Even she, who had been horribly mistreated by Leonora, had forgiven her. The loathing in Wardoor's words seemed unfounded... unless he was hiding something. Was that something what Leonora had been trying to tell her?

But at a ball was not the time to delve into such an inquiry. Isolde cleared her throat. "When will we expect you to call? I wish to discuss some important matters with you." "Soon, my dear, if you'll allow me to address you as such." His words were slurred and he smelled of hard liquor. "I so look forward to our marriage and our wedding night."

He winked, and Isolde narrowed her eyes.

She watched as he took another glass of brandy from a passing footman, saluting her with the amber liquid before drinking it down in one gulp. There was something not quite right with his lordship, and with sickening dread Isolde couldn't help but think it had nothing to do with the drink he held in his hand.

"I think it would be best if we were to spend a little time together before we're married. You've been acting quite the stranger these past few weeks."

He rolled his eyes, dismissing her concerns. What is wrong with the man?

"Alas, it shall not be tonight, as I have another more pressing event to attend. A private party by strict invitation only, you understand, but I'm willing to call later in the week, if that would suit you."

Isolde resolved to find out what was going on. "Well then, I hope you have a pleasant evening, my lord." She dipped into a curtsy, before making her way back toward Alice.

Her sister took her shaking hands. "I've made a terrible mistake." Again, another gentleman from her set was about to make a fool of her. And worse was, if she married Wardoor she would have to live with that mistake for the rest of her life. It was not to be borne.

"What did he say?" Alice looked back to Wardoor and then to her. "What did he do?" She pulled her over to some vacant chairs, and they sat. "Tell me everything."

Isolde didn't know where she should begin. "For starters, he's drunk beyond anything I've ever seen in a gentleman. He couldn't have sounded less enthused to stay here and spend time with me, and he didn't even ask me to dance! He even seemed bored by my request for him to call." Tears threatened, and she swallowed the lump in her throat. The contract may have been signed, but she was a sister to a duke, and nothing was irreversible until she actually married him.

Alice nodded, a slight frown between her brows. "Perhaps in an hour or so he'll sober up a little and you'll be able to have a proper, adult conversation."

"I think not," Isolde said, shaking her head. "He's not staying at the ball. In fact, His Lordship made it perfectly plain that he had other events to attend. Events that were private and strictly by invitation only. I can't help but feel he was being coy and yet sarcastic at the same time, like he was laughing at me not knowing the truth behind his impending party."

"Surely you must be wrong. He was so set on gaining your hand. His feelings and words seem so out of character—almost like he's a different man altogether."

It was exactly what he was like, very similar to how Leonora had behaved in Society at times. Pretty face, beautiful clothing and jewels, but with a mouth and reactions that were crass, without thought, and cutting in the extreme. "I'm willing to marry a man who attends his clubs, has a mistress even; so long as in Society I'm given the respect that is due to me as a wife and a daughter of a duke. But I will not be made a fool and treated like an annoying fishwife who's dismissed and ignored. Tell Mama that I have a megrim of some sort and that I've returned home. I do not need looking in on." Isolde had to see what he was about. Leonora had hinted at something, and she was determined to find out, now, before it was too late.

She stood, and Alice clasped her hand, halting her steps. "Where are you going? I don't like the sound of this."

"I'm going to follow Wardoor to his party and see for myself what he's up to. If I cannot get the truth from him, I shall see it with my own eyes."

"Are you truly going to follow him? You'll stand out, dressed in a ball gown."

"No, I'll change and return here. From his tone it seems he's happy to stay at the ball for a little time longer, and I know which carriage is his. I'll hire a hackney to wait across the street until he leaves."

Alice stood and walked her toward the entrance foyer. "What if something happens to you? We won't know where you are. I don't think you should go."

Isolde's attention snapped to her betrothed, now lounging against a wall, a delicate little debutante with cheeks the color of a red rose, speaking with him. The poor girl looked shocked and a little out of her depth. "I know I said I would marry for convenience, not love, and I'm fine with that choice. But I cannot marry a man whose temperament is so changeable. I feel something is happening with him that I'm not aware of, but Leonora was. I have to know the truth of his character."

"I don't know why the troublemaking wench just didn't tell you what it was. Leonora was always so willing to strike at you in any other way. It makes no sense."

Isolde realized that, in a way, it did. For if Leonora was aware of Wardoor's secret, it was just another attempt to laugh at her. Once married, there would be no turning back. And had Leonora not died, she would've thrown that fact into Isolde's face at any opportune moment.

Isolde summoned her pelisse and waited while the family carriage was brought around. "I will be home well before dawn." Her sister's unease was palpable, and she hugged her quickly. "All will be well, darling, and by tomorrow I shall know what to do, I promise."

---

*T*he incessant knocking at his front door pulled Merrick from the estate business he was still going over, even at this late hour. Sleep eluded him, so most nights he worked until he nodded off, usually where he sat.

The knocking continued, and since he'd sent his staff to bed, Merrick walked out into the foyer and opened the door, only to see Lady Alice Worthingham standing on his front step, a dark hooded robe covering all but her face. He noticed her paleness first, and then the worry that held her normally pretty features rigid.

"Lady Alice, what are you doing here?"

She walked straight past him and shut the door without a word, before rounding on him like a hellion. "Isolde has not returned home as she promised me she would. I tried to tell her not to go, but she wouldn't listen." Alice growled. "She's says I'm stubborn, but really, if the truth were to come out, I think everyone would agree, she's the most stubborn of us all."

Merrick held up his hand, halting the young woman's tirade. "Stop, and start again. Where is Isolde?"

Alice sighed, throwing him an annoyed glare as if it were his fault she was here in the first place. "She followed Wardoor this evening, or last night, since his bizarre behavior lately has made her question their understanding. She has not returned home. And at the ball, she promised me she would be back well before dawn."

Unease crept along his spine as he walked back into his library, throwing on his overcoat and grabbing his hat. "Did she have any idea where Wardoor was headed?" Merrick's mind raced as to where Wardoor could be, and, having been distant with the fellow since his attention to Isolde, realized he didn't have much of an idea. Damn it.

"The only words that his lordship said were that he was invited to another event that was strictly invitation only. I got the impression that Isolde didn't like the tone he used in regard to the forthcoming entertainment, along with Wardoor's manner. I believe my sister does not trust him and will decide her future with him depending on how her investigation went this evening."

Merrick strode to the foyer, pulling Alice with him. "I will check the clubs for Wardoor and the few other locales where he might be." He clasped Alice's shoulders, meeting her worried gaze. "I will bring her home, I promise you. Now leave, and wait for further instruction from me." Isolde's sister nodded and walked quickly back to her carriage. He stood there until it rumbled away on the cobbled road, before he walked quickly to the corner and, spying a hackney cab, hailed it.

Settling back in the squabs he called out the direction, having an awful premonition that where he would find Wardoor, and possibly Isolde, was not somewhere any woman should ever be. And certainly not a duke's daughter.

CHAPTER 15

"**W**e're here, miss."

Isolde stepped out of the carriage and quickly paid the man. "Did you see what direction the gentleman went whom I asked you to follow?"

The large, somewhat scruffy driver pointed down a darkened alley that looked less than savory. "You'll find what ye're looking for down that way."

Isolde pulled her cloak closer about her and used the few inns and houses that ran along the wharf to light her way. Laughter carried out from one particular building farther along the dock, and she quickly made her way toward it, hoping the carriage driver had not led her on a merry chase and she was, in fact, near where Wardoor currently was.

Thankfully, her betrothed had done just as she assumed and had stayed at the ball for another two hours before summoning his vehicle to leave. If Isolde had thought his lordship would attend another ton ball, or an event at one of his clubs, she was sorely disappointed and somewhat relieved. For where they were headed only proved to her Leonora's words were true.

Wardoor had secrets.

Isolde walked down the alley, her nose crinkling in disgust at the stench of rotting rubbish and unwashed bodies. A little way along the alley a man stood, arms crossed over his burly chest, looking about the street as if he owned the whole neighborhood. Not one person dared to engage him, and the few who walked past went with quickened steps and lowered eyes. Isolde, however, would have none of that, and, walking up to him, met his gaze head on.

"Open the door, please," she said, smiling a little, which seemed to help her cause, for although he stared back with indifference, he soon moved, and, reaching behind him, opened the door. Relief curled through her at gaining entrance, for she'd not known if a secret password or payment was required, and she'd brought only just enough funds with her to get a cab back home.

At her first glimpse of the interior of the house, all thoughts that it was a whorehouse or just a very poor acquaintance of Wardoor's were erased. This was certainly no place she'd ever thought to darken the threshold. That her betrothed seemed to like such seedy establishments angered her beyond reason. That his lordship had made her come down to this unfortunate area of London to see for herself what he was about was beyond forgivable. Even if he was unaware of her outing.

There were bodies strewn everywhere, some asleep, some smoking, while others draped themselves over the opposite sex and did things Isolde had never witnessed. The sweet, sickly smell of opium greeted her as she walked into the room, along with the realization that there were people present from all levels of Society, all mingling, enjoying one another as much as the addictive drug they smoked.

In this den of hell, men of influence mixed with scullery maids and prostitutes, while women of rank sank further into their addiction and, if anything like Leonora, would eventually shorten their lives by many years.

Isolde moved through the room, taking note of faces—most unknown to her, some known to her very well. Seeing them at a ton ball or London event would make the future meeting awkward, on her side, at least. She doubted they would remember her here, so sunk into the depths of debauchery were they.

Moving to the opposite side of the room where there were fewer people, Isolde tried to blend into the furniture as much as possible. There was no sign of Wardoor, and relief coursed through her that perhaps she'd been wrong. Too judgmental and untrusting to believe what others told her as truth.

But her relief was short-lived as a gentleman, one she knew all too well, strolled down the stairway, a whore hanging from his arm.

Never had she seen Wardoor look so disheveled. At the ball earlier, he'd looked less than polished, but this—this was a side to him she had never wanted to see.

He looked like a man just out of bed. His shirt hung open right down to his chest and his cravat was completely missing. As for his jacket and waistcoat, they were gone as well.

He laughed, gazing about the room, and Isolde noted his eyes were blank of any emotion, just glassy mirrors into a soul that was possibly too far gone for her to help. A servant rushed to Wardoor's side, pouring him a large glass of wine. The couple moved to a nearby abundance of pillows that sat upon the floor.

Isolde shook her head, unable to believe that Leonora had been right in what her betrothed loved to do when not satisfying the ton and their need for titled gentlemen. Isolde had thought Leonora's words were just another hateful way to injure her, and perhaps they had been, but they'd also been the truth.

No matter how much that truth hurt, her eyes did not deceive her. Wardoor was addicted to opium, just as Leonora had been.

This lifestyle his lordship was so fond of was not what she wanted for herself or her future children. She didn't want to be a wife who turned a blind eye to the goings-on of her husband, and she certainly didn't wish to be married to a man who could come home at any time, demand his right of her body and give her the pox. Such a situation was too awful to even imagine. This betrothal could not go on.

When they'd first discussed a marriage of convenience, she'd thought it would be one in which he would have a mistress, enjoy his clubs, as men do, and not demand too much of her in the marriage bed. But she would not condone, nor agree to live with this man if he continued to partake in this opium den and the depraved activity that was happening before her. This could not be her future.

A woman staggered past her, laughing when she bumped into her. Isolde righted her gown and studied the intoxicated girl, who couldn't be any older than her youngest sister Victoria. The woman stopped, blowing sweet, sickly smoke into Isolde's eyes and making them water.

"I ain't ever seen you 'ere before. First time, love? Is ye going to lose ye opium virginity to us, hey? We so love deflowering women in this place." The stench from her mouth fought with the woman's body odor. She was poor, if her work-worn clothing and dress that was two sizes too small were any indication. "Come, luv," she said, slurring the words. "You can sit over here with me."

The woman dragged Isolde closer to where Wardoor lounged within a group of people.

They came to an array of silk pillows, similar to what her

betrothed was sitting on, the show of decadence with this type of fabric at odds to the location. Not wishing to delve further into the how or why of this place, she sat.

The woman waved to a servant, who came over and passed her a long pipe. Taking a long draw, she sighed out the smoke, smiling at Isolde with what resembled relief and pleasure.

"Ere, have a taste of heaven." The woman gestured the pipe toward her. "If only to remove yourself from the hell in which we live."

Isolde stared at the wooden and silver object, tentatively taking it to appease the young woman. Should her brother ever find out she had come here, he'd rightfully send her hightailing it back to Scotland. When she'd embarked on this little adventure, she'd merely wanted to see the truth for herself and then leave. And as of now she'd not seen enough of what Wardoor was about to leave, but to be forced into smoking a substance she didn't want to had never entered her mind.

She wiped the end of the pipe that had touched the other woman's mouth and took the smallest inhale of smoke she could. She coughed, her eyes watering. Others around them laughed just as a bout of dizziness swept over her.

Isolde leaned against the wall for support as those about her started to dance in her vision. She looked toward Wardoor, hoping to attain his attention and have him help her home. Surely, if only she could make him out in the crowd, he would help her, possibly explain his actions. Going to stand, her legs refused to do as she bid; instead, they were numb and heavy and in no way willing to move, no matter how much she tried to make them do so.

The other woman took the pipe and inhaled deeply, before blowing the smoke into her face again.

"Don't do that," Isolde said, swiping the smoke away.

Laughter rang out, and her stomach turned. For a mortified moment Isolde thought she would be sick on the floor.

"The light-headedness will pass, love, and so, too, will your stomach upset. Just sit back and enjoy the ride. It gets good soon."

This was no joyful occasion, and it certainly was no heaven-on-earth. She managed to sit up, found Wardoor, and blinked. He sat on the cushions, a woman's hand down the front of his breeches, while a bare-chested man kissed him deeply, her betrothed's hands clasped tightly into the other man's hair. Isolde blinked and watched as her betrothed kissed his way down the man's neck, his chest, before untying the frontfalls of the man's breeches and kissing the end of his manhood.

This could not be happening.

"I need to leave. Help me, please." She was going to be sick. Never in her life had she seen anything like what was happening before her. That her fiancé was partaking in such escapades was more than she could stomach.

The woman merely grinned and blew more smoke in her direction. Isolde slumped against the wall, a lamb to the slaughter amongst all these wolves. What a fool she'd been. She should've just asked Wardoor, demanded the truth from him, and made her decision from there.

And now she was stuck here, unable to leave and a target to the fiends about her. A shot of fresh air alerted her to the fact that the front entrance door opened. Maybe if she slept for a little while all would be well. Isolde let the heaviness of her eyes enable the darkness to swamp her just as the sound of her name being called floated past her senses.

"I'm here," she said, smiling as arms lifted her from her pillowed seat and carried her, in what direction she neither knew nor cared, just so long as the hard, muscular chest she was cradled against didn't go anywhere. It was rather nice and smelled delicious, too. Much better than the flowery smoke of the poppy seed.

"I have you, Isolde."

The voice was familiar, comforting, but she couldn't place it. Instead, she let sleep take her and prayed come morning she would still be cradled in her knight-in-shining- armor's embrace.

———

*M*errick looked about the opium den as he headed toward the door, Isolde cradled safely in his arms. He spotted Wardoor, in what would only be termed a very compromising position, and shook his head.

What was the man thinking? Or for that matter, what wasn't he thinking?

But for now, he needed to get Isolde into fresh air and home, safe and sound with her family. He would deal with Wardoor another day.

His heart had not slowed since he'd seen Isolde's sister into her carriage only hours before. He had visited all the gentlemen's clubs he knew Wardoor frequented. Having no luck at any of the establishments, only a few smug grins and sly comments, he'd gone on his way.

Thinking back to Leonora's words and her declaration that his lordship was just as fond of opium as she was, Merrick had traveled to the only opium den he knew. What he'd found upon arrival would be burned into his consciousness for the rest of his life.

That Wardoor was indeed present was no surprise, but the slumped-over, vulnerable figure of Isolde was something he never wished to see again.

Fear unlike any he'd known—that she'd been attacked in some way, was possibly hurt—had coursed through him.

Merrick pushed the thought aside, not wanting to delve into what could've been, for she was safe now, held securely in his arms, where he'd never allow anything to happen to her.

Merrick looked down and noted her parched lips. People in the den moved out of his way, with the deadly glare he was bestowing.

Reaching the outside, he called for his driver, and, making the vehicle, stepped in with some help. Merrick settled Isolde as best he could against the squabs and cradled her on his lap. "Hanover Square, Mayfair. And quickly, mind."

"Right ye are, Your Grace." The driver shut the door and climbed up on the box. The carriage lurched to one side for a moment before the flick of the ribbons marked their exit, and the vehicle picked up speed along the wharf.

Merrick reached across to the opposite seat and clasped the carriage blanket that was folded there. He wrapped it about her, relieved to see the color start to return to her face. Isolde's breathing became deeper, and he realized she'd fallen asleep in his arms.

Crossing the Thames, they were soon on the outskirts of the affluent locale in which they lived. They had made good time back to Mayfair; not a surprise given the late hour.

Unable not to, Merrick watched Isolde, pushing a lock of hair from her face to see her better. He shook his head, imagining that this sweet, innocent woman could've fallen victim to cutthroats, rapists, thieves—anyone looking for an easy target.

That her family had not known where she was traveling to, had the worst happened to her, no one would've ever known where she was. And after seeing the condition of Wardoor, well, the gentleman would've been no help in finding her. The bastard would likely not even remember his own name, never mind who else had been at that opium den.

For the second time in his life, Merrick could've lost her

—the woman who would forever hold his heart in the palm of her hand, no matter where her future led. The thought trickled ice through his veins and he pulled her closer to his chest, needing to feel her warm flesh, the beat of her heart against his own.

She didn't wake as the carriage rocked to a halt before the Worthingham's London townhouse. Lights blazed from the establishment, and no sooner had the driver jumped down to open his door than the front door swung wide. Isolde's brother ran down the steps, his brow furrowed with worry.

The duke swore as he came up to them. "You found her?"

"We'll discuss her whereabouts once we've settled her inside." With some difficulty, he alighted from the vehicle, and, with quickened steps, carried her indoors.

The duchess made a sound of distress before coming over to check on her daughter. Her aged hand touched Isolde's cheek with care, and he noted Isolde smiled a little at the contact.

"Where is her room?"

"This way, Your Grace," the duchess said, ushering him toward the staircase.

"Please, no formalities tonight. Merrick will do perfectly well."

She nodded, smiling a little, and for the first time since the eve of his ill-fated marriage to Leonora, Merrick received a genuine glance. He swallowed the lump that formed in his throat and followed the duchess. Behind him, the duke beat out orders to the staff for a tisane, cold compress, and chilled water. The servants scattered, all busy with their jobs as they went to do as he bid.

Making the first floor landing, they headed down a passage, and the duchess opened a door and showed him into Isolde's room. Merrick strode to the bed and placed her onto the sheets, the blankets already pulled back for the night.

The duchess fussed with her daughter, touching her face. That she was distressed was evident on her furrowed brow, and he stepped toward her, touching her arm. "She'll be better by morning, Your Grace. I promise you."

"Where did you find her? When Alice told me of her absence, we had no idea where to look. Josh went out to check the balls that were still entertaining, but he returned home without her." The duchess sat, asking the wide-eyed maid to come and help her with Isolde's gown.

"I believe what I have to say should be said in private, Your Grace. I will await you downstairs."

She studied him a moment, and understanding dawned in her eyes. "Very well. I shall be down soon."

Merrick left and waited for the duchess, and within half an hour he was seated in the library. Isolde's brother, the Duke of Penworth, stared at him from across his large mahogany desk, the duchess at her son's side.

"Where did you find my daughter?"

Her tone was to the point and, if he wasn't mistaken, a little annoyed. "I found her in an opium den. The people with her, or at least one woman, were forcibly blowing the smoke into her face, bringing forth the effects of the drug. I do not know why she was there, and with your permission I would like to stay and speak to her tomorrow to ascertain why she would act so recklessly."

The duchess leveled him with a piercing stare, and Merrick shifted in his seat under such scrutiny. It had been a long time since anyone had made him feel like a boy in short coats.

"As much as I'm appreciative of your help tonight, Your Grace, there is nothing more you can do here. I suggest you go home and get some rest. We will send word if she wishes to see you to thank you for your assistance this evening."

Anger ignited within him, and he shook his head, not sure

he was hearing her words correctly. "I know what you think of me, and I know that you believe what happened the night before I married Leonora was something I wished for. But you would be wrong. I loved Isolde. I wanted to marry her, and the one woman she trusted most stole that future from us. I think you forget that Lady Alice sought my help this evening, after Isolde had doubts regarding her understanding with Wardoor. Rightful concerns, after what I witnessed this evening."

The muscle at the duke's temple flexed as he played idly with a paperweight on his desk. "We will speak to Alice as to why she went to you, and Isolde, too, as to why she followed Wardoor to such a locale."

"Alice came to me because she knows, when it comes to Isolde, I will always be there for her." And he would be there forever, no matter what happened. It did not matter if she married another, or no one at all. Merrick was determined to win back some sort of friendship, if only to be near her and part of her life.

Isolde's brother leaned back in his chair. "Alice mentioned that Isolde was looking to see what Wardoor was about. That she suspected him of something. Was his lordship at this opium den tonight?" The duke ran a hand over his unshaven jaw. "We've not seen him since the announcement of their betrothal was made public, and even I'm starting to wonder if he's suitable for my sister."

There was no way in hell Merrick would allow Isolde to marry such a man as Wardoor. How he had not noticed that his friend had fallen to such a low baffled him. Wardoor had been one of his closest friends since Eton. That his life had spiraled to such depths was not what he had wanted to ever see. "I think you shall find that once Isolde is awake and coherent, the understanding she has with his lordship will be at an end."

"So Wardoor was there? Why did he not assist my sister?"

Merrick chose his words carefully, knowing, in time, he would discuss what he beheld Wardoor doing and why. Help him, if he could, to remove himself from such a lifestyle. A mistake he'd made with Leonora that he would not repeat with his friend. "He was otherwise engaged. In fact, I believe Wardoor was not even aware Isolde was present at the establishment."

"This is beyond unconscionable." Her Grace paced behind her son, her silk skirts flying about her ankles. "When I see Wardoor next, he'll be lucky to remain living."

The duke threw his mother a startled glance but didn't deny her words. "We will speak with Isolde and Wardoor, as soon as possible. But now," he said, standing, "It is really very late, or early, I should amend, and we all need our rest. We thank you for your assistance, Moore, and as we stated before, Isolde will send word when she's up for visitors."

As much as he wanted to stay, he nodded and stood. "Very well," he said, walking toward the door but halting at the threshold. "I would like to know why Isolde was at the opium den. And, although I have my suspicions, I wish to know for certain, before I confront Wardoor about his conduct this evening."

The duke nodded. "That, Your Grace, is something we would all like to know."

Merrick left the house, the cool night air hitting his face. He rubbed his eyes, blinking to rid himself of the fatigue. The reddish glow of dawn pierced the night sky and, entering the hackney cab, he called for home to where bed beckoned.

If he never had another night like the one he just lived through, he would be a happy man. Not since his son's disappearance in the East End had fear for another crippled him and left him anxious beyond reason.

As for Wardoor, well, the man would be lucky to escape

with his appendages intact, among other things. How dare he treat Isolde with so little respect, or himself, for that matter? Wardoor should have been cheering from the rooftops that he'd secured her hand, and yet, the misbegotten idiot was slumming in opium dens and engaging in sexual acts that could get him hanged.

It wasn't to be borne. Wardoor was skating on very thin ice, and his actions tonight would not go unpunished. Nor would Merrick allow Isolde to enter a marriage that was a mirror image of what his own had been.

Regrettable misery was not something he wished anyone to live with—least of all, Isolde.

CHAPTER 16

A knock sounded at the door, and Isolde turned to see a footman enter with the silver salver. "My lady. A missive just arrived for you."

She took the note. "Thank you." Breaking the seal, she recognized the writing immediately, and anticipation skittered across her skin.

Lady Isolde,
I need to see you. When can we meet?
Regards Moore

S he frowned down at the note, wondering when, in fact, she could do as he asked. Over the last few days her family had cosseted her to the point that Isolde had had to lock her bedroom door just to gain some peace and quiet.

Out of love they doted on her, out of the fear that she had

been injured more than she was, but it still made the attention, which was beyond suffocating, unbearable.

The clock on the mantle chimed eight, and she threw the note into the fire before heading upstairs.

"My dear, you're not ready! We're to attend Almack's tonight. Did you not receive my note?"

Isolde stared at her sisters as they waltzed down the stairs; Alice's and Victoria's gowns were the epitome of beauty and youth. "I'm sorry, Mama, I did not." Not that a night at Almack's was something she wished to attend, in any case.

Not now that Merrick wished to see her. Needed to see her… "You go and have fun without me. If I should change now, I would only hold you up, and I must admit, I have a slight headache, still." The reminder of her ordeal worked as she wished, and her mother strode over to her, feeling her forehead.

"Straight to bed, my dear. We'll not be home until late, so do call a servant should you need a tisane. And if it worsens, please have a servant fetch us from the ball. I will return home immediately."

"Why so late? I did not think you liked to stay overly long at Almack's."

Her mother adjusted her silk gloves, walking over and checking her hair in the foyer mirror. "We've been invited to the Marquess of Booth's ball afterward, which I hoped to attend. Do you think you shall be well here on your own? You know I would stay if you wished it."

"I will be well." Isolde smiled, in part as the idea of what her night would entail popped into her mind. To be alone with Merrick once more filled her with such tumbling emotions to make her dizzy. Would they talk as they once had, long into the night and about all things that interested them? Would he look at her with such longing that she would be hard-pressed to deny him his every wish? Isolde ushered her mama toward the door. "There is no need for you to look in on me when you return. I shall be asleep, and no doubt the headache will have passed by then."

"If you're certain, my dear," her mama said, a slight frown marring her normally perfect brow. Again she reached out and touched Isolde's forehead. "You do feel a little warm…" Victoria came over and kissed Isolde's cheek. "We shall miss you tonight, but please get some rest. We have a new wardrobe to purchase tomorrow from Madame Glasse."

Alice squealed at the mention of the famous French dressmaker, her sister clapping her hands in excitement. Isolde inwardly cringed. The last thing on her mind was shopping, for the whole purpose was to complete her trousseau.

Unfortunately, the morning after her travels to an opium den had left her with a very vague memory and, for the life of her, she had not been able to recall what had occurred. Her brother Josh had been persistent with his questioning, as if he knew a little of what had happened but wouldn't elaborate, wanting her to remember and fill in the gaps herself.

And it was only this morning that it had come back in full clarity. All day the thought of what she'd seen Wardoor do with the whore and the other gentleman had haunted her. Shame had washed over her that she was betrothed to such a man. That the life he currently lived was the one he would still live when married to her.

Thankfully, her brother was away from home this day and she'd not been questioned, but come the morning she would have to inform them all that the wedding would never take place and that Wardoor could go to the devil, if he wasn't there already.

"I look forward to it," she said, bidding them good night. Isolde waited for the front door to close before heading back to her room to change. She dressed quickly into a light muslin blue gown and black cloak, pulling the hood over her head to disguise herself.

Isolde snuck down the servants' stairs, and not seeing anyone about, slipped through the front door and started down the street. It was only a short stroll to Merrick's townhouse, and at this time, no one was about to see her, most of the ton already out at the many balls and parties London hosted nightly.

She came around a corner, and a slight breeze ruffled her cloak and she shivered, pulling it closer about her body for warmth. A light drizzle of rain started to fall from the moonless sky, and only the few lights off the grand homes of Mayfair lit her way.

For a time, Isolde stood a little way up the street and stared at Merrick's Hanover Square residence, hoping to summon enough courage to visit him. She was an unmarried woman, after all, and should she be caught doing such a scandalous thing, nothing would save her reputation. A smile lifted her lips at the thought. She no longer saw such a scenario as a bad thing, but possibly her own chance for a happily ever after. After all, Merrick had invited her, stated he needed to see her, and with that thought, she took a step toward his home.

Since her adventure, she'd been lightheaded and nauseous, enough so that the family had stopped their at-homes over the last few days. Moore had sent missives requesting to see her, and she'd refused them. Not that she didn't want to see him, for she did, but she'd simply not been well enough to see anyone.

Isolde frowned, not liking that he could've seen such a request as a rebuff, for it was the last of those things. That he'd helped her escape that dreadful opium den, had taken action as soon as her sister begged him to, was something for which she'd never be able to thank him enough.

Noting a couple walking toward her, Isolde turned and strode with purpose down the darkened alley that ran down the side of the home. She slipped in through a side gate and walked toward the terrace and the library doors that led out onto the flagstones.

A small glow of a candle flickered through the curtains, and light shone from the upstairs rooms. Isolde snuck up to the door and peeked in through the small gap that she found. Merrick sat at his desk, his hand busy scrawling words across parchment, and she smiled at the vision he made.

She knocked, the sound so minute that she doubted he heard it, until he paused, looking around the room. Moore turned back to his documents, seemingly dismissing the noise, and then resumed his work. Isolde knocked harder still, and this time he stood, frowning in her direction, although she doubted he could see exactly who it was disturbing his night.

Her mouth dried at the sight he made as he strolled toward the terrace doors. His shirt front hung open, showing off the hint of a formidable chest that she remembered well, his hair was down and disheveled and, if she wasn't mistaken, a little damp. Had Merrick bathed in the last hour or so? The thought of water cascading over his body made her envious of the soap that would've lathered his skin, left it smelling clean and delicious...

Isolde stepped back as he made the threshold and swallowed her nerves as he pulled the curtain aside and stared at her. Shock registered on his face, then a hint of pleasure, before he opened the door, looked about outside, and quickly pulled her inside.

"What are you doing here, Isolde? I thought—are you

well? I've been worried, having not seen you since I left you with your family."

She smiled, shutting the door and closing the curtains to ensure privacy. "Everything is fine, I assure you." Now that she was here. Was she brave enough to tell him she sought his company? That she wanted to come alone and thank him for what he'd done for her? Taking a deep breath, she fortified herself to be strong, to speak to him as they once had—openly and confidently. "Truth is, when I received your missive I knew I needed to see you, as well. To personally thank you for your assistance the other night. I don't ever wish to think about what could've happened had you not arrived."

"Well," he said, "you should probably thank your sister. For had she not the inclination to find me, I don't wish to think about what would've happened, either."

His lips lifted in a teasing grin, and her stomach fluttered. "Well, sincerely, I thank you."

"You're more than welcome, but I must admit to being a little curious as to why you would seek out Wardoor at such a venue. Why not just confront the man about your concerns?"

She walked farther into the room and could feel him following close on her slippered heels. Her stomach was tied up in knots, and her mind raced with what to say. They had been friends once, and after all that had passed between them, it was the one thing she missed most. And now, even though he'd recently buried Leonora, had become a father again, he'd taken the time out of his busy life to save a woman with whom he was no longer affiliated.

Isolde sat and met his steady gaze. "I feel I owe you a great debt, and apology, and thanks all at the one time. Even with all the pain your family has suffered these past weeks, you rescued me from myself. For it was my fault, and I take full responsibility for my actions that night. I allowed gossip to cloud my judgment, when I simply should have asked the questions I needed answers to. I should never have gone down to the docks to find them."

He sat beside her, and Isolde became aware of just how much Merrick was lacking in clothing and how very close he was. Her mouth dried and she fought to keep her eyes above the line of his shoulders and not devour his chest and bare lower arms.

"Above all else, there is one thing that I wish to know." Isolde turned a little to face him.

"What? I'll answer anything," she said.

"Of what did you suspect Wardoor?"

Isolde looked over his shoulder, not really focusing on anything other than the hazy memories of her night of regret. What a silly little fool she'd acted and in a way that could've cost her life. "Before Leonora passed away, she hinted that I didn't know Wardoor as well as I thought I did. She never mentioned anything in particular, but it was enough to make me doubt him."

Merrick's troubled gaze made her stomach churn. "Please tell me what you know of his life," she asked.

He ran a hand through his hair. "It is as you feared when you went looking for him. He's afflicted with the same demons that Leonora was."

Isolde had seen it for herself, but hearing it spoken out loud made it real. And because of Wardoor's affliction, she would call off another understanding. Again she would be cast into a scandal not of her making. She bit her lip to stem the threatening tears. "I'm a good person, Merrick. Why do bad things keep happening to me?"

He sighed. "I do not know. You do not deserve it."

Isolde was quiet a moment as she fought to find the words to speak as she must. "His Lordship kissed a man and not just on his lips, but elsewhere. A place that I never imagined proper between two people. And all the while, a woman was busy with his person, too." That Merrick didn't seem shocked told her he'd seen it, too. "Leonora had hinted I should not worry about him having a mistress. At least I know now what she meant by that." She paused. "What are male mistresses called, do you know?"

Merrick shut his eyes, shaking his head. "It is true what she said, but until I witnessed it for myself the other evening, I had refused to believe it." He took her hand, and she welcomed the comfort. "I'm so sorry, Isolde."

She shrugged, swallowing hard at his heartfelt words. Tears blurred her vision, and she fought to keep her emotions under control. "It seems I'm doomed when it comes to marriage. I feel I cannot trust anyone and have no talent for reading someone's true nature. And on top of it all, I'm going to be crucified by the ton for breaking off another betrothal. No gentleman will think I'm capable of marriage."

"You can trust me," he stated, forcefully. "And I will not allow anyone to speak ill of you. This is not your fault."

Isolde met his gaze and read the sincerity in his eyes. She wanted to believe it to her very core. She wished he stated the truth. And perhaps he did. Maybe it was a simple case that she'd been born under an unlucky star, forever doomed when it came to romance. "Can I trust you? Really?"

"Yes, you can." His thumb rubbed against her palm, sending delightful tremors to travel up her arm. The air thickened with long-denied need. "I never meant to betray you. As for Wardoor, I'll ensure he makes no trouble for you when word breaks of your separation."

"Thank you, Merrick." The sound of a servant in the foyer caught Isolde's attention, and she remembered her other reason for calling this evening. "I know you're in mourning and not about Town at the moment, but I came here also to see if you're all right. Is there anything you need or that I can help you with? It's the least I can offer, after what you did for me."

Merrick pulled away and sat back, and the moment their contact was lost, she missed him.

"I'm hoping to close up the London home and go back to Mountshaw for the foreseeable future. The children will be better out of the city, and there is nothing to keep me here. As I'm in mourning, I cannot attend any entertainments, and I'm tired. Tired of everything, I suppose."

She pushed away the pang of sadness that assailed her, knowing Merrick wouldn't be at the balls and parties she would attend once the trouble with Wardoor was settled.

How she would miss him. A knock at the door made her tense, and Merrick stood, walking over to answer it. He spoke quietly to a woman before coming to sit back down.

Isolde fiddled with her cloak. "I apologize for not letting you know of my visit. I had the opportunity to slip away unnoticed and well…" She shrugged. "I took it."

"I'm glad you did." He gestured to the foyer. "That was my daughter's nursemaid. Lily is being a little terror tonight and isn't settling. She wanted to know if I wanted to check in on her while she's awake."

Isolde sat forward, having not seen the baby yet. "May I meet her?" She blurted the question before she'd had a chance to really think about her request. Would Merrick want her to? And the fact that she was desperate to meet the little girl made her wonder why she was so interested.

"I would love you to. Follow me. I'll take you to her now."

Isolde walked along with Merrick up two flights of stairs before they headed toward a room on the second floor. A door stood ajar, and the flickering candlelight bathed the passage wall in a soft yellow glow.

A maid sat on a chair, slowly rocking the crib in which

the child lay. Through an adjoining door, she could see William asleep, a toy soldier clasped tight in his fisted hand. A small fire burned in the grate, and the room was filled with pretty white furniture. The windows faced west and ran almost the length of the room, making the space feel large, but homey. Isolde walked up to the crib and gazed down at a little girl who fussed with her blankets, kicking her little legs as if she were annoyed with her whereabouts. "She is beautiful, Your Grace." Isolde ran her finger across her chubby pink cheek.

"May I hold her?"

Merrick cleared his throat. "Of course. Her name is Lily." He picked up the baby and handed her over. Lily was the most adorable little cherub Isolde had ever met. She took in all her features, noting her perfect little eyelashes and sweet nose. "Oh Merrick. She's just too sweet." Tears sprang to her eyes, and she blinked them back quickly. She chuckled to hide her embarrassment. "You know I'm absurdly jealous of you. How lucky you are."

He rubbed a hand over his daughter's head, pushing back the little bit of hair she sported. "I know I am." Merrick sighed, sitting down on a nearby chair. "You're a natural with children. I always thought you would be."

She smiled, laughing when little Lily clasped her finger and wouldn't let go. "Well, I am the second oldest in the family, so I've been around a few babies in my time." Isolde sat, holding Lily on her lap. "I cannot believe the miracle of life. How wondrous to make something so amazing."

"She's a good baby, considering her rough start. I did not think she would be."

"You mean Leonora's addiction to opium and such. Has it affected Lily at all, do you think?" The baby yawned and Isolde kissed her little cheeks, nuzzling her a little.

"I do not think so, but she can be a little unsettled some

days. We've consulted the doctor, and he's assured us that she'll grow normally with a proper diet and care."

Isolde hoped so. "She's lucky to have you as a father." Isolde inwardly cringed at her words, forgetting for a moment that Merrick was, in fact, not the father of this precious little girl.

He smiled, nodding. "She has my name and my love. Nothing will ever harm hers or William's future. Nothing."

"I'm glad for it." The wet nurse returned, and Isolde handed the baby back before watching Merrick wish the little girl pleasant dreams. They walked back downstairs in silence before entering the library once again.

With the click of the door closing, the air in the room thickened and charged. Alone, Isolde fought the urge to go to him, wrap her arms about his neck, and kiss him to distraction. Desperately, she wanted to taste him again, to feel the hunger that fired her blood each and every time they touched. To be alive in his arms and take what she wanted, instead of waiting for things to happen, to behave and always act as a lady ought. "I should return home. I want to ensure I'm back before Mama returns from her entertainments."

He smiled, walking toward her. "Will you come again?" His words were laced with need, and his eyes darkened with desire.

Isolde bit her lip as she thought over his question. Would she visit him again, alone? At night? Should she be caught, her reputation would be ruined, for sure. Especially, since she was about to cry off a second marriage. The prospect was more appealing than ever, but then reason pulled her back toward proper decorum.

About to tell him no, she met his intense gaze, and the words fell away unsaid. What was right, what Society expected, could go hang. "I will," she said, unable to force her feet to move, to leave. She was playing with fire, going against the rules, and it was madness and marvelous all at the same time.

---

*W*ith each step that Merrick took, Isolde shuffled back. For so long he'd allowed her to slip through his fingers, to be always at arm's length, but no longer. Under her own volition she'd come to him, not during a chance meeting at a ball or a stroll in the park, but alone, at night, and in his home. It had to mean something.

Another step, another shuffle.

"What are you doing, Merrick?"

His name on her lips was an elixir that he longed to taste. She came up against the settee, and she clasped its back, stopping herself from going over the seat. Her emerald eyes blazed with wariness, but beneath their vigilance was a weakness that he, too, fought to deny. To give in to. "Do you have any notion how much I want to kiss you?" He touched her wrist, running his finger along her cloaked arm. "Show you how much I've missed every ounce of your being?"

A shiver rocked her body, and he breathed deeply, not wanting to alarm her as to how close he was to madness. In time, he would win her again, but tonight wasn't the night. They had spoken for the first time in years as friends, allowed each other back into their lives, and it was just as precious as his children who lay sleeping abovestairs.

"I know your struggles, Merrick, for they are mine, too." Their eyes met, and he stepped against her, but there was no leaning away, no shuffling to the side. Isolde stood her ground and raised her chin, taunting him, if anything, to do as he willed.

He pushed the cloak from her shoulders, absently hearing the thump as it pooled at their feet. Her dark locks were in disarray from the cloak, and he pushed away a tendril of hair that fell over her eye. "I've longed for this for so long."

She licked her lips, and need roared through him, hot and consuming. "Let me kiss you. Please," he begged when she watched him, as calm and poised as ever. A front, for there was no doubt Isolde wanted him, just as much as he yearned for her.

Her gaze dropped to his lips, and he swooped down and kissed her. Hard. The long years apart, the denied thirst, crumbled any decorum, and the kiss was beyond tame. As if they had never been separated, Isolde kissed him with an intensity that left him reeling and grappling for purchase.

Time ticked by as the glide of her tongue sent his blood thrumming and met with sweet sighs and gasps. Merrick threaded his fingers through her hair, feeling it fall over his hands and against her back. He broke the kiss, taking in her disarrayed beauty that was for him only. "You're so beautiful. I've missed you so much."

She pulled him back to kiss him again, and he groaned, his hand sliding down her back to settle on her derriere, yanking her against him. He kissed away her shocked gasp, undulating against her, pushing them both toward a conflagration of pleasure. He pushed her on, teasing and tempting her to be with him like this forever.

"Merrick," she sighed. "Stop. We have to stop." She pushed against his chest, and, reluctantly, he stepped back, his breathing ragged as if he'd run a mile.

"I should go." Isolde picked up her cloak and strode toward the library doors, pausing at its threshold to look at him. "I missed you as well," she said, leaving him without another word.

A smile lifted his lips as elation bloomed through his soul for the first time in five years. Where there was passion, there was hope, and he would do anything, be anyone she wished, if it meant she was his and he was hers once more.

Forever.

---

*I*t took Isolde almost a week before she was able to sneak away to see Merrick again. Her family had traveled to the theater, a play which Isolde hadn't wanted to see, so it wasn't hard to evade the outing.

Her sister Alice had lingered longer in the foyer, looking at her as if she suspected something, but, pulling on her gloves, had left with all the others, and Isolde walked to the mews and had their groom summon her a hackney cab.

London this evening was shrouded in rain, a relentless torrent that Isolde had thought would stop her mother from attending the theater, but the lure was too much to be foregone because of a little dampness.

The cab was summoned quickly, and it wasn't long before the familiar streets of Mayfair passed as she made her way to Merrick's home. She told the driver to drop her off on the side street and walked the short distance to the alley from which she entered Merrick's yard.

Pulling her cloak close, she pushed the small metal gate open and walked toward the terrace and library doors. She stood on the flagstones, unable to knock on the door, torn between what she wanted to do and what she ought to do.

What am I doing here? Although she knew very well what she was doing. Where was the shame she ought to feel at such an escapade? That there was none was telling indeed. She had always played by the rules, but that had always ended with heartache and despair. Maybe she ought to try another way and see if the outcome would be more favorable.

The library was darker than the previous time she'd been here, and for a moment she wondered if Merrick was out, or abed already, before movement near the fire caught her attention and she spied him seated before it.

Isolde knocked, and he looked at the door, his face one of expectation. He smiled when he observed her, and all misgivings vanished into the cold night air.

Although the moment she stepped into the room she was not the least chilled; if anything, heat bloomed across her skin and sizzled with a longing she'd denied herself for too long. "Good evening, Your Grace."

He laughed, and her stomach tightened. "My lady. You come again."

She followed him toward the fire and sat on the little footstool he pulled out for her, one that matched his own. Only a few candles burned in the room, giving the space a seductive, romantic air. "I have." She frowned. "But I shouldn't have. I'm not acting as a lady should."

He watched her, his fingers idly running across his lips. The action pulled her gaze to that part of his body, and heat pooled at her core and with it the realization that she wanted to kiss him again. Wanted to feel the passion and fire he'd wrought in her last week.

She looked back to the fire and cleared her throat. "I'm sorry I haven't been able to call sooner. It's been a busy week. I hope William and Lily are doing well."

He smiled at the mention of the children, and the pulsating tension between them eased a little. "They're very well. William is looking forward to getting back to Mountshaw. Lily is putting on weight and is settling better this week."

"I'm so glad," she said, truly thankful the little girl hadn't suffered for her mother's addiction. And that William was going forward, continuing to be a happy, polite child, was a welcome reprieve. "We will miss you when you leave. I hope you'll allow me to visit you."

Merrick met her gaze. "I think we both know that will be impossible. You will, after all, marry one day. I hesitate to believe your new husband would wish to stay at a house where your ex-betrothed lives."

"And if I don't marry but visit you anyway, will you allow me to stay?" The question was more forward and telling than anything Isolde had said in years. A muscle worked on his jaw, and he looked pained. She took a fortifying breath, sick of being the perfect duke's daughter. Always doing right by the expectations of others. She'd had her fill of it. "Merrick?" she asked when he didn't answer.

"I don't believe that would be wise."

She chuckled. It wasn't wise, and for once that's exactly what she wanted. "Do you not want me to stay?" Disappointment stabbed sharply that he'd distance himself after their kiss. What was wrong with the man? She was all but throwing herself at his head.

He turned to her, taking her hands in his. His thumb ran over her skin, sending shivers down her spine. "May I ask you something, Isolde?"

A small frown line marred his brow, and she wanted to wipe away his concern, not let him worry about things as much as he did. "By all means. Anything."

"Is it true that you're willing to enter the marriage state without love or affection? That a marriage solely for the procurement of children is all you wish?"

Embarrassment washed through her that she'd wanted a marriage such as Merrick had explained. To hear the truth of her wishes out loud made them sound heartless and cold. Which, in fact, they were, but nothing out of the ordinary for others of their set. "I thought I did. Certainly, I would not be the first woman to do so."

He cringed, and she gazed back at the fire, hating the guilt that entered his eyes. "Promise me that you'll marry for love, Isolde. You deserve better than mediocre."

"I…" Isolde bit her lip, unsure if she could keep such a promise. To love again meant to risk her heart. After the painful years of separation from Merrick, she wasn't sure if she could put herself through such emotions again. "I couldn't risk loving and losing another as much as I loved and lost you. People marry all the time for no other reason than to achieve position, beget funds, or heirs. I did not love Wardoor, and should his lifestyle have been less risqué, I would've married him."

Merrick's mouth turned up in distaste. "You would've allowed Wardoor to have a mistress? That once married, as long as you had children and a secure future, you would've given him free rein to do as he pleased?"

Anger spiked through her that Merrick would chastise her so, when her options, no matter how wealthy she was, were still confined. "What do you suggest I do, Moore? Marry for love and be heartbroken when he sleeps with someone else? When I marry, I would rather keep my heart locked away and free from that kind of pain."

"You cannot make all men pay for my actions. Your father made me marry Leonora for the very reasons you were willing to accept Wardoor. Let me assure you, they do not make for a happy union."

She gaped at his words. "You broke my heart. I do not have a whole one to give to someone else." This conversation and night were not going where Isolde had wanted. She should leave.

"You must not hold yourself back from love, Isolde. A small part of you will not let go of the hurt I caused you and because of it, you will regret any marriage in which you enter. I do not want that for you." He paused, softening his tone when he said, "You must learn to trust again. Without it you'll have nothing."

"There is no one whom I love, so the point is moot. Without love, I do not need to learn to rely on that emotion." She stood, distancing herself from him.

"And if I asked you to marry me, would you learn to love and have faith in me again?"

This conversation was not happening, and Isolde's mind whirred with thoughts as to how to escape. "Are you asking me to marry you?"

"Depends on your answer."

Nerves assailed her at the thought of Merrick being her husband. The sensations he'd always been able to raise in her were unlike anything she'd ever known, but did he mean it? And more importantly, did she want him to mean it? "My family would never allow me to marry you. Not after everything that's happened between us."

"Blast your family and Society. What do you want? Think ahead to when you're alone, married, years from now, and unhappy. With a husband who cares little for your feelings, or those of your children. Will you wish that you'd chosen differently?"

She paced before the fire, unable to think straight. What Merrick said was true. She would hate a marriage of convenience. But up until a few minutes ago, that was all she could see for herself. Merrick had not voiced his desire to marry her, and she'd not allowed herself to dream, to hope that one day they could have the future they both wanted. "You cannot speak to me in such a way."

He rounded on her, towering over her like a bear before a large morsel of meat. The breath in her lungs expelled, and she fought hard to breathe evenly.

"I want you, Isolde. I've wanted you from the very first

moment I laid eyes on you at that country dance, and I will want you up to the day that I take my last breath."

Tears welled in her eyes, and she blinked quickly. "Oh, Merrick..." Her mind raced along with her heart. This was too wonderful and dreadful at the same time. How many hours had she lain awake at night, wishing he would visit her? Wishing she had stayed and fought Leonora for his hand. Wishing she had listened to his excuse that she'd come to believe as truth.

"If you do not marry me, I want you to go into whatever alliance you choose with your eyes open, because once you're married, it is forever, Isolde. As I had to face, and accept, only too well."

She swallowed the lump in her throat, hating that the man before her was the only one she'd ever met who could rile her up and bring forth any true emotion. "I will know my future husband well enough, but I'm a modern woman, not a simpleton. I know my husband will wish to be free and do as he pleases most nights. And I will not stop him from doing so, as long as he does not stop me from having the life that I want."

"Really," he said, stepping closer still. "And pray, what do you mean by that?"

"Only that...that is to say..."

"Does that mean you would have an affair with another man once a golden band sits about your finger and protects you from the Society you hold so dear?"

His breath was but a whisper away from her lips, and she wanted to lean closer still and touch them to hers. Desire smoldered, just waiting for a flame to bring it to life. "You're reading more into my words than you ought."

He scoffed. "Do not fool yourself that freedom beckons at the signing of a marriage register." Merrick paused, his gaze dark with intent. "I will not allow you to marry for anything other than the purest love." His touch skimmed along her arm, and a charge of desire spiraled deep in her belly.

"And you think you can stop me?"

He threw her an amused glance, nodding. "Yes," he said without hesitation.

"Merrick," she said, placing a finger against his lips, "shut up and kiss me." Isolde wrapped her arms about his neck and took control, doing it herself when he stared at her, shocked. He gasped, whether to say something or to deepen the embrace she didn't know, but what did it matter when she was kissing the man who'd haunted her dreams for the last five years.

A heady sense of power and desire coursed through her veins, and she opened to him, kissing him with a desperate, ravenous need. He wrapped his arms around her and held her tight. This close she could feel his desire, and the knowledge of it only increased her own. Delicious heat pooled between her legs, and the decision reverberated in her mind that this was right. And nothing and no one was going to stop her from getting what she wanted.

Not ever again.

---

*I*t took Merrick a moment to catch his breath when the woman he'd longed to taste, to hold and love, kissed him without restraint. And yet, with every delicious moment, devouring her mouth wasn't enough. He wanted more. So much more.

The smooth glide of her gown beneath his hands tempted and teased him. His arms slid lower to caress the most sensual, perfect bottom he'd ever known a woman to have.

She moaned her acquiescence, nibbling his bottom lip and making him as hard as the statue of David. Shivers stole over him, and he pulled back to collect some perspective. "You cannot kiss me like that and marry another. I'll not allow it."

She clasped his face, her emerald eyes sleepy with desire. "I don't want to talk about my fictional future husband."

Merrick couldn't agree more. He pulled her closer still, allowed her to feel what she was doing to him, what she made him crave. Her. Only her.

He shuffled them toward the settee, hauling her down onto his lap as he sat, while never breaking the kiss. The slide of her tongue against his left his heart thrumming a beat of need he'd only ever had with Isolde. She was everything to him, and if she'd allow it, he'd take her. Have her and be dammed the consequence. Or thank God the consequence, for marriage is what he'd demand from the action.

"Touch me, Merrick."

The need in her voice undid him, and he growled, only too happy to do as she bid. "Where would you like to be touched, my lady?"

Isolde bit her lip, moving so she straddled his legs, shuffling up her dress a little to allow her more movement against him. "Everywhere." She clasped his hand, pushing it up against her breast. "And anywhere."

The breath in his lungs expired. For a moment, Merrick was unable to speak or move. She wiggled, and the slight brush of her mons against his cock awakened him from a dream he'd never thought would come to reality.

Sliding his hands down her legs, he enjoyed the smoothness of the silk beneath his palms that was rivaled by her own skin. Soft and warm, he slowly slid the gown up her legs to pool about her waist.

"You undo me." He licked his lips, noting Isolde wore no drawers. God damn it, he would be lucky to survive the night.

"Please."

Her plea, another wiggle against him, could not be denied. He clasped her hip, running one finger across her lower abdomen and toward the dark thatch of curls between her thighs. How he wanted to free himself from his frontfalls and slip into her hot core, to embed her on him and bring them both to climax.

She shivered above him as his hand grazed her curls, sliding slowly over her flesh, teasing and stroking as he delved further. She was so wet, hot and ready for him, he could almost feel her aching need.

"Oh my, that's…" She clasped his jaw, lifting him up to look at her. "That feels so wonderful, Merrick."

He slid one finger into her. So sweet and tight. He stroked her slowly, watched as her eyes glazed over with lust, her head dropping back as she enjoyed the music he played against her flesh.

Her hands splayed into his hair as her movements became more frantic, her body undulating, mimicking an act that the pliant woman in his arms had never experienced. A blessing and curse, for who would not wish Isolde to be loved, to enjoy love such as they were now.

"I want you." The words came out raspy and breathless. "Let me have you," he begged, unable to hold back the desires he'd harbored for so long.

She looked at him, coming down to kiss him, her hands sliding down his chest to fumble with his pant buttons. "I want you as well. So much."

Sanity prevailed for a moment, and Merrick understood that no matter how ready Isolde was for him, such a position would not be best for her first time. He clasped her ass and flipped her to lie on the settee, settling over her.

Her fingers resumed their frantic unbuttoning, and

within moments his cock sprang free and into her eager hand. She looked up at him in shock. "Oh, it's so soft."

He laughed and groaned when she started to play with him.

"I have a notion that I'm going to enjoy what we're about to do," she said, grinning like a minx. And there she was, the teasing, laughing woman he'd fallen in love with at a country dance. How he'd missed that carefree smile.

"I aim to please," he gasped, trying to hold himself together as her untutored hand slid about him, squeezing a little.

He supported himself on his arms, watching her watch him. Her legs open to him, her breasts rising against her gown with every frantic breath. He placed her hands above her head. "Hold the armrest," he said.

Her green gaze widened, but she did as he asked. He glided his cock against her core, running it over her swollen nubbin and aching heat. She oohed beneath him and he couldn't stop teasing them both for a moment longer. It had been so long since he'd wanted a woman. So long since he'd had Isolde in his arms that he never wished it to end. Desperate as he was, she lifted herself to place him at her core, pushing the head of his penis into her heat.

"I want to go slow for you. The first time often hurts," he said, fighting for breath.

She clasped his arms, her nails biting into his flesh. "Merrick, my patience is starting to wane. I will flip you onto your back in a moment and do the deed myself, if you do not hurry up."

He grinned. How remarkable she was, and how much he had missed her. All the years that they had been apart were too long. "I will be as gentle as I can," he promised. Merrick slowly pushed against her just as a knock sounded at the door. Isolde stilled in his arms and he swore.

"Your Grace?" Another tap, louder this time. "Lord William is awake and asking for you. He's..." His servant paused. "Had a nightmare and wishes to see you, Your Grace."

His gaze caught Isolde's. "I'll be right there," he replied, his voice strained and harsher than he wished. Merrick took a deep calming breath before pulling away from her.

She sat up, trying to right her clothing, her eyes tinged with disappointment.

"I'll be back. Please do not leave."

She caught his hand as he stood, tugging him back to sit beside her. "I must leave. It's getting late, and William needs you. I don't want you to rush with your boy just so you can come back to me."

He frowned, hating the thought of her leaving after what they'd been about to do. "I wouldn't do that to him, but I also do not wish for you to go."

She didn't reply, only leaned up and kissed him sweetly on the lips. Fear spiked through him at the finality of the gesture. "Go, Merrick. I will see you again. I promise."

He stood, looking back at her at the door and knowing that when he returned to the room, he would find it empty.

CHAPTER 17

*I*solde woke up with a start, the soft cotton sheets haphazardly spread about her bed, the blankets piled at her feet and floor. "Another bad dream? You've been waking me up all week with your nightmares."

Isolde looked toward her armoire and noted Alice going through her dresses, holding a blue silk gown against her body in contemplation.

"What are you doing in my room?"

"I want answers." She hung the gown back up and strolled toward her. Her sister's gaze fixed on her with a determination she'd often seen on her elder sister Elizabeth's visage prior to her marriage to Henry.

Isolde swallowed. "What sort of answers? I don't know anything." Not anything she wished to disclose, in any case.

"I came home early from the theater last night, and you were not here. I searched everywhere, by the way, just in case you try to come up with some pitiful excuse."

Heat bloomed on her cheeks, and Isolde grabbed the sheet, holding it up against her mouth. "I went for a walk in the garden. Nothing amiss with that." If only that were true.

The thought of what Merrick had done to her, of his touch, his kisses, his hard...

"Where were you, Isolde?" Alice crossed her arms over her chest, one brow determinedly raised. "I want to know."

"Away from my room. As I said." She shuffled from her bed, walking to the window to take in the weather—no sign of rain today.

Alice spied her gown thrown carelessly across a chair in her dressing room. She strode over to it, lifting it up as if to inspect it before smelling it. "This has the distinct odor of maleness."

Isolde laughed, but even to her own ears it sounded brittle with guilt. "Don't be absurd. You cannot smell a man on my gown."

"How long have you been sneaking out to meet him? And by him I mean, His Grace, the Duke of Moore."

When did Alice become so damn nosy, and for that matter so damn smart? Isolde rolled her eyes. "Moore? Do be serious, Alice. I've just broken my engagement with Wardoor, so why would I allow courtship so soon, pray?"

"I know you are, for you were certainly not home when I arrived last night. And you were not in the gardens. Now," Alice said, raising her brows, "know that I won't tell anyone your secret so long as you stop whatever destructive thing it is you're doing, before it's too late."

"It's not destructive."

"Ah ha! So you are sneaking out to meet someone. I demand you tell me at once or I'll be forced to tattle to Mama, and that'll not do you any good at all."

"You wouldn't dare." Isolde rounded on her sister, glaring at her smirk and the careless shrug of her shoulder. The last thing she wanted was her family knowing of her rekindled friendship with Merrick. They loathed him after his treatment of her five years ago and had not forgiven his sins.

Even when she had explained that he was not at fault, that he had been tricked, along with herself, they still found it difficult to be pleasant and cordial in public.

"I will, if you do not own up to what you're about. There cannot be a scandal afoot in this house, unless I'm part of it." Alice stood in wait, expectation clearly written on her visage.

Isolde sighed. "I've merely called on Moore a couple of times to see how he and the children are getting on after Leonora's passing." Isolde slumped onto the chair behind her writing desk, waiting for the inevitable scolding that Alice was sure to give. Many would say their seeing of each other was too soon after Leonora's death. That Isolde was pushing in on a family that was in mourning. Taking advantage of them. She frowned.

Am I?

"We've always suspected you loved him, even all these years later."

Mortification swamped her. Was she so obvious to everyone? "You did not."

"Is it true?" Alice came and stood before her. "But I would caution you on it. You could marry someone with no past to cloud your judgment. There are other men besides His Grace who could make you happy, if only you tried."

The words were reminiscent of what Merrick had said the night before. But Isolde had given her heart to him many years ago, and she didn't want it back. "I know you mean well, and I will think on your words." Isolde sighed. "I simply visited Moore to thank him for his help that disastrous night, and because I felt for him and the children after the duchess's death. It cannot be easy losing a spouse, even if the marriage was not a love match." At her words, guilt pricked her conscience at having been about to sleep with a man who was still in mourning. She was the worst kind of person, who should be ashamed of herself, but the thought of Merrick's lips, demanding and ravenous upon her own, his strong capable arms pulling her close... Well, she bit her lip, if only she could do more of the same.

"Are you going to visit him again?"

"No." And she wouldn't. There could be no more secret meetings. Each time she was with the duke it became harder and harder to stay away, to remain unmoved by his presence. She'd caused the family enough grief with the debacle of her love life. If she were to single out Moore, allow him to court her, London Society would have a fit. Not only had he married her best friend, but he was still in mourning. What a conundrum. "We're friends, nothing more. His Grace is to return to Mountshaw very soon, for his children's sake. I simply wished to see him before he left, to ensure all was well." Isolde looked down at some parchment to hide the heat that bloomed on her cheeks at the lie.

When did I become so scandalous?

Alice's eyes narrowed. "If you say so, but you would tell me if what you say wasn't your true thoughts, wouldn't you? All we wish for you is happiness."

"I am happy." Isolde smiled and noted her sister's stance relaxed a little at the falsehood she'd not caught. "I'm more than content, in fact. And as for the duke, I was simply being a friend. Nothing more, I assure you."

Alice watched her for a moment longer and then nodded. "Very well. I'll not delve further into the matter, and I will take you at your word, but know this, sister, the family would never wish for you to settle for anything other than what you want. No matter what has happened in the past. That is done with. It's time to move on into the future and all the wonders that said future will bring."

Isolde stood and, coming around her desk, hugged her sister. "I know and thank you. For a younger sibling, you're more intelligent than I thought."

Alice feigned insult. "I have my moments. You never learn anything in this Society if you're smart. One must feign stupidity at times. There is nothing a gentleman or the matrons of the ton hate more than an intelligent woman who can say more than yes, no, and thank you."

Isolde laughed, and Alice walked from the room. The moment the door closed, tears sprang to her eyes. She swiped at them—useless, unhelpful things. Crying would not help her now. Only a leap of faith would do that. And, right at this moment, Isolde was unsure if such a thing were possible, especially when it came to Moore, the man who'd already broken her heart.

---

*A*gainst Society's rules, Merrick attended a Shakespearean play for no reason other than Isolde would be there. He sat in the ducal box alone. Much to his surprise, he spied Wardoor for the first time since his night at the opium den, seated on the opposite side of the theater, his head dipped in quiet conversation with a party Merrick didn't recognize.

A gentleman dandy in the pit shouted at one of the actors, and Merrick's attention was temporarily diverted to see who was making such a racket. The play continued on as normal, and it was soon reasonably quiet once more.

Merrick leaned back in his chair and took in Isolde's splendor, her delightful pink satin and cream silk gauze gown that fell about her like a second skin. She was perfection personified, more beautiful than he'd ever seen her before. The thought of undoing the laces of the gown and stripping it from her body and kissing her sweet-smelling flesh, watching as she blushed under his touch, bombarded his mind, and he adjusted his seat.

He ignored the mumblings of his theater neighbors who made it known they did not approve his attendance. Words such as scandalous, heartless, unpardonable, were mentioned, and he ignored them all. If they knew just how terrible his marriage had been, that his wife was a mistress to many, perhaps even their own husbands, maybe their defamation of him would cease. With such thoughts, the never-ending guilt assailed him that Leonora had done what she had out of desperation to gain his attention. If she'd been a bad wife, he, too, had been a bad husband. And if that was the case, he deserved their censure.

Applause rang out as the curtains swung shut, and the lamps were turned up during intermission. Merrick stood, and walking from his private box, made his way to the Worthinghams'. The curtain was open, Lord and Lady Kinruth paying their regards, when he bowed to them all. The Duchess of Penworth threw him a steely glare, her annoyance at his presence obvious to all who stood around him.

He bowed. "Good evening, Your Grace, Lady Isolde." Merrick clasped her hand, bowing over it and kissing it lightly. A shiver of awareness made her hand shake and he met her gaze, wishing they were alone so she could kiss away his uncertainties of not being worthy. Help him forget how cruel he'd been to his deceased wife.

"Your Grace," she said in return, standing. "Are you enjoying the play?"

"I forget there is even a play as the theater holds so many other delights this evening."

She blushed, and Lord Kinruth coughed, covering his grin with his hand. "I didn't think you would attend," he said.

"As you can see, I have." He noted the absence of Isolde's brother and her younger sister Victoria, and yet Lady Alice was there, her gaze one of contemplation.

"Out, while in mourning, Your Grace. Correct me if I'm wrong, but have the rules of polite Society changed so much to allow such a thing?" the duchess asked, watching him with contempt.

"Mama," Isolde said, blushing furiously. "I'm sure His Grace has reasons for attending this evening."

"I'm sure he does," the duchess mumbled, taking her seat and giving them her back.

"I find myself equally surprised you're here but glad that you are." Isolde moved them to the back of the box to give them privacy. "I did not think gentlemen attended such entertainments when in mourning."

He cringed, knowing how true that was. "You're absolutely right, but I couldn't go another day without seeing you."

Isolde looked up at him, her beautiful green eyes widening at his words. How he wanted to take her into his arms and astonish her and her family even more. "I've shocked you."

She nodded, biting her lip. "You have, Your Grace, but not in a bad way."

"Merrick—no titles between us," he whispered. He watched her with something akin to desperation. He needed to see her again, alone where there was no one to interrupt them. "When will I see you again? Just us?"

She looked back toward her family, and Merrick noted that although they spoke with others who visited their box, their attention constantly diverted toward them. "We cannot." She frowned. "You're newly widowed, and I've just broken my betrothal. The scandal would be too much, if we were caught. I have to think of my family and yours."

Merrick could understand her concern. Hell, he had his own demons that haunted his every waking hour. He did not deserve a second chance, to be happy once more, not after his part in making Leonora's life a living hell. But must they continue to be apart, if only to please others? To always do what was right and expected of them? He thought not.

The pain in Isolde's eyes told him, more than words, that she loved him, wanted the same as he—for them to be together. If only they could make the choice and the ton could go hang with their so-called standards that left so many unhappy couples within that social sphere.

Hidden by Isolde's gown, Merrick reached out and clasped her hand. Her fingers entwined with his, and her lips lifted in a knowing smile. "Please, Isolde." He would beg if necessary and be damned who was about. The theater staff started coming in to turn down the lamps, signaling that the second act was about to begin. "Please think on it."

Isolde slipped her hand free and patted the lapels on his jacket. "I will. I promise."

Merrick stood back and allowed her to pass, not leaving until Isolde had regained her seat. He didn't return to his box but left the theater and sat in wait in his carriage for the entertainment to be over. And then he would see what Isolde's choice was and if he had any chance of winning her back.

CHAPTER 18

*T*hey returned from the theater late, and Isolde potted about her room, as sleep eluded her. Merrick's plea, and her insomnia, made his request hard to deny.

There was nothing more she wished than to lose herself in his arms. To let him sweep her off into the dream of them, but she could not. The risk was too great, for everyone, and she would not, no matter how much she cared for Merrick, place her family in the midst of another scandal.

The clock on her bedroom mantle chimed midnight and with it another day beckoned, filled with balls and parties that she no longer found interesting. With her betrothal to Wardoor at an end, and no other gentleman about town she wished to pursue, the Season loomed long and boring. Isolde rubbed her forehead, wondering what she should do versus what she wanted to do.

What a conundrum.

Isolde blew out the candles and slid under the blankets. The sheets were cool, and she rolled over, looking out toward

236

the moonlit night. Not being able to sleep, she opened the drapes to see the stars, but with the moon so large on the horizon, it muffled the stars' brilliance and took all the glory.

A creak of the floorboard outside her bedroom door made her start, and she sat up, clasping the blankets to her chest. No light shone under her door to explain the noise, and it was well past the time that the servants would be about.

Fear crept up her spine as her door silently opened, before the ghostly figure of a man she'd never thought to see in her own room quickly stepped into the space, shutting the door behind him. The flick of the lock sent tendrils of desire spiking through her.

"What are you doing here?" She didn't move, just watched as he made his way toward her, the cloak, shrouding all but his face, dropping to the floor.

"If you'll not come to me, I will come to you." The deep baritone made the air in her lungs still.

Merrick was all muscular beauty and dark features that left her shivery with need. "Josh will murder you if he catches you here. You must leave." She kneeled on the bed, pointing toward the door. He ignored her, coming to stand at the foot of the bed. So close she could almost touch him.

She wanted to touch him. To slide her hands against his perfect frame and marvel in his strength.

He pulled at his loosely tied cravat, dropping that, too, on the floor. He threw her a seductive grin that promised a night full of pleasure and sin. "I'm not going anywhere."

Oh my… "Merrick, do be serious." The mattress dipped as he, too, kneeled on the bed. Unconsciously, her hands reached out to touch his chest, his muscles flexing under her contact, and she swallowed the need that coursed through her hot and fast. A small voice at the back of her mind warned her that this was wrong. To travel down this path led to scandal and possibly broken dreams.

"Your brother is otherwise engaged. I checked on his whereabouts before coming here. As for the rest of your family, they're asleep. No one will interrupt us."

Heat pooled at her core, as his words and the meaning behind them became perfectly clear. "And pray tell, what exactly would they interrupt?"

His gaze raked over her and all thoughts of anyone but the two of them vanished. "Tonight, my beautiful Isolde, I intend to ruin you."

Isolde clasped the hem of his buckskin trousers and pulled him close. Merrick's hands came around her back, hauling her against his chest. Hard muscular planes met her through her light silk shift, and she shivered. Had it been only a few days since she'd been in his arms? Each hour had seemed a lifetime...

Merrick smiled, playing her like a pianist played a piano, to perfection and for his own enjoyment. He traced the line of her shoulder, flicking a tendril of hair out of the way before leaning down and kissing her beneath her ear. Isolde closed her eyes at the softness of his touch that left an ache in her chest. Yes, he knew exactly how to play her perfectly. "I've missed you, Isolde. You promised to come see me again. You lied."

His words were said with playfulness, but Isolde didn't miss the steely tone. "I wanted to come. I did, but..."

"No more excuses." He pushed her onto the bed, and she bounced, a laugh bubbling up inside her. Merrick watched her, a wicked edge to his gaze, before he crawled over her, pinning her to the spot. "Take off your shift, Isolde."

Heat bloomed on her chest. "I cannot. I..."

"If you do not, I'll rip it off. Unless you're up to explaining your ruined unmentionables to your maid..." His hand ran up her stomach to clasp the underside of her breast. Their eyes met in the moonlit room as his fingers clenched about the shift, slowly pulling it down until her breast was bared.

The cool night air made her nipple harden before he stroked her breast with an expertise that left her warm and achy. Isolde moaned as he leaned down and kissed her pebbled flesh. The feel of him there was so right in every way. Before their betrothal, they had only kissed, a risqué touch every so often, but nothing like this. Nothing like this kaleidoscope of sensations that were rioting inside her. How could they ever make up for lost time? She clutched his hair, her heart overflowing with the rightness of what they were doing.

"Merrick," she gasped, her voice breathless. "Kiss me."

With a little love bite to her breast, he moved up to meet her gaze. "As my lady wishes." He took her mouth in a fierce kiss, and there was no turning back. The years spent apart fell away, and Isolde embraced all that he offered. She'd dreamed of such a night, and now it was finally here; Merrick was in her arms, just as he should be.

He sat back, and clasping her shift, ripped it down the front. Stunned, Isolde didn't move, before she laughed at her ability to make him lose restraint. His heated gaze raked her body before halting at the apex of her thighs. Isolde writhed under his attention, wanting him to touch her where he looked.

Merrick ran a finger along her thigh, across her stomach, before sliding over her sex. She bit her lip, slick and achy, his touch when it went farther still, made her breath hitch. It was too much. Her body no longer her own.

Merrick let out a guttural groan, his touch sliding against her flesh became more insistent, more delicious. "I want you. Let me make love to you, Isolde."

She lifted one of her legs to wrap about Merrick's waist,

pulling him down with her foot. She clasped his face, the slight prickle of a day's growth tickling her palms. She adored him, had missed him beyond anyone or anything in her life. She nodded. "Yes. You may."

*A*t her words, Merrick ground his hips against her heat, the need to take her, to make her his, beyond anything he'd ever experienced before. He moved to grasp her ass, helping her to push against him. The contact shot blood to his cock, and he hardened further. He took a deep breath, fighting for control. "Tell me you want me, Isolde." He needed to hear her say the words. Needed to know she longed for him as much as he did her. In some small way, he needed reassurance that what they were doing wasn't wrong. That he deserved her after all that had passed between them, after how he'd treated his wife. All the mistakes and wrongs he'd done over the years.

"I want you, Merrick."

Her whispered reply made his soul soar. She was his, and he was hers. Always had been and, from this day forward, always would be. She fumbled with the buttons on his front falls, and the breath in his lungs stilled. Her saucy gaze met his before she slid her hand into his pants and stroked his cock. More confident this time and with a little knowledge of what he liked.

Holy hell, he'd never survive the night. He'd dreamed of making love to her, making them of one body as they'd always been of one mind. His breathing irregular, he pushed into her touch, wanting for this to never end.

"Help me." Isolde understood his plea and aided him in pushing down his breeches. Free of restraint, he came over Isolde and kissed her hard, enjoying the delicious friction of his member against her sex. Her hands came about his nape, her eyes heavy with unsated desire.

"Stop teasing me, Merrick."

Her words broke what little restraint he had left, and he took her in one smooth stroke. Isolde stilled beneath him, and he fought not to move, to give her time to adjust to him. His breath came out ragged and fast against her neck, and he kissed the little mole beneath her ear, soothing her as much as he could. "I'm sorry, my love."

Her fingers threaded through his hair, dragging him back to look at her. "I'm not." The pad of her thumb brushed his lip. "Don't stop. Don't ever stop."

Isolde's long, slender legs wrapped about his hips, pulling her to him, and he rocked into her. She fit him perfectly, the sweetest thing he'd ever possessed. Never would he have enough of her, and he'd known that from the first day they'd met. Isolde was his soul mate, his one true happiness in the world, and always would be. Her hands clawed at his back, and he reveled in her pleasure. The smooth glide of their lovemaking increased, and with each thrust it became fiercer, overwhelmingly uninhibited. She bit her lip, and he muffled her moan with a kiss. Nothing else mattered but to give her pleasure, make her as crazed for him as he was for her.

"Merrick," she panted, the air of her breath whispering against his cheek.

Their gazes held, and he pushed her on, took them toward a pinnacle of pleasure. He repeated her name, how much he loved her, had longed for her always. "You're everything to me," he said, kissing away a tear that slid down her cheek. "I love you, so very much."

Her mouth opened on a sigh, and her shattering release pulled his own forth. Tremor after tremor rocked through to his very soul, and he lost himself for a moment within her arms. They lay like that a minute, both panting, neither willing to move. Merrick rolled beside her and smiled as she nestled into the crook of his arm.

"I know you love me, but I can't help but wonder if it's enough."

"What do you mean?" Unease ran through him at her words, and he remained silent as he waited for her response. "You are probably the only person in the world who knows me better than my own family. And you know I always try to do the right thing. I captured your heart at a country dance, without even having to have a Season in Town. How very clever of me, don't you think?" She threw him a self-deprecating look.

"I believe it was I who courted you that night, not the other way around."

Isolde clasped his hand. "I'm not the oldest of my siblings, but they all look up to me. I'm the sister who always sees both sides of any situation, doesn't judge or give criticism, but looks on things with both pros and cons and then decides which way would be best. I removed myself from Wardoor, my second betrothal, which the ton is unlikely to forgive or forget. I cannot bear to think what my family or Society will say if I marry you. A duke still in mourning, his wife not two months gone."

Merrick sat up to lean on the headboard. "What are you saying? That you will not marry me? I've ruined you, Isolde," he reminded her.

She sat up also, kneeling beside him. "You must see it's not possible. Not at the moment, at least."

Words eluded him for an instant, before he said, "When then?"

"A year. You'll be out of mourning, and by then the ton will have forgotten about my engagement with Wardoor, or at least, found something else to amuse them."

Merrick slid from the bed, anger coiling about his insides.

"Why do you care what the ton thinks? Are you not the same woman who only weeks ago told me I deserved to be happy? That Leonora's death wasn't my fault?"

"Yes, but—"

"There is no but in this decision. I love you, Isolde. I want you to be my wife. No more waiting for when Society thinks we should marry. I want to marry you now." He stared at her a moment, willing her to let everyone who had no bearing on them to go hang. "Marry me, please."

She shook her head. "I want to marry you, Merrick. I do, but I cannot. Not yet. You have to give us time. Please," she said, following him to where he stood, heedless of their nakedness. "Just do this one thing for me. I've put my family through so much already. I can't foist an understanding with you on them. My brother will need time to come around. You know he still thinks you guilty of your crime against me with Leonora."

Merrick pulled on his pants and grabbed his shirt, throwing it over his head, heedless if it was on backward or not. "I'm sick of paying for other's mistakes, other's choices. You know the truth of that night with Leonora. What does it matter what your brother or anyone believes?" She crossed her arms over her chest, and he clenched his jaw, pain severing through him like a sword. "Do you love me?"

Her silence was deafening. Merrick walked to the door, pausing when he grabbed the handle. "You know where I am when you're ready, or when you believe Society is." He left without another word, striding down the hallway, heedless of how loud his footsteps were. He shook his head, not believing what had just occurred. Isolde was well known for her strong conviction, and if she believed this was the correct course for her, no one, not even he, could talk her out of it.

At the base of the stairs he turned and headed toward the back of the house, and the servants' stairs that led to the kitchens below. Twelve months loomed ahead of him, unbearable months that he couldn't be with her. How would he ever survive it? He cringed, knowing he would, for when had he not done what Isolde wished? He would do it for her, even if it was intolerable.

CHAPTER 19

The following week, Merrick lounged in a settee at Lord Statton's home, the gentleman hosting a coming-out ball for his daughter, Madeline, and Moore's first cousin. It was an event that, even in mourning, he refused to miss, no matter what gasps and glares he received from the ton.

The fire crackled in the hearth as he waited for Wardoor, whom he'd summoned to join him. The rumor mill about town was rife with scenarios as to why Isolde had cried off from the wedding. The most disturbing whisper was the one he wanted to discuss above all else—his love had endured enough heartache over the past five years. He wouldn't allow any more to darken her soul.

And then, once Wardoor was dealt with, he would try to amend his mistake with Isolde. He should not have walked out on her after they'd just made love. Was he insane? Isolde was entitled to her beliefs, even if they were the opposite of his own, and he should have respected that more.

I love her.

Wardoor stumbled into the room, and Merrick stood,

frowning when two women who could only be termed whores strode in after him. Their gowns gaped at the front, their hair askew and knotted. "I do believe I summoned only you, Wardoor. Your friends may leave."

His friend sent him a mocking grin. "Ah yes, you did, but I find that I may need a good tumble whenever I wish, now that I'm no longer betrothed. I'm sure you've heard." He gestured to the women. "Here are my relieving wenches."

The women giggled, one seating herself on Wardoor and, for a moment, Merrick was given a show of his friend grinding himself against the woman's sex. It was enough to make him sick.

Merrick noted the cane beside Wardoor, and he gestured to it. "You need a stick to walk these days? How much did you drink today?"

Wardoor grinned. "I fell off my horse, if you must know. My ankle took the brunt of the fall, and that is why I need the cane. No other sinister reason for it, I assure you." He kissed the second whore deeply. "Now, to what do I owe this pleasure? You've not sought my company for some weeks, so I'm all ears as to why you wish to reacquaint yourself with me now."

Merrick ignored the remark, or the fact that Wardoor had probably fallen from his horse due to drink or opium. "I'm here merely to ensure you apologize and that you do not cause Isolde any trouble. There are rumors. Absurd talk, to be honest."

"I have nothing to apologize for," Wardoor said, plying one of the whore's breasts.

Merrick scoffed, but wondered if his lordship had memory lapses similar to what Leonora had experienced. Did his friend even know why Isolde had cried off? "I know you're addicted to opium, Wardoor. And I know you visited an opium den in the East End some weeks ago, because I observed you there myself. Your conduct is the reason why Isolde broke your understanding. She followed you to find out what you were about."

Wardoor paled, his gaze unfocused and with not a small amount of confusion. "I do not attend those sorts of establishments."

Merrick shook his head. What a dreadful way to end up, a peer of the realm, brought low by scandal and vice. "I know you were there, Wardoor, and what you were doing. But that's not all." Merrick rang the bell, and the butler strode in moments later. "Please bring your two burliest footmen. These ladies need an escort back to their own establishments."

The butler bowed. "Yes, Your Grace."

"You have no right to remove my guests." Wardoor sat forward, glaring.

"I have every right. This is my uncle's home, and they're not welcome here. And considering what escapades you partook in that night in the opium den, and the company you kept, I think you'll do exactly as I ask."

Wardoor pulled at his loosely tied cravat. "I ah…"

The door opened and in strode two footmen just perfect for the employment Merrick had tasked for them. "Take the ladies and hire them a hackney back to the East End. Pay the driver and ensure they return to their establishments safely."

Merrick watched as the women were taken away, vile words spewing from them as they were walked through the foyer. "You have a problem, one that is the same Leonora had, but, my friend, I will not make the same mistake I did with Her Grace. I wronged Leonora, but I will not wrong you, as well." If anything could be salvaged from this situation, Merrick would ensure it was Wardoor. The man before him, a broken shell of who he'd once been, was not his friend. But in time, he would be again.

"You have no proof of anything, and as for Isolde, well, it seems the lady has an aversion to men and marriage, in general. With my understanding broken, that makes two so far for her." Wardoor leaned back in his chair, smirking.

Merrick took a calming breath, seeing his baiting for what it was, a means to remove himself from this situation and place the blame on others. Well, it would not do. Not this time. "I have, at the ready, quill and parchment for you to write an apology to Isolde, whose only crime was trusting in your word. I also require you to sign a document my lawyer had drawn up that stops you from suing Isolde for breach of promise. Once you've done this, you shall be taken to one of my country estates where a doctor is waiting to ensure your addiction to opium is broken. You are a marquess. You have people who rely on you for their livelihood. I will not allow you to throw all that aside for nothing." Merrick met Wardoor's gaze and read the pain that lurked in his glassy eyes. "I've known you since Eton. You're my closest friend, and because of that friendship, I'm not going to let you travel down into the pits of hell without some fight in pulling you out."

Wardoor ran a hand over his jaw. "Perhaps your responsibility toward me would cease should you know the full truth."

Merrick crossed his arms, knowing everything there was to know about the man, and still he would not leave him alone in this. "I know everything. I know that when you're so high on opium you allow women and men to please you sexually. I know that your estate has suffered because of your affliction. And I know that you may have fathered my daughter."

A sheen of sweat broke out on Wardoor's brow. "You know that?" He paused, frowning. "How?"

The memory of how Merrick had learned such a thing

and the tragic circumstances that had followed made his stomach knot. "Leonora told me the day Lily was born. It was one of the reasons we argued." Merrick sighed, seating himself across from Wardoor. "I didn't wish to believe it, but after seeing you at the opium den, I realized that when you were under the influence of such a drug, you were capable of anything."

Wardoor cringed. "I did not know what I'd done. You were my friend, and I would never betray your trust so, had I known what I was doing. Leonora told me that we'd been together, and that I was the one who got her pregnant, but it was never confirmed. For what it's worth, I'm sorry, Moore. You did not deserve that."

"Ah, but I did," the duke said, in all honesty. "I pushed Leonora away, into the lifestyle she lived, and her death is on my hands. And for a time, I didn't believe I deserved happiness, not until Isolde showed me otherwise. I will forever regret my actions toward my wife, but I am determined to make it up to her through our children. I will raise them well, ensure they are respectful, productive people in the world. And I will save you from yourself. I will not fail in this."

"And if I don't wish to be saved?"

"You do. Deep inside, the man I respected is still there, and I'm determined to have him back beside me as my closest confidant." Merrick stood, gesturing toward the door. "Outside is a carriage and two very persuasive gentlemen who will take you to one of my country estates for recuperation. Do not try to fight this, Wardoor, and do not make a scene."

Wardoor stood, stumbling a little. "Tonight, with your highhandedness, I cannot thank you, but I will do as you ask, and we'll see." He went over to the desk and sat. Merrick watched him pen a letter of forgiveness to Isolde, and then sign the document his lawyer had drawn up. Merrick escorted him out to the carriage and watched as it rumbled down the street and out of view.

---

*I*solde stood, mouth agape, against the library door, as the conversation inside met her ears. She should not have sought out Merrick, but after their parting the other night she needed to explain that her wish to wait was in no way linked to the feelings she had toward him. If she could, she would marry him tomorrow.

Wardoor was Lily's father! Had slept with Leonora! The words made her gasp, and she covered her mouth with her hand lest they hear her eavesdropping. She shook her head, baffled and hurt for Merrick. Surprisingly, he sounded calm, almost accepting of such deception, and she loved him even more for it. Wardoor and the duchess had not been themselves for some time. Both of them had needed help; sadly, for Leonora, that help had never come.

The two men spoke for some time before Merrick told Wardoor of the plan for his recovery from his addiction. Isolde prayed that it would work, for she believed Wardoor was a good man, a great one, especially if Merrick had once considered him his closest friend.

The door to the foyer opened, and she could hear Wardoor leaving before Merrick walked back into the library, shutting the door firmly behind him.

Isolde pushed through the doorway, and her heart thumped hard at the sight of Merrick standing at the desk and slipping two letters into his coat pocket. He was too good, even for her, perhaps. Even after all that Wardoor had done to him, he would stick by his friend and help him in his time of need.

There were few who would ever sacrifice pride to do such a thing.

"Merrick," she said, at a loss for words. "I'm so sorry. I had no idea Wardoor was involved with Leonora." Unsure of what else to say, she shut the door, pausing for a moment before turning to meet his steady gaze.

He leaned against the desk, crossing his arms over his chest. Isolde's gaze ran over his form, the wide shoulders that were accentuated in such a pose. His slender waist and long muscular legs. She'd been such a fool to think she could live without him for another year. What had she been thinking?

"You heard everything?"

She nodded, hoping he wasn't too angry with her. "I did, but not on purpose. I came looking for you, and I heard you talking with Wardoor, and well…"

He smiled, holding out his hand for her. She quickly crossed the room. "I don't want there to be any secrets between us," he said, "but I'm also weary of our past. I want us to move forward, to start a life together."

"I know you do." And she did, too, more so tonight than any other time. The muffled music of a waltz floated through to them. "Dance with me, Merrick."

He placed her hand on his arm and walked them toward the ball. The room was overflowing with the upper ten thousand. Couples took their places on the floor, and the room was awash with colorful silk gowns. Merrick walked them onto the floor and pulled her against him, closer than he ought.

The dance began, and the duke spun her into the steps, guiding her every move. He smiled down at her, and butterflies took flight in her belly.

"I will wait for you, if that is what you wish. I would do anything to have you," he whispered, his gaze intense.

Isolde swallowed the lump in her throat and took a calming breath. "You deserve more than that, Merrick. Some weeks past I stated you deserved love, no matter what had happened in your life. Or who had hurt or failed one another. But then I didn't follow that through with any action. Instead, I turned about and said you had to wait, and that was wrong of me. You should not have to wait anymore. Neither of us should. I think our time apart has been quite long enough."

Merrick waltzed them to a stop in the middle of the room, the other couples continuing the dance around them. Merrick clasped her chin, lifting her gaze to meet his. "Are you saying that you will marry me now and not twelve months from now?"

Isolde smiled, nodding. "That is exactly what I wish." The music faded to a stop, and whisperings from the gathered throng surrounding them commenced. Gasps sounded when Merrick bent down on one knee before her. Her vision blurred, and she sniffed, trying to stifle her tears.

"Will you marry me, Lady Isolde Worthingham? And become my duchess?"

A laugh bubbled up inside her. Looking up, she noted her mama to the side with wide eyes, looking on with the rest of their set. She returned her gaze to Merrick and nodded. "Yes. I will marry you."

He stood and, without hesitation, kissed her before the ton. Kissed her, slowly and with such promise that all her concerns floated away. He leaned back, still holding her face. "Let the gossips talk and take their pound of flesh. It won't be long before another scandal grabs their attention, and our nuptials will be forgotten."

"I have always been a little too well-behaved," she said, grinning. "I think it's time I do what I want. Something that will make me happy."

"I think," Merrick said, kissing her again and this time leaving her breathless, "that you're absolutely correct."

Isolde wrapped her arms about Merrick's neck and ignored the scandalized onlookers. No matron or grumpy lord could ruin this moment for her. The man in her arms was the love of her life, and now that life could commence. "There is something I need to tell you, Your Grace."

Wariness clouded his gaze. "What's that?"

She kissed him, smiling when someone yelled out for smelling salts for a collapsed guest. "Only that I love you. Even through all the times that I hated you, I loved you still. Will adore you, always."

A muscle worked in his jaw, and she could tell by his misty gaze that he was fighting for composure. "I thought I'd never again hear those words from you."

"From this day forward, you're going to hear them often, for they're true." Merrick picked her up and spun her about, both of them laughing and oblivious to the stunned disapproval of the ton.

Tonight was theirs, and damn anyone if they did not accept their union. The choice was not Society's to make and, from now on, Isolde would never be swayed by the opinions of others. Only the man she would marry could convince her to think otherwise, and something told Isolde he had no desire to change her.

Just as she would never change anything about him.

---

*I*t was Merrick's turn to be summoned. He sat in the Morning Room at Whites, the room closed off to all other members, as the Duke of Penworth stared at him with what Merrick could only assume was distaste.

He deserved it, he supposed, especially after declaring himself so publicly last night, before all of Society, and forgetting throughout it all to ask permission for Isolde's hand. He schooled his features, wanting to smile at the memory of only a few hours ago, when finally, Isolde had promised to be his and not in a damnable twelve months' time, but weeks only.

Merrick met the duke's gaze. Not even the gentleman's dislike of their union would put a stop to it. Nothing would, and Merrick would make sure of that this time.

"Well," the duke said, crossing his legs and steepling his fingers on his lap. "Do explain what happened last night. You can imagine my surprise when my mother returned home and told me of Isolde's betrothal. Not a month since her last one ended."

Merrick fought not to laugh. Instead he frowned. He didn't wish to put the duke any further offside than he already was. "I know Isolde has explained what happened at Mountshaw on the night before our wedding, and no matter your thoughts on who was to blame, or who was not, there was always a constant throughout the years, and that was my love for your sister. Her understanding with Wardoor was a mistake, and I must admit to being relieved it is no longer so. I know you are aware of the circumstances behind this."

"I am aware, but it does not change the fact that I have not, nor will I ever, forgive you for what you did to her five years ago. The pain that she lived through was as devastating as our father's passing. I will not allow you to hurt her so again." The duke's steely tone was menacing.

"I swear on my life that I will never hurt Isolde again. I never meant to the first time. I love her. So very much. Please give us your blessing." Merrick remained outwardly calm, but his heart raced. Would the duke cause trouble, or was the man willing to put aside his own grudges and allow Isolde to marry whom she wished?

The duke's brow rose mockingly. "Would you break the understanding if I did not approve?"

Merrick took a calming breath, not liking the turn of this conversation. The last people he wished to be at odds with were Isolde's family. "Neither you nor anyone else shall stop me from marrying your sister. Nothing." Merrick held his gaze, his eyes narrowing as his temper rose. Never again would he live another day in abeyance of someone else's wishes or desires. Isolde was his, and he was hers. There was naught else to it.

The duke watched him a moment before taking a sip of his brandy. "I will give my blessing, but only because I love my sister and wish to make her happy. But be warned, Moore. Should any rumor or whisper reach my ears of her being less than pleased, I will claim my pound of flesh and enjoy it while doing so. Do you understand?"

As much as Merrick disliked a peer of the realm talking to him in such a way, he allowed the insult to pass. If it meant that Isolde could marry him with her family's blessing, a notion he knew she wanted, then he would swallow his pride and allow the duke his warning. He nodded. "I accept your decree."

The duke sat forward and held out his hand. Merrick shook it. "I'm glad we're in agreement."

So, too, was he. "Likewise," he said, finishing off his drink as a silent toast that his final hurdle in gaining Isolde's hand was cleared.

CHAPTER 20

*W*ith the help of her mama and her sisters, Isolde stood still as the heavy golden silk gown slid over her head and settled about her form. The bodice had gold thread and beading throughout that shimmered in the morning light. It was heavy and the most beautiful dress she'd ever worn, and to think that this was the dress she would promise herself to Merrick in, filled her with happiness.

Her mama placed a diamond encrusted necklace set in gold about her neck, along with the small matching tiara that was part of the ducal collection. Isolde looked in the mirror and couldn't imagine that this was her. That finally, her wedding day to Merrick had arrived. Already the day was beyond perfect and nothing, she was sure, could ever top it.

Her heart pumped fast in her chest. In under an hour she would be marrying the man she loved beyond reason. Their future left her dizzy with anticipation.

"Isolde, my dear," her mama said, taking her hand, a pensive look on her face. "We haven't spoken much about what happened with Moore and yourself during the Season, but I need to know. Before you say your vows and your life is unable to be altered from your choice."

"What is it, Mama?" It had taken Isolde some days for her to get her brother to calm down enough to hear reason and see sense, and eventually he had, but only after an in- depth discussion with Merrick at Whites. Her mother had come to accept what had happened between Moore and Leonora on the night before their nuptials and was willing to move on. Although it meant Isolde had to tell the truth of Leonora's and Wardoor's affliction, and it was with that admission that finally her family had relented and supported her choice. So her mother's concern now was baffling.

"I wanted only to check with you that you're certain. No matter who was at fault, there have been many hurts between you and Moore. Maybe even more than you're capable of forgiving entirely. I need to know, before you give yourself to him, that this is what you want. I would hate to see you unhappy in your marriage and be unable to change the situation."

"Oh, Mama." Isolde pulled her into an embrace. "Merrick is who I want, who I've only ever wanted. I will not be unhappy. If anything, I will be incandescent with joy."

Her mama's eyes welled with tears. "As pleased as I am to hear this, the talk about town is very unkind. For some time, maybe even years, you may be seen in a very poor light. Merrick is still in mourning, and you broke an engagement to a very eligible young man. Are you sure this is the path you want to walk along?"

Isolde, with full clarity and sureness, nodded. "I am so very certain. I do not care what Society will say; I know they're fickle and they will soon move on to some other unfortunate soul. But I will no longer live my life to please anyone but myself and those I love. You may be sure I shall not lose any sleep over what anyone says about our union."

The duchess smiled, clearly relieved by her words. "Very well, I shall not mention the situation again." She stood back, looking at her. "You're so beautiful, my dear. I hope you know how proud of you I am. Perhaps your father acted rashly the night before your wedding, but his main goal was only ever to see you happy. He was always so protective of you all; if his choice to keep you apart from Merrick was wrong, he would be sorry for it. I wish he were here to walk you down the aisle."

She smiled at her mama, swallowing the lump in her throat at the mention of her dearest father. "Thank you. That means the world to me."

Alice, who stood silently to the side, watched Isolde with a contemplative look. When her mama and Victoria went to fetch the small posy of flowers, she joined Isolde at the mirror. "You make a beautiful bride. All of London will be here today to see you marry Moore." She paused, smiling. "Are you excited?"

Isolde pulled her thoughts back from what the wedding night would entail and how much delight she would have as Merrick tried to get her out of this dress. For the past few weeks, Isolde had made Merrick promise to behave, and he had, damn it. And now, all she could think about was what he had planned for them when they were finally alone.

"You have no idea how thrilled I am that today I marry the man I love. It's been a long journey for both Merrick and me." And they deserved their happiness now.

"You must love him very much."

Isolde met Alice's gaze before pulling on her ivory silk gloves. "I do. He's the best of men. The only man for me."

Alice leaned closer to ensure privacy. "Are you nervous about your wedding night? Moore is even more handsome than he was when you first were betrothed. I should imagine his kisses are most seductive."

Isolde laughed, feeling heat burst on her cheeks. "That is enough, Alice. You're teasing is wasted on me, especially as you know I've not been the most virtuous fiancée. Now, help with the train of this gown. It's time to go."

Victoria came in and passed her a small posy of hydrangeas. "Shall we be off? We don't want to be late, even though some of the girls this Season have been saying that to arrive at the church late is quite the thing to do."

Her mama clasped her arms, kissing her quickly, while checking that each of her daughters had all the jewels and required pieces to their gowns to proceed to the church.

"I'm so very happy for you and do believe Moore will treat you well and spoil you as much as you deserve. You will be happy, Isolde. Now, let's be off."

"I shall, Mama. I'll be perfectly content."

The carriage ride to St James was quick and without incident, which was pleasing. She was determined that nothing would happen that would keep her from marrying Merrick. Not one thing or one person.

Josh greeted them at the steps of the church just as the carriage rocked to a halt. Her little brother grinned down at her as she alighted from the carriage, and taking her hand, placed it on his arm. "You look beautiful, sister."

Isolde smiled. "Thank you, brother." They headed toward the double doors that stood closed to the morning sun. From the steps, Isolde could see a few lingering guests entering the church to take their seats, the floating sounds of a piano reached them each time the door opened.

"Is Moore here?"

Josh chuckled, kissing her cheek quickly. "He's inside and, I might add, looking extremely nervous. You need to put the poor chap out of his misery and say I do before he expires of anxiety."

She chastised herself at the overwhelming relief that

Merrick was inside. It had been a quiet fear, that as much as she'd tried to push away, kept niggling at her mind—that something would happen to keep him from being here this day. That he would change his mind, or some entity would step in and steal him away again.

But no one had stopped the wedding, and now no one would, for they were both here, both eager and ready to commit to their love before God.

Making the church's threshold, Isolde paused for a moment to allow her sisters to set her dress before the long walk down the aisle to Merrick would commence. The pianist started to play and, with a flourish fitting for a duke's daughter, the double doors were opened and the congregation stood.

The other guests faded in Isolde's vision, for at the end of the aisle stood Merrick, the radiant affection beaming from his handsome face. Tears welled in her eyes at the sight of him, hands clasped and his attention wholly fixed on her.

Coming up beside Merrick, Josh placed her hand on Moore's arm, and she smiled, laughing as he pulled her overly close to his side, his hand firmly fixed atop hers.

The reverend smiled at them, clearing his throat and looking toward the congregation. "We are gathered here today in the face of this company, to join together His Grace, the Duke of Moore and Lady Isolde Worthingham in matrimony, which is an honorable and solemn estate and therefore is not to be entered into unadvisedly or lightly, but reverently and soberly. Into this estate, these two persons present come now to be joined. If anyone can show just cause why they may not be lawfully joined together, let them speak now or forever hold their peace."

Isolde swallowed, waiting to see if anyone dare yell out that the marriage should not go ahead, but silence reigned and she smiled, relieved beyond reason.

The reverend continued. "Who gives this woman to be married to this man?"

Josh stepped forward, his face of serious concentration. "I do."

Isolde listened and said the appropriate words as the marriage ceremony moved forward with no difficulty.

"I love you," Merrick said, leaning down to whisper against her ear.

Tears smarted behind her eyes, and she fought not to let her emotions get the better of her. "And I you, forever and a day."

"And I now pronounce you man and wife," the priest declared, smiling.

And because shocking the ton once this Season wasn't enough, Merrick kissed her thoroughly before them all. And just a little bit scandalously, too.

EPILOGUE

*I*solde walked about the grounds of her sister's Scottish castle and admired its beauty. Elizabeth, who was in her late stages of pregnancy, had invited them to stay at Muirdeen before heading off on their wedding trip.

Merrick and she had left London and its wagging tongues behind, only a day after saying their vows. The gossipmongers were beyond put out over their marriage so soon after her broken engagement to Wardoor and because Merrick had married during his period of mourning. They had decided to break their journey to the Continent by visiting Scotland and the beautiful Highlands. Isolde wanted Merrick to see Avonmore and all its beauty. Furthermore, she wanted to celebrate their nuptials with her sister Elizabeth, who hadn't been able to attend the wedding so close to her time.

The heather was in full bloom as Isolde strolled through it, picking it absently as she made her way back to the castle. Lady Lily lay asleep in her arms, her perfect dark eyelashes sweeping across her rosy cheeks. Little William ran about before her, his own bunch of heather gaining size with each passing moment. Isolde looked out over the lands before Muirdeen Castle, a locale that could, she admitted, rival that of her own Scottish estate.

But here at Muirdeen her sister and her dearest little nephew lived, and so it was probably slightly better than Avonmore.

Merrick came out of the castle and gazed about, seemingly looking for her. She made her way over to him, inwardly thanking providence that he was now hers.

"Are you looking for me, Your Grace?" A gust of wind lifted her skirts, and she had to hold them down with her hand lest he see her unmentionables...again. She blushed. "I thought you were tasting whisky today with Henry." Isolde pulled the knitted blanket about Lily's face to keep the wind away.

"I've partaken in all the whisky I can handle," he replied, grinning, before he kissed his daughter's head.

"Really?" That certainly didn't sound like him.

"No." He laughed, taking her hand. He lifted it slowly and kissed her palm with a lingering look. His face had day-old stubble around his jaw, and handsome didn't come close to how he appeared.

"I came to seek you all out. I missed you."

She went into his arms, reaching up to place a small kiss on his cheek. "We missed you, too. But it's been only about three hours since I saw you last, and William has been keeping me company. Haven't you," she stated, catching her son's eye.

"I have, Father, and look," William said, foisting a posy of heather toward his papa. "I have heather for Lily. I'm going to have Nanny put it in her room until you return from your trip."

Isolde noted Merrick's proud stare. "You're a good boy, and I hope you behave for Auntie Elizabeth and Uncle

Henry. If you do, we shall bring lots of presents back for you both."

William started to hop on the spot, his eyes bright with excitement. "Will you, Papa? Oh, can I have a toy theater? I read about one, or at least Nanny did in one of your papers, and I would love to put on a play for you all."

"You'll have to wait and see," Merrick said, ruffling his son's hair, who went back to picking heather, a smile breaking across his delightful face.

Isolde caught Merrick's gaze, and they stood looking at each other for a moment before Beth waddled out of the castle doors, waving them over.

"Your Grace, how very kind of you to leave my husband asleep and snoring in the library. And that he smells of liquor tells me you enjoyed your visit to the distillery."

Isolde laughed as Merrick tried to look contrite. "Do forgive me, Lady Muir. I did try to curtail our partaking of the drink, but it really is very good whisky. The best I've ever tasted, in fact."

Beth laughed and gestured for them to come inside. "Come, dinner will be served in the next hour, and we should get changed. Nanny has a bath ready for the children, also. And if I'm not in the dining room on time, please come looking in the library, for I'm surely still trying to wake my husband."

Isolde laughed and taking Merrick's hand, proceeded indoors and headed toward their room upstairs. They bade the children good night, but not before undressing William and depositing him into the bath. Isolde kissed both children before making her way to her room. The castle's old stone staircase circled about, and coming to the second floor, they walked along the long passageway, both quiet with their own thoughts.

Isolde's maid, Fanny, dipped into a curtsy when Isolde

dismissed her for the night, smiling at Merrick as the young woman's face lit up at the kind gesture.

Merrick stood beside the dressing table, slowly undoing his cravat when his gaze lifted and their eyes met in the mirror.

Pleasure spiked through her as she watched him. Watched as he looked at her like a lion looked at its prey. Ravenous and without remorse.

"Do you need help with your cravat, Your Grace?"

His eyes darkened with passion and butterflies took flight in Isolde's stomach. "I've got this." He turned and strode over to her but not touching her, just stood there, undressing himself before her and teasing her senses.

"I've thought about having you to myself in this room all day." His whispered words sent spirals of desire coursing through her blood.

The room was shadowed in the afternoon light, twilight upon them in this part of the world and, with the small windows that the rooms had, shadows danced in every corner.

Merrick's lips came down hard on hers, and she clutched at his shoulders, wanting, needing to be as close as she could.

His tongue swirled with hers, and need, hot and heavy, buckled her knees. "We have only an hour, my love," she gasped as he ground against her.

He groaned. "That shouldn't be a problem."

*M*errick had to have her. Now. Pain tore through his body at the thought of stopping. It was too late for that. He picked her up, and she wrapped her legs about his hips. Her heat scorched him. Her body, open and willing, made him wild with need.

He strode toward the door, the closest purchase he could

find, and pushed her up against the wood paneling. She fumbled with the front falls of his breeches until they were together, skin on delicious skin, body against aching body. He slid against her center, feeling her readiness and inflaming his own.

"You're so beautiful. I want you so badly it hurts."

Their gazes met, and it slammed into him how much she was enjoying herself. The wild urgency he read in her gaze drove him to distraction, and he had to take a deep breath lest he lose control and disgrace himself against her slick heat.

"I have to have you, too."

Merrick took her with little finesse. She gasped, her eyes closing slowly in ecstasy. His hands slipped about her ass, holding her against him as he relentlessly pumped into her hot core. The door creaked behind them, their labored breaths forgotten as they lost themselves in each other.

"Oh yes. Merrick," Isolde gasped, her hands wrapping about his neck and holding him close. "Don't stop."

He couldn't. She was the perfect fit for him. The moment she came, her body clamping around him and pulling him toward his own pleasure, was too much. He didn't stop, just took her again and again as she climaxed in his arms, her moans muffled by a kiss.

"Would you be averse to eating in our room this evening?" He nibbled her neck and steadied her when she wobbled in his arms.

She met his gaze, grinning. "Not at all. That sounds perfect."

He slid his hand about her breast, and she shivered in his arms. Always so willing, so loving and responsive to his touch. How he loved her and all that she was. "What will your sister think of us missing dinner? You're turning into a scandalous wench."

She kissed him, her hand sliding down his stomach to his nether region, helping him place it back into his pants. He gritted his teeth, enjoying the moment far more than she'd ever know. "Careful love, or I'll not allow you to leave this room ever."

Again she drove him to distraction, her soft kisses against his neck sending delectable shivers down his spine. "Then my work here is done." She smiled up at him. "I do believe I'll enjoy being locked up in this castle room with you. How long do you think we could remain just so?"

"Forever, if I had my way, but alas, I received word that our ship to France will dock next week and so I'm sorry to be the bearer of bad news, but we'll be leaving the delightful Highlands for the Continent sooner than you thought."

Her eyes widened with surprise and excitement. "France. I cannot wait even that long."

"And Switzerland, followed by Italy. I want to explore the world with you, make up for the time we lost."

She reached up, hugging him close. "Oh, thank you, Merrick, for fighting for me, for loving me as much as you do. I cannot imagine my life without you, William, or Lily now."

Merrick picked her up and strolled over to the bed. "Nor I, and you're most welcome, the pleasure is all mine."

She threw him an impish grin. "And mine, too," she said as he kissed her soundly. They did not make the dinner, as planned.

Dear Reader,

I hope you enjoyed, *Only a Duke Will Do*, book two in my To Marry a Rogue series!

I'm so thrilled you chose my book to read, and if you're able, I would appreciate an honest review of *Only a Duke Will Do*. As they say, feed an author, leave a review!

If you'd like to learn about book three in my To Marry a Rogue series, *Only a Viscount Will Do*, please read on. I have included the prologue for your reading pleasure.

Alternatively, you can keep in contact with me by visiting my website or following me online. You can contact me at www.tamaragill.com or email me at tamaragillauthor@gmail.com.

Tamara Gill

ONLY A VISCOUNT WILL DO

TO MARRY A ROGUE, BOOK 3

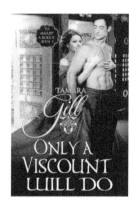

Lady Alice Worthingham never conforms to Society's norms. Ever. She loves adventure, new experiences, and approaches life with a sassy attitude Society can take or leave. But even for her, robbery by a highwayman is a bit much.

. . .

Lord Arndel, Lady Alice's neighbor, is playing a dangerous game--acting the proper viscount by day and the Surrey Bandit by night. And to brazenly steal from the woman who's captured his attention is no mean feat, or the wisest of moves.

When Lady Alice learns the truth, the viscount finds that when a well-bred woman seeks revenge, she'll make a gentleman thief pay for his crimes with everything...including his heart.

PROLOGUE

*C*allum squinted, the light in the room blinding as the blindfold was ripped from his face. He blinked, growing accustomed to the brightness in the room.

He didn't recognize any of the men staring at him, but he could understand the menace that glistened in their eyes. Callum rolled his shoulders, the bands about his wrists leaving his hands almost numb.

"Who the hell are you?"

The man behind the desk, a rotund, balding gentleman, stared at him nonplussed. "I'm a moneylender. One who's come to collect."

Two more burly men came into the room and stood behind the man at the desk. They crossed their arms over their chest and Callum understood the unspoken threat. "I don't owe you any funds."

The man laughed. "*Tsk tsk*, a minor detail that you'll soon be remedied of. *You*, Lord Arndel may not owe the money, but you have inherited the debt of your late cousin, along with his title." He shrugged. "I'm sorry to be the bearer of bad news, but the debt your cousin owed me is perhaps more than you can pay, and, therefore, just as your cousin was asked to do, you, too, shall have expectations toward us that will be met."

"I'll do nothing you ask of me. I have no idea of this debt that you speak, and I fail to see why I should inherit it."

"All true," the man said, his eyes narrowing slightly. "And yet you do inherit the debt and you shall do as we say or your sweet, loving family shall be, how do I say this," he said, tapping his chin, "hurt."

Callum swallowed, the need to hurt the bastard increasing tenfold. If only he wasn't tied up, he'd pummel the man within an inch of his life. How dare he threaten his child? "You touch my daughter, even one hair on her head, and you will rue the day."

"You will rue the day if you think I am joking, my lord." The moneylender took a sip of his amber liquid, placing the glass down as if he had not a care in the world, and hadn't, in fact, just threatened a man and his family with who knows what horrendous consequences. "Before your cousin died, we had a contract written up, in case his demise was earlier than foreseen. Now that you've inherited the estate and title, we have forwarded the contract to your solicitor, and I'm sure in the coming days he will ask for an audience with you."

"How much is the debt?" With any luck it wouldn't be as much as he feared, though his cousin Robert had lived a misbegotten lifestyle full of vice and debauchery, which apparently involved large wads of blunt.

"The debt is in the vicinity of eighteen thousand pounds. More than I know you have."

Callum tried to take a calming breath and failed. The room shrank, and for the first time in his life he thought he might pass out. "Eighteen thousand pounds...no doubt you thought nothing of lending such sums to a man who you knew would never be able to afford such debt. How dare you act so criminally."

The moneylender laughed, his gut shaking in mirth. "Alas, my lord, if it hasn't escaped your notice, I *am* a criminal and I will get my money back, and with your help." He reached into his desk drawer and pulled out a file with a multitude of papers within it. "Would you like to know the details of the services that will render me happy?"

"Do I have a choice?" Callum asked, his words cutting, severing any hope he may have had of his and his family's future.

"In this folder is a listing and drawings of jewels that I want you to procure for me. Each piece is of high value, made of the finest quality jewels and will make me so rich that you may even see me gracing the ballrooms of the *ton* in the years to come."

Callum doubted that very much, nor did he want to think about what the moneylender's words meant. He wracked his brain for a way to remove himself from the situation, to walk away without debt nor any links to the man before him, but his mind came up blank. There was no way out for him. He had no money of his own; he had the estate only and most of that was entailed and untouchable.

"You, Lord Arndel, shall steal these jewels from these rich toffs, and deliver them each month until the debt is paid. And just to sweeten the deal, some of these jewels are worth up to a thousand pounds, so do not despair that I'll be requiring your services forever."

"You want me to become a thief, stealing into these people's homes, people who I shall see most nights at Town events and such? Damn you. I shall not do it."

The moneylender gestured to one of his guards, who then went and opened a door, mumbling to someone inside the dark space. Rage unlike any he'd known consumed him when they carried out his daughter, her body limp in the man's arms.

"What have you done to her?" he roared, standing and throwing the chair his hands were tied to against the wall. A satisfying crack sounded and he did it again, the chair giving way, enough so he could pull his hands free.

As he went to his daughter, the second burly man tackled him to the ground, his weight and solid punch to his lower back winding him. "Tell me what you've done?" he wheezed, his gaze blurring with the horrible realization that they may have killed his little girl.

"She's alive, for now. Too much liquor in her tea, unfortunately. Knocked her out cold." The man laughed and Callum promised he'd kill the bastard. Maybe not today with his daughter's life still in the fiend and his cronies' hands, but one day. One day, the man laughing down on him would pay for daring to take her from his home.

"In one month's time the first jewel is due. There will be no sneaking into their homes. You must wait for them to be attending a ball, or traveling to or from their estates after a jaunt. It is at these times you must strike, steal their valuables, and bring them to me."

"So I'm to be a highwayman?" The absurdity of the situation was too much for his brain to register. Just when his life had taken a positive turn, and now this. He fought to move, to get up. The moneylender gave one curt nod and the man took his knee off the middle of his back. Callum ran to Amelia and wrenched her from the second guard's hands, hating the fact these bastards had been anywhere near her, had stolen her from right under his nose with nary a problem.

"Fine," Callum said, holding his daughter tight. "I shall do as you ask, but if you ever come near my child again I will kill you. Even if I hang before all the *ton*, do not doubt that I will allow you to live, should you hurt one hair on her head."

The moneylender threw him an unamused glance. "I will have no reason to hurt anyone should you do as I ask, within a timely manner."

"Give me the list." The man held it up and Callum ripped it from his grasp, striding to the door. He stopped when one of the guards stood before it, his arms crossed over his chest.

"Let Lord Arndel pass. Our business today is complete."

Callum strode from the room, his steps faltering when a bevy of half-naked women stood along the walls, watching him, some of their eyes beckoning him to join them in the rooms behind them. How dare the bastard take his daughter into such an establishment. Amelia mumbled in her sleep and Callum frowned. What liquor had they given to her? What if they'd killed her by accident? If his cousin Robert wasn't already dead, he'd kill the man himself for placing his daughter into such a predicament.

Stepping free of the building, Callum made his way out of the circular square that had buildings in dire need of repair and headed toward where a busier road lay beyond. He would get Amelia home and then he would decide what was to be done and how he would face the next few months under the order of such a man as he'd just left.

It wasn't to be borne, and yet somehow it must. Callum couldn't see a way out of the situation. He was beholden to him until he paid off a debt that wasn't his.

Damnation.

Want to read more? Get Only a Viscount Will Do Do today!

LORDS OF LONDON SERIES
AVAILABLE NOW!

Dive into these charming historical romances! In this six-book series, Darcy seduces a virginal duke, Cecilia's world collides with a roguish marquess, Katherine strikes a deal with an unlucky earl and Lizzy sets out to conquer a very wicked Viscount. These stories plus more adventures in the Lords of London series! Available now through Amazon or read free with KindleUnlimited.

Lords of London

KISS THE WALLFLOWER SERIES
AVAILABLE NOW!

If the roguish Lords of London are not for you and wall-flowers are more your cup of tea, this is the series for you. My Kiss the Wallflower series, are linked through friendship and family in this four-book series. You can grab a copy on Amazon or read free through KindleUnlimited.

LEAGUE OF UNWEDDABLE GENTLEMEN SERIES AVAILABLE NOW!

Fall into my latest series, where the heroines have to fight for what they want, both regarding their life and love. And where the heroes may be unweddable to begin with, that is until they meet the women who'll change their fate. The League of Unweddable Gentlemen series is available now!

LEAGUE OF UNWEDDABLE GENTLEMEN

ALSO BY TAMARA GILL

Wicked Widows Series
TO DREAM OF YOU

League of Unweddable Gentlemen Series
TEMPT ME, YOUR GRACE
HELLION AT HEART
DARE TO BE SCANDALOUS
TO BE WICKED WITH YOU
KISS ME DUKE

Kiss the Wallflower series
A MIDSUMMER KISS
A KISS AT MISTLETOE
A KISS IN SPRING
TO FALL FOR A KISS
KISS THE WALLFLOWER - BOOKS 1-3 BUNDLE

Lords of London Series
TO BEDEVIL A DUKE
TO MADDEN A MARQUESS
TO TEMPT AN EARL
TO VEX A VISCOUNT
TO DARE A DUCHESS
TO MARRY A MARCHIONESS
LORDS OF LONDON - BOOKS 1-3 BUNDLE
LORDS OF LONDON - BOOKS 4-6 BUNDLE

To Marry a Rogue Series
ONLY AN EARL WILL DO
ONLY A DUKE WILL DO
ONLY A VISCOUNT WILL DO

A Time Traveler's Highland Love Series
TO CONQUER A SCOT
TO SAVE A SAVAGE SCOT
TO WIN A HIGHLAND SCOT

Time Travel Romance
DEFIANT SURRENDER
A STOLEN SEASON

Scandalous London Series
A GENTLEMAN'S PROMISE
A CAPTAIN'S ORDER
A MARRIAGE MADE IN MAYFAIR
SCANDALOUS LONDON - BOOKS 1-3 BUNDLE

High Seas & High Stakes Series
HIS LADY SMUGGLER
HER GENTLEMAN PIRATE
HIGH SEAS & HIGH STAKES - BOOKS 1-2 BUNDLE

Daughters Of The Gods Series
BANISHED-GUARDIAN-FALLEN
DAUGHTERS OF THE GODS - BOOKS 1-3 BUNDLE

Stand Alone Books
TO SIN WITH SCANDAL

OUTLAWS

ABOUT THE AUTHOR

Tamara is an Australian author who grew up in an old mining town in country South Australia, where her love of history was founded. So much so, she made her darling husband travel to the UK for their honeymoon, where she dragged him from one historical monument and castle to another.

A mother of three, her two little gentlemen in the making, a future lady (she hopes) and a part-time job keep her busy in the real world, but whenever she gets a moment's peace she loves to write romance novels in an array of genres, including regency, medieval and time travel.

www.tamaragill.com
tamaragillauthor@gmail.com